J.C. and the Bijoux Jolis

THE ROUSSEAUS, BOOK #3
THE BLUEBERRY LANE SERIES

KATY REGNERY

SPENCER
HILL
PRESS

Please visit www.katyregnery.com

First Edition: November 2016
Katy Regnery

J.C. and the Bijoux Jolis: a novel / by Katy Regnery—1st ed.
ISBN: 978-1-63392-094-1
Library of Congress Cataloging-in-Publication Data available upon request

Published in the United States by Spencer Hill Press
This is a Spencer Hill Contemporary Romance, Spencer Hill
Contemporary is an imprint of Spencer Hill Press.
For more information on our titles visit www.spencerhillpress.com

Distributed by Midpoint Trade Books
www.midpointtrade.com

Cover design by: Marianne Nowicki
Interior layout by: Scribe Inc.
The World of Blueberry Lane Map designed by: Paul Siegel

Printed in the United States of America

The Blueberry Lane Series

THE ENGLISH BROTHERS
Breaking Up with Barrett
Falling for Fitz
Anyone but Alex
Seduced by Stratton
Wild about Weston
Kiss Me Kate
Marrying Mr. English

THE WINSLOW BROTHERS
Bidding on Brooks
Proposing to Preston
Crazy about Cameron
Campaigning for Christopher

THE ROUSSEAUS
Jonquils for Jax
Marry Me Mad
J.C. and the Bijoux Jolis

THE STORY SISTERS
(coming 2017)
The Bohemian and the Businessman
The Director and Don Juan
The Flirt and the Fox
The Saint and the Scoundrel

THE AMBLERS
(coming 2018)
Belonging to Bree
Surrendering to Sloane

THE ATWELLS
(coming 2019)
Blueberry Lane Books #21–24

Based on the bestselling series by Katy Regnery,
The World of...

The Rousseaus of Chateau Nouvelle
Jax, Mad, J.C.
Jonquils for Jax • *Marry Me Mad*
J.C. and the Bijoux Jolis

The Story Sisters of Forrester
Priscilla, Alice, Elizabeth, Jane
Coming Summer 2017
The Bohemian and the Businessman
The Director and Don Juan
The Flirt and the Fox
The Saint and the Scoundrel

The Winslow Brothers of Westerly
Brooks, Preston, Cameron, Christopher
Bidding on Brooks • *Proposing to Preston*
Crazy About Cameron • *Campaigning for Christopher*

The Amblers of Greens Farms
Bree, Sloane
Coming Summer 2018
Belonging to Bree
Surrendering to Sloane

The English Brothers of Haverford Park
Barrett, Fitz, Alex, Stratton, Weston, Kate
Breaking up with Barrett • *Falling for Fitz*
Anyone but Alex • *Seduced by Stratton*
Wild about Weston • *Kiss Me Kate*
Marrying Mr. English

For my friend Kerry, who, after three years, still reads everything I write.
I appreciate you.
xo

And for Meital and Kim.
I would have been lost without you two.
xo

A note to readers of
The Rousseau books

J.C. and the Bijoux Jolis shares and exceeds the time frame of *Jonquils for Jax* and *Marry Me Mad*, beginning at the wedding of Étienne Rousseau to Kate English.

CONTENTS

Prologue

August 1939
Marseilles, France
"You are . . . exquisite," sighed Monsieur Montferrat, peeking at her from one side of the canvas before hiding behind it once again. "*Magnifique*."

"*Merci*," said eighteen-year-old Camille Trigére softly, wishing she could flex her arms and roll her neck to get the kinks out.

A bead of sweat that started at the nape of her neck swerved around her collarbone to rest precariously on the tip of her left nipple. It was hot this summer. *Merde*, but it was hot.

Still, to be immortalized by a famous painter like Pierre Montferrat was an honor for a very new and inexperienced portrait model like Camille. A hundred years from now, when she was long gone, this portrait, which Monsieur had titled *Les Bijoux Jolis*, would hang on someone's wall, somewhere in the world.

Immortalité.

It was worth a moment's discomfort to live forever.

"Do not move. Not even an inch," said Monsieur Montferrat, pulling at the gray goatee on his chin as he stood to admire her, a glass of muddy-gray water in his hand. "I must refresh the water."

She watched until he had left the small studio, then stretched her arms over her head eagerly, massaging the feeling back into her hands. For over four hours, she'd held the same pose of "young nude wearing emerald necklace," and she was tired, damn it.

Casting her eyes toward the open doors that led to a small terrace, she wondered if her old friend and new lover, Gilles Lévy, was already waiting downstairs to walk her home. The sun was quite low. It must be after four.

Camille and Gilles had known each other forever, growing up in the same neighborhood and attending the same synagogue throughout their shared childhood. Lately, the France of their early years was shifting, however, with conservatives and socialists whom Camille's father had once considered mainstream now speaking out against the Jews of Marseilles and aligning their politics with worrisome new ideas filtering into France from Germany.

The shift was subtle—Camille saw it in the way that Monsieur Ragout had stopped taking Jewish piano students this summer, too busy for one more student, though very little lesson music wafted down from his third-floor studio on Rue Saint Dominique. In Camille's own life, the shift had been slightly less subtle and infinitely more personal: Monsieur Montferrat, upon meeting her in July, had commented, "How curious! You don't have the *look* of a Jewess."

His initial inspection had made her uncomfortable enough to reconsider the monthlong modeling job, but she'd accepted despite misgivings. Although her father would skin her alive if he found out what she'd been doing every day, she hoped to make enough money to run away to Paris with Gilles this fall. He had a second cousin willing to share his deux-piéces with the young lovers. Struggling artist Gilles said they'd find work at a local café during the day, and every night he would paint her in the moonlight before sweeping her off to bed to make love until dawn.

When Monsieur Montferrat slipped back into the room, Camille's arms and hands were perfectly in place, though her smile may have been a bit more dreamy.

"It's almost five," he said, flicking a glance at the terrace doors regretfully. "I suppose you have to go soon."

"*Oui*, Monsieur. Gilles will be here at five. How much longer today?" asked Camille politely as the artist stood at his canvas, surveying his work.

After several long moments of staring at the portrait, he looked up at her and sighed. "We're finished."

Camille sat up immediately, grabbing her chemise and panties from under the divan and wiggling into them, always self-conscious of her naked form when Monsieur Montferrat was finished painting. She shrugged her light-blue cotton dress over her head, smoothing the clothing back into place, relieved that she was fully covered once again.

"Shall I come again tomorrow?"

Monsieur Montferrat raised an eyebrow as he smiled sadly at her, slipping around his painting carefully to take his place behind her. Gathering her black hair in her hands, Camille lifted it off the back of her neck and stood still, waiting for him to unclasp the necklace so she could go.

His rough fingers rested on the damp skin of her neck. "Do you know what's happening in the world, *belle* Camille?"

"Monsieur?" she murmured, surprised by the distressed tone of his voice.

"Madness," he cursed softly. "The world is going mad, *petite*."

Camille liked Monsieur Montferrat.

He was gray and wrinkled like her grandfather, but he had been kind to the young model: respectful, not leering; patient as she learned how to maintain a pose for hours on end; and always kind to her, talking of art and music during their long afternoons together. But his outburst made her uncomfortable and eager to leave.

"Monsieur," she said gently, "my friend will be most anxious."

She felt his fingers working the clasp of the ornate emerald necklace. She'd worn it every day for twenty-nine days while her parents believed she was minding Gilles' twin nieces on the other side of town.

The heavy jewels slipped into the crevice of her breasts as Monsieur Montferrat lifted the two sides from around her neck, then raised them over her head. Camille breathed a sigh of relief as he stepped away, and she reached down to tug on her shoes, quickly buckling them.

"You needn't come back, Mademoiselle Trigére," said the artist, crossing the room and placing the priceless necklace back in a black velvet box, which he locked in the bottom drawer of a desk.

"Monsieur?" she whispered, fearing that she had displeased him in some way.

Turning to face her, his smile was rueful. "The portrait is finished."

He beckoned her to stand beside him, and she stepped around the easel to look at the canvas she'd never been permitted to peek at before now.

Her painted body, pale and pink, was stark on the dark-green velvet divan on which she had posed, but she quickly realized that she was merely a palette for the necklace around her throat. The gems caught the afternoon light, facets gleaming, white-gold settings shiny and bright. The centerpiece of the painting was the necklace, and Camille had a sense of disappointment as she realized that her immortality would be forever overshadowed by the jewels she'd worn around her neck. Yet still . . .

"It's beautiful," she said softly.

He collected an envelope full of francs from the shelf at the bottom of his easel, holding it between them, searching her eyes with his. When he finally spoke, his voice was urgent. "Don't go to Paris, *petite*. Go to London. Or better, New York. *Oui, belle* Camille, go to America. *Maintenant*. Now. Promise me."

"America?"

"*Oui*. As soon as possible."

Troubled by the wild look in his eyes and ever more eager to leave, she took the envelope from his fingers. "You have been kind to me. *Merci*."

"Promise me," he begged her in a whisper, "that you will have a good life."

She stepped forward to press her lips against his papery cheek. "*Adieu*, Monsieur."

Her footsteps echoed down the metal stairs of the tiny apartment building, and she flung herself into Gilles' arms, heady with freedom, as soon as she reached the sidewalk.

"*C'est fin!*" she told him with a beaming smile, offering him the envelope of money that would secure the next step of their shared future.

"Paris, here we come!" he cried, covering her mouth with a lusty kiss.

From the lonely terrace of his apartment, Monsieur Montferrat watched them link hands and scurry joyfully away, wondering just for a moment what would become of the young Jewish girl in the painting . . . the beautiful young woman in his final portrait, *Les Bijoux Jolis*.

Chapter 1

If the best man and maid of honor are both single, thought J.C. Rousseau, taking another peek at Kate English's best friend, Libitz Feingold, *it's practically an unwritten rule that they should pork.*

And if anyone on earth looked to be in dire need of a good, hard, thorough fucking, it was Mademoiselle Feingold.

As the priest droned on about the blessing and sanctity of marriage, the groom—J.C.'s younger brother, Étienne—elbowed him subtly in the side, and J.C. straightened, clearing his throat and shifting his glance away from Kate's skinny, tiny, perpetually annoyed-looking friend.

She was definitely, positively *not* his type—she wasn't even breathing the same air as his type—so why had he kept stealing glances at her over Étienne's wedding weekend? Fuck if he knew. There was something intriguing about her, but he couldn't quite put his finger on it.

While he generally preferred blondes or redheads with long, luxurious hair, Libitz had short, jet-black hair she wore in a close-cropped pixie cut that could have looked masculine on a larger woman or twee on someone as small as Libitz. But he had to admit, she somehow pulled it off, looking both feminine and chic.

J.C. was partial to women with big tits and hips he could hold on to while he fucked them from behind. Libitz? Well, her "bits" were small and her hips were nonexistent, much like her ass, which didn't have the usual curve and swell that made his mouth water.

She was practically boy-shaped under the champagne-colored silk bridesmaid gown she wore today, and yet he couldn't stop staring at her.

Maybe it was her massive dark-brown eyes that took up half her face like a Margaret Keane portrait come to life . . . or the creamy-looking texture of her olive-colored skin . . . or the fact that her lips were almost perfectly bow-shaped and plump enough to pillow around a man's cock and take him to heaven. Or maybe it was that she just seemed so fucking ambivalent about everyone at the wedding except for Kate, whom she affectionately called "KK." He wondered what it would take to impress her—literally, to make an impression—but damned if he knew. Last night at the rehearsal dinner, he'd discovered that she was utterly immune to his charm.

"You must be the famous Libitz," he'd opened, taking his assigned seat beside her and flashing his sexiest grin. After all, if she was his chosen conquest for the weekend, there was no time like the present to work his wiles.

Wearing a simple black sheath dress with aqua circles, seventies-style mod makeup, and oversized silver and crystal chandelier earrings that almost brushed her thin shoulders, she'd turned to him and blinked those wide, all-seeing eyes.

"And you . . . *must* be kidding."

Taken aback, he'd stared at her for a second before chuckling. "Wha—I mean, how's that?"

"Let's start over," she said, cocking her head to the side. "Here's your line, Romeo: 'Hi, I'm Étienne's brother, Jean-Christian. It's nice to meet you.' Want to give it a try?"

He cleared his throat, his smile fading. "Hi, I'm Étienne's brother, Jean-Christian. It's nice to meet you."

She locked eyes with his, her lips neutral, tilted neither up nor down. "Hi. I'm Libitz Feingold, Kate's best friend . . . and it's not cold enough."

"What?" asked J.C., feeling completely turned around.

"It's not cold enough in hell for me to fall for someone like you," she said, then shifted back around to talk to the person on her other side.

Well, fuck me, thought J.C., taking another gulp of beer as he tried to figure out if he was insulted or impressed. After a moment, he nudged her in the side with his elbow, and she looked at him over her shoulder, her expression annoyed.

"Yes?"

"I hear the temperature's dropping there," he said casually, then added, "because they're expecting a visit from you."

"Ha!" she chortled, a genuine grin brightening her eyes for a moment before she quickly reined it back in to practiced ennui. "Is that right?"

He shrugged, tipping his bottle of beer back as he held her eyes, challenging her to come back at him with something clever. "So I heard."

"From all the friends you've got there?"

He almost spit his beer out. Damn, but she was quick.

"Truce?" he asked, placing his beer on the table and holding out his hand.

She stared at his hand for a moment, then looked away, leaning forward to pick up her champagne glass and bringing it slowly to her lips. "No, thanks. Mama didn't raise no fool."

"You're unreal."

She shook her head, that bored look still in place. "Nope. I'm real. I'm just not a good target for charming scamps looking for trouble."

"A target? Shit. Who got to you?" he asked, feeling a little abused by her insta-judgment of him without actually getting a chance to know him in person. Not that she was wrong exactly. But getting into trouble with the right person could be a hell of a lot of fun.

"The list is long and distinguished," she shot back.

His eyes widened and his lips wobbled.

"Oh, God," she said, shaking her head as her cheeks bloomed an appealing pink under her makeup, "I walked right into that one didn't I?"

"Yes, you did," said J.C. with what he hoped was a disarming grin. "All together, now . . ."

"*So's my Johnson*," they said at the same time, quoting the rebuttal line from *Top Gun*.

"Hey, look at that," he said, still smiling at her. "You *do* know how to have fun. I was beginning to worry."

Her smile instantly faded. "You're not as cute as you think you are."

"Yeah," he said, nodding as he finished the last of his beer, "I am."

She rolled her eyes and presented him with her full back, their conversation apparently over.

"Jean-Christian!" muttered Étienne, elbowing him in the side again as the priest gave him a dirty look.

"*Père*?" he asked, wondering what he'd just missed.

The priest sighed with exasperation. "The rings, my son?"

Fuck.

J.C. patted down his pockets, finally remembering he'd placed the two gold bands in his inside pocket and winking at Libitz as he handed them to Étienne. She rewarded him with a scathing look, shaking her head with disgust as the priest continued the ceremony by blessing the rings.

Damn, but he couldn't catch a break with her. It was frustrating as hell.

He was good looking. He *knew* he was. For a fact.

Just last week, his sometimes-fuckbuddy, recent divorcee Felicity Atwell, told him that he was a "real-life Gideon Cross." And while he had no idea who the fuck this Cross fellow was, hearing her purr the words "sexy and powerful . . . just like Gideon" into his ear while he thrust inside of her had made him come twice as fast.

Thankfully, Felicity was out of town this weekend, visiting friends in Scotland, so inviting her to the wedding as his date hadn't been an issue. But frankly, he wouldn't have invited her even if she was in town. He'd never promised her anything, after all. Theirs was a conscience-free, commitment-free arrangement of convenience, and either of them could walk away from it at any time. It was his favorite type of relationship, in fact: no expectations, no assumptions, no feelings. Just two mutually consenting adults who occasionally had drinks or dinner or fucked. It was perfect.

Perfect because J.C. had no interest in committing himself to one woman when the world was full of delicious ladies of every color, shape, size, and age. Perfect because J.C. didn't want the pressure of living up to one person's expectations of him. Perfect because he didn't want to be on either end of a two-person relationship when feelings that were meant to last forever would inevitably start to fade.

He'd watched it with his own parents: his father's disinterest in his mother as she aged from a graceful and nubile ballerina into a middle-aged mother of four. He'd been witness to his father's philandering, even included regularly when his father went to meet a paramour in the city. He'd been so familiar with the Morris House Hotel, in fact, that the concierge and bartenders knew his name. The first time J.C. had ever gotten drunk, it was at the Morris House Hotel, in the lobby bar, where Monsieur Rousseau had handed the bartender his gold card and told him to "babysit" J.C. while he disappeared for an hour.

Faced with his wife's hostility when they returned home, his father would slap thirteen-year-old J.C. on the back and use father-son bonding time as the excuse for them missing dinner or coming home so late on a Saturday afternoon or Sunday evening. Her face, a mixture of brittle and betrayed, would search J.C.'s eyes for a truth he was unable to offer. After a while, he couldn't look into his mother's eyes without flinching, so he stopped. He stopped looking into them altogether.

And he promised himself he'd never, ever make a woman look that way at him. And the best way to achieve that goal? Stay loose. Stay free. Enjoy women, as his father had, without the caustic damage to a disillusioned wife while using his young son as an alibi.

"Do you, Étienne Xavier Rousseau, take this woman, Kathryn Grey English, for your lawfully wedded wife, to live together after God's ordinance in the holy estate of matrimony?"

"I do," said Étienne softly, his voice gravelly with emotion.

"Will you love her, comfort her, honor and keep her in sickness and in health, and, forsaking all others, keeping yourself for her only, as long as you both shall live?"

Étienne's head jerked in a small nod before he whispered, "I will."

"Kathryn Grey English, do you take Étienne Xavier Rousseau to be your lawfully wedded husband, to live together after God's ordinance in the holy estate of matrimony?"

Kate English locked her gaze on Étienne, her eyes full of tears, her lips tilted up in a smile so sweet and genuine, it was unbearable to see, and J.C. had to look away.

"I do," she said, her voice soft and tender.

"Will you love him, comfort him, honor and keep him in sickness and in health, and, forsaking all others, keeping yourself for him only, as long as you both shall live?"

"I will," she murmured, her voice breaking just a little.

It was a promise.

A promise J.C. had no doubt she meant. He could hear it in the sweet seriousness of her voice. He could see it in the glistening vulnerability of her eyes. She meant it.

But hadn't their mother meant it once upon a time? Hadn't their father meant it too?

It baffled J.C. that Étienne had somehow managed to move past their parents' fucked-up marriage to find a committed, loving, stable relationship of his own. But then again, J.C. had never allowed Étienne to be the one to join their father in the city. He'd always shoved his brother aside and volunteered to go instead. And besides, at age fifteen, Étienne had been sent off to military school in the Deep South, only home for a few weeks at Christmas and in the summertime. He'd missed a lot of their parents' wildly dysfunctional relationship, and the twins—his sisters, Jax and Mad—had had each other for comfort. J.C. had had both the exposure to his father's infidelity and no one with whom to process it.

Not that it mattered at this point. He'd chosen how he wanted his life to be—free of the sort of emotion that could break your heart or someone else's—and for the most part, he was happy with the way things were.

Looking past Étienne and Kate, he checked out Libitz again, wondering what it would take to get under her skirt . . . because fuck, but he loved a conquest, and he sensed that fucking Libitz would pay off in spades. Angry chicks were always nuts in bed, and she was the angriest he'd ever seen.

Kate had mentioned that, like him, Libitz had an interest in art. In fact, if he recalled correctly, she had a gallery in New York while he was in the process of opening his own gallery in Philadelphia. Now that was an interesting bit of information, because one of the few things in life about which J.C. allowed himself to feel genuine passion was art. He loved it. He fucking loved it.

It was honest.

It was raw.

It was ugly.

It was beautiful.

It was real in a way he could never be, and yet it allowed him to experience infatuation, repulsion, lust, and even love in a way that kept him, and others, safe. Art combined every emotion he didn't allow himself to feel and offered it up in a beautiful, untouchable package. He could feel *about* it and *for* it, but it couldn't hurt him and he couldn't hurt it. It was an almost perfect relationship and, aside from that with his siblings, the only other to which he felt truly and wholly committed.

But conveniently, there was also no harm in using art as a topic to woo a woman trying to appear disinterested in him.

Like most serious women stuck in their own heads, he suspected that if he could get Libitz to talk about business—*her* business: art and galleries—she would feel powerful and equal. If he was right, it would also make her defenses fall, and maybe she'd think she was seeing another side of him through his enthusiasm for a shared passion. Of course he could never extend such emotion to her, a living, breathing human being with a heart capable of breaking. But that wouldn't be an issue. Before they fucked, he'd make sure that she—like every other woman on the face of the earth—knew that Jean-Christian Louis Rousseau offered nothing except his eager tongue, his fat cock, and the desire to make her come all over both.

Libitz felt his eyes on her again, but she refused to look at him.

Between Kate and Kate's cousin Stratton, whom Lib had known for most of her life, she knew all she needed to know about Jean-Christian Rousseau, and very little of it was favorable. She knew from Kate that Barrett was sometimes referred to as "the Shark" in business circles, but as far as Libitz was concerned, the only shark at the English-Rousseau wedding today was the one staring at her.

Wait. Staring at her?

No.

Eyefucking her, same as he'd been doing since last night when he sidled up to her at the rehearsal dinner and tried introducing himself with so much innuendo, she almost couldn't hear his words through the cloud of smarm.

Jean-Christian was a predator, plain and simple, and every lazy eye blink, every sexy smirk, every deep breath he took was premeditated to make a woman rip her panties down the middle and mount up with abandon.

And the thing was, Libitz had no problem with that.

Though she wanted, one day, what KK had found in Étienne, she had no illusions that it was going to happen anytime soon. She'd dated boys from prep school, from summer camp, and from college. She'd met them through well-intentioned mothers at her parent's temple; through sorority sisters whose boyfriends had brothers; through J-Date, an online dating service for young Jewish singles; and occasionally at posh hotel bars, where she wasn't above a quick fuck in a coatroom if she felt like it.

Libitz was no prude, and despite her longing, she had no fanciful ideas about a happily-ever-after around the next bend. Whatever romantic bones she had in her body were protected so far beneath the surface, she wasn't even positive they still existed. If she hadn't hidden them away, after all, her veritable parade of Mr. Wrongs would have surely crushed them all to dust.

No, Lib didn't mind that Jean-Christian Rousseau was on a mission to screw every human being with a vagina in a ten-mile radius, but she refused to be added to his list.

Why?

Mostly because of Kate. Kate English. KK. Libitz's best friend since kindergarten, where their desks and coat hooks had been side by side because of their last names, English and Feingold. Neither girl had been blessed with siblings, but they'd quickly chosen each other as their adopted sister for life. Through six years of elementary school and seven years of middle and high school, where Libitz was one of four Jewish kids at Trinity Prep in Manhattan, KK and Lib had remained inseparable. There was nothing that Lib wouldn't do for Kate. Nothing.

And she certainly wouldn't dream of jeopardizing her long-term relationship with Kate's new family by fucking her best friend's brand-new brother-in-law. He wasn't some random guy she met in a bar who could give her a nice anonymous fuck. She was going to know him for the rest of her life, which made him complicated.

Not just complicated.

Forbidden.

But that didn't mean it was going to be easy to refuse him.

Jean-Christian Rousseau was the epitome of a beautiful bastard—a gorgeous specimen of a male, a man so eminently fuckable in every way, it physically pained her that she couldn't let it happen when she'd lowered the bar for far-less-deserving men.

Letting her eyes flick to his for just a moment, she scowled at him and watched as his dark-green eyes lit with amusement. Deep inside, under the bridesmaid dress and the silk lingerie she'd bought for Kate's wedding, she felt a heat, a blissful pressure in her core, her muscles clenching and relaxing as she turned away from her nemesis, feigning disgust.

Well, partially, anyway.

He was brutally hot. It would be impossible to be disgusted with his tall, muscular body, Henry Cavill good looks, sexy smile, slight French accent, and easy, charming manners.

But when Libitz looked just beneath the surface of the stunning packaging, disgust wasn't far behind or difficult for her to find and grasp. He was also an opportunist, a sexist, and a possible misogynist. From all accounts, he ploughed (literally) through women like a wrecking ball taking out fifty-seven floors with a single swing. It happened fast, and he was long gone after the destruction.

How did she know this?

Well, she knew what she'd been told by Kate and Stratton—that his list of conquests was substantial, leaving more than one disappointed woman behind—but more importantly, she knew his type: beautiful, charming, self-centered, self-serving men who thought with their dicks.

How many hearts had he broken?

A million, she'd bet. Or more.

And the funny thing was? If you asked him, he'd probably say, "None." He probably assumed that because he wasn't interested and made it clear, it staunched any interest or expectations on the side of his partners. Stupid, selfish man. Women didn't work like that.

At any rate, it wasn't her business how many hearts he'd broken, only that hers would *not* be among them.

Unfortunately, however, with a man like J.C. Rousseau, the stronger she was in her refusal, the more ruthless he would likely be in his pursuit. At this point, after two solid days of rolling her eyes and ignoring his come-ons, she was a juicy bone and he was a dirty dog with one thought in his very teeny, tiny mind: to eat her whole.

Libitz just hoped the weekend ran out of time before it all came to a head, because she had experience with men like J.C. Rousseau, and when they didn't get what they wanted, it rarely ended well. For whatever reason, he'd chosen her as his target for the weekend, and she sensed that he wasn't going to back off . . . which meant that eventually he'd run out of patience, call her a "bitch" or worse, and either cause a scene or create a rift between himself and his new sister-in-law, who wouldn't stand for Lib's abuse.

And that was the antithesis of everything Libitz wanted both for Kate and for herself. She wanted KK to have a happy life with her new family, smooth and full of love at this tender beginning. And Lib, who also wanted a permanent place in Kate's new life, didn't especially want to piss off her brother-in-law out of the gate.

She glared at him as Kate and Étienne kissed and the crowd cheered with applause, because she resented him for putting her in this position.

Why couldn't he find someone else to bother?

Sighing with annoyance, she collected herself just in time to watch Kate and Étienne turn around as the priest announced that they were husband and wife. She beamed at her friend with a lifetime's worth of affection and offered the bride her bouquet.

I love you, mouthed KK to her best friend before turning to her new husband with a look of such utter and complete happiness, Libitz's heart clutched with longing.

She stood, nearly limp with yearning, watching as Kate and Étienne laced their hands together and walked up the aisle to Mendelssohn. Her eyes burned. Her lips quivered.

Luckily, J.C. was there to shatter the magical spell woven by Kate's happiness.

"Hey, Elsa," he said, nudging her bony hip with his elbow, "ready to go?"

"My name isn't Elsa," she said, fixing a smile on her face as she reluctantly took his elbow and started down the altar steps to the middle aisle of the church.

"Really? Because I could have sworn you were an ice princess."

"Ah! You're referencing a character from a Disney cartoon movie. Meant for children. Right about at your level, huh?"

He waved with his free hand at someone he knew before tipping his head closer to hers. "Actually, I just thought I'd bring things down to your level, Princess. Basic and cold."

She chuckled acidly, winking at a friend from Trinity. "Any woman who doesn't do a split on your dick is an ice princess, huh?"

"*Quoi!* Did you just say 'dick'?"

"You heard me," she said through clenched teeth, waving at her mother.

"You're going to make me hard," he murmured.

"No great feat there," she answered back, relieved to be nearing the rear vestibule of the church.

"You know we're sitting together at the reception, right?"

When they'd cleared the sanctuary, she whipped her arm away and faced him. "Must be my lucky day."

"It could be. If you'd just let it happen," he said, leaning so close to her, she could feel his warm breath on her cheek and the throb of her pulse in her throat.

Why do you have to be so fucking hot?

"Not cold enough," she whispered near his ear, forcing herself to take a step away from him even though his soft, seductive words came perilously close to making her rethink her resolve not to fuck him.

A door opened to their left, and they turned in unison to see Kate emerging from a small bride's room at the back of the church, where she'd fixed her lipstick and veil.

"Lib!" she cried. "I did it! I'm married!"

Libitz held out her arms and gathered Kate in her embrace as she narrowed her eyes at J.C., who stood behind Kate, beaming at Libitz with a wolfish glint in his eyes. "You did it, KK. You're a Rousseau now."

Chapter 2

J.C. inadvertently avoided Libitz for most of the reception, trapped with family visiting from France who wanted to catch up with him while his parents greeted the hundreds of guests in the receiving line. He kept an eye on her, however, watching her face relax from uptight to merry around a handful of Trinity friends by the bar. She laughed a lot, keeping a knuckle on her hip while her other hand held a glass of Cabernet at an exquisite right angle. At first glance, she appeared *all* angles, this petite, prickly woman—sharp and obtuse, acute and right.

The softness in her, he learned through observation, was concentrated in her face—in her almost-too-big brown eyes and pillowed lips, in the rounded peaches of her cheeks when she smiled, and in the warmth in her expression when she chuckled with a friend.

She was angular, yes, but not wholly without curves, he realized, even if they weren't the obvious ones that he was used to. Something about that realization made him feel . . . fortunate. It was a little bit like how he'd felt the first time he'd seen a Picasso up close—like he was seeing something very precious that not everyone got to see, something special that could be easily missed if one didn't take an extra moment to look closely.

One of her prep-school chums put his arm around her slight shoulders, pulling her close for a photo, and J.C. flinched, a sudden burst of acid souring his stomach as he instinctively flexed the knuckles of his left hand.

"Looks like someone stole the march on you, Jean-Christian," said his second cousin Luc, a Montferrat relation on his mother's side.

J.C. shifted his gaze away from Libitz and her handsy fucking admirer. He wasn't familiar with the expression his much older cousin had just used. "Sir?"

"You look ready to fight off Satan."

He scowled. "What do you mean?"

"Narrowed eyes." He flicked a glance at J.C.'s hand. "Clenched fist. Scowl. *Cherchez la femme*."

Cherchez la femme? It translated directly to "Look for the woman," but J.C. sensed it was a French idiom—one with which he was unfamiliar. He searched his cousin's amused eyes, trying to figure out what the hell he was talking about. Look for the woman? *What* woman? Libitz? Ha!

Luc chuckled knowingly and J.C.'s scowl deepened—not because of a woman, but because Luc was using archaic expressions that didn't mean jack shit, and it was annoying. But as bad luck would have it, Luc was not only his elder but a guest.

J.C. relaxed his fist and shrugged. "Not sure what you mean."

Luc's eyes trailed deliberately to Libitz and then back to J.C. "Ah, but I think you do."

He followed his cousin's glance and found Libitz standing about a foot away from the guy who'd been mauling her a moment before for the camera. Releasing a breath he hadn't realized he was holding, he gestured to the bar with his chin. "I need a refill. You?"

"No, thanks." Luc cocked his head to the side. "But good luck."

"With what?" asked J.C., feeling beyond irritated as Luc winked at him before wandering away to chat with more Montferrat and Roche cousins across the room.

"*Casse-toi*," J.C. growled in Luc's direction before heading toward the bar.

Swirling the ice in the bottom of his glass, he shook off the awkward exchange with his cousin, waving to a friend with whom he'd been at Princeton but not bothering to stop and chat. He ordered a scotch on the rocks, then pivoted slightly to find the frosty maid of honor standing to his right with her back to him.

Turning back to the bartender with a grin, he ordered a lowball glass full of ice.

"With . . . ?"

"Nothing," said J.C. "Just the ice."

The bartender gave him a look but filled a lowball glass with ice cubes, placing it on the bar beside the scotch. J.C. nodded his thanks and picked up both. As he passed by Libitz, he "accidentally" spilled several of the cubes into the concave of her back.

"Ah!" She gasped in shock, whipping around to face him. "Did *you* do that?!"

"What?"

Her eyes shot to the glass of ice in his hand, wiggling to release the cold cubes from where they must have lodged between her lower back and the dress.

"Did you just put ice cubes down my back?!" she asked, her voice just shy of a shriek, intense in expression but low in actual decibel.

Damn, but she's fiery.

He shrugged, taking a sip of scotch. "One might have slipped from the glass as I turned around, but I certainly didn't—"

"Save it," she hissed as two cubes plunked on the ground by her satin shoes. "Follow me."

Without excusing herself from her friends, who had watched the exchange with interest, she hustled away, her heels clacking furiously along the edge of Le Chateau's ballroom. Without thinking, J.C. followed her, barely able to conceal his grin as she made her way through a set of open doors at the end of the room that led outside. She didn't stop until she reached the ornate cement balustrade of the West Terrace. When she turned to face him, her arms were crossed, her face fierce.

He placed the glasses on a table just outside the door, then straightened, staring back at her in the moonlight.

"What do you want from me?" she demanded.

"What do I . . . *want*?"

"You've been staring at me and coming on to me for two days. And despite the fact that I'm *clearly* not interested, you show no signs of stopping. So what'll it take? What do I have to do to get you to cut it out and leave me the fuck alone?"

It was a good question.

Such a good question.

But unfortunately, he was too distracted to give her a quick answer. Her huge spirit was in such contrast to her tiny body, for a moment he wondered how she contained it. This close and this alone, the physical differences between them were startling: she wasn't more than five feet tall and couldn't weigh much more than one hundred pounds, while J.C. cleared six feet and weighed in at almost two hundred pounds.

Reminded of a line from William Shakespeare's *A Midsummer Night's Dream*, he whispered distractedly, "*Though she be but little, she is fierce!*"

She dragged a sharp breath through her lips, and her eyes flashed and narrowed, but she didn't respond, holding her pose, staring up at him, waiting for him to answer her question. He chuckled softly at her bravado. If he wanted to, he could break her in half like a twig, and yet there she stood—eyes furious, arms crossed, so fucking pissed, so fucking indomitable and strong, she was . . . magnificent.

And again he wondered, as he had last night, *What would it take to make an impression on you?*

Without consciously coaxing the image to mind, he had a sudden mental fantasy of tongue fucking her—of her laid out, spread eagle–style on his bed, her tawny skin bare, her smart mouth open in a perfect *O* as he razed her tender clit with his teeth then shoved his tongue between her legs to lave the inside of her sex until she screamed.

That would make a fucking impression, ice princess, wouldn't it?

Two fingers appeared an inch shy of his nose and snapped twice. "Earth to Jean-Christian."

Merde. He flinched in shock, stepping back from her. "Don't fucking snap at me."

Her hands landed on the nonexistent flare of her hips as she fearlessly stared up at him. "Then answer the fucking question!"

His cock jumped at her bossy fucking tone, blood sluicing from all over his body to unexpectedly stiffen it. Letting his eyes drop to her breasts, which looked slightly bigger because her arms were crossed under them, he deliberately gaped for several seconds before raising his glance slowly and smirking at her.

"Ask me again."

"What. Will. It. Take. For. You. To. Leave. Me. Alone?"

This time his eyes fixed on her pink lips, which were glistening and glossy in the dim light.

"A kiss," he murmured, the words coming from nowhere.

"What?"

"A kiss. Yeah," he said, leaning into the idea quickly and stepping closer to her, so close she had to tilt her head back to look up at him. "Give me a kiss and I'll leave you alone."

"That's ridiculous," she answered, though her voice was slightly weaker than it had been a moment before. "I'm not going to kiss you. Choose something else."

"No."

She took a sharp breath, averting her eyes from his for a moment before looking up at him again.

"I won't *give* you one. But if it'll get you off my back, you can kiss me."

"What's the difference?"

"Giving versus taking."

"But I don't just want to take," he said, his voice dropping to gravel. "I want you to give too."

"Why?" she asked, her forehead creasing with annoyance.

His heart thumped faster, and his cock, which was already pressing uncomfortably against the zipper of his tuxedo pants with intense arousal, throbbed. "Because I want you to participate."

A small noise—so small, he would have missed it if they hadn't been standing so close—issued from her throat, and when he flicked his glance downward for a moment, he realized that her chest, small though it was, heaved with every breath she took, her nipples straining against the thin, silky fabric of the bridesmaid dress.

He dragged his eyes back up her body, lingering on the pale skin of her delicate throat, stopping at her lips, which were softly parted, then finally slid his gaze to hers.

"So?" he prompted. "What'll it be?"

"One kiss," she confirmed.

To start. He nodded.

"One kiss and you'll leave me alone for the rest of the weekend," she said, her eyes dropping to his lips as she wetted her own.

"Sure. But you won't want me to . . . leave you alone," he teased, unable to keep his lips from grinning as her arousal became more plain to him.

She jerked her eyes back to his, the fire in their depths telling him she'd let him rot in hell before ever asking for another.

"One kiss," she said. Raising her angular little chin, she nodded once. "Fine."

The closeness of him—the proximity of his body—was making her breathless.

Fuck him for oozing sexy from every pore, like if she licked his skin, he'd *taste* like it. This would be so much easier if she wasn't attracted to him, because she could give him one kiss and walk away from him forever like it never happened. But she had a dreadful, aching feeling that if she kissed Jean-Christian Rousseau, it would be an experience she'd never be able to forget.

Unfortunately, it was too late for misgivings.

She'd already agreed.

And besides, she needed him to leave her alone. Her relationship with KK trumped all, and it certainly trumped a cheap fuck at a wedding with her brand-new brother-in-law. They weren't going to "happen"—no how, no way—and the sooner he understood that, the better.

Taking a step forward, she raised her palms and slowly, slowly placed them on his chest, first the pads of her fingers, then the heels of her hands, until finally they rested, flush and full, against the crisp white linen of his shirt. Beneath her right palm, she could feel the thundering of his heart, and she furrowed her brows in confusion, wondering why it was beating so fast if this was just a game to him and she was just a plaything. Before she could muse on the topic any further, however, she felt the curve of his finger under her chin, lifting her head back so that she gazed up at him.

His eyes, so dark-green as to appear black in the moonlight, stared down at her, searching her eyes for a long moment—much longer than needed for a kiss that meant nothing—as he repeated softly, *"Though she be but little . . ."*

It was her favorite quote of all time, and one that she had had professionally painted in chic white script on her powder-pink bedroom wall years ago when she moved to New York City. Hearing it now, issuing from his lips a second time in a handful of seconds, made her heart clutch and stutter unexpectedly, and she gasped a breath of surprise, holding it as his lips descended, with unerring precision, to hers.

. . . she be fierce.

His mouth sealed over hers as he swallowed her exhalation of breath, his tongue exploring the seal between their lips with an unexpected gentleness that made her fingers curl lightly into his shirt, and she stepped tiptoe onto his shoes to even out their height difference and press her body closer to his.

She felt the hard ridge of his erection immediately, and his hands, which had been cupping her face, slid down her back to cup her ass, forcing her closer so that the soft inward curve of her sex cradled the bulging hardness of his.

Ring.

Their kiss became hotter and more desperate, Jean-Christian's tongue sliding against the length of hers as his hands kneaded her backside, pushing her close as he thrust against her hard enough that she felt the pressure of his rigid cock, through layers of clothing, against her clit.

Ring.

Something's ringing. The thought slipped into her mind for a moment, then exited just as quickly as his palm, wide and sure, slid up the left side of her body, stopping just under her breast. He tilted his head, changing the angle of their kiss, and Libitz arched her back, inviting him to touch her more intimately.

Ring.

His hand slipped boldly into the bodice of her dress, the heat of his palm covering the flesh of her breast as his thumb and forefinger found her painfully erect nipple and rolled it. Fire spread like lava, red-hot liquid heat, deep inside her body, invading her core and saturating her sex. She moaned into his mouth, returning his thrust as he clutched her ass and pushed her forward into his cock again.

Ring.

"Fuck!" he bellowed, ripping his mouth away from hers.

Panting with need as she opened her eyes, she felt his hand slip quickly from her breast as he reached into his back pocket for his phone. With one hand, he pressed a button on the screen and held it to his ear, while the other held her to him, an uncompromising band around her waist.

"*What?*" he roared, his eyes fierce as they stared into hers from an inch away, his massive erection still straining against her pelvis. "This better be good, Jax," he grated out. "I'm *with* someone."

She couldn't hear his sister through the line because her blood was rushing so fast in her ears, she could only hear its whooshing, accompanied by the wild beating of her heart.

"Walk," he growled, tightening his arm around Libitz, his breath hot where it landed in jagged pants on her cheek and nose.

Libitz's hands were trapped between them, still flattened on his chest, but now, as she realized what had just happened—how far from a single kiss in the moonlight they'd wandered—she pushed against him, trying to shove him away.

His eyes narrowed and he tightened his arm again, refusing to yield.

"*Moi*? *I'm* the asshole?" he said into the phone, though his eyes nailed her, and Libitz wondered if he was speaking to her as well. She pushed at the muscles of his chest again, but his arm flexed around her, trapping her against him. "Try again."

"Release me," she hissed.

He looked angry, his eyes boring into hers as his slick lips tightened into an unhappy slit. Struggling to back out of his arms, she mashed her heel into his shoes, and he finally loosened her, covering the phone with his palm.

"What's the problem?"

"No problem."

"We don't have to stop."

"Yes," she said firmly, "we do."

"Why?"

Because you're my best friend's brother-in-law, and I want to be in her life forever, and fucking you on day one isn't going to do either of us any favors. Besides, she hadn't expected to lose herself so completely in his kiss. Her brain was still swimming. Her body was still pulsating. She'd barely escaped, and now that her eyes were open again, she needed to get away from him.

"We agreed on one kiss," she said. "We kissed. It's over."

"It doesn't have to be."

Her body throbbed with need, but her mind was more and more in control and issued a final warning that she couldn't ignore: *He is the worst possible candidate for a fling. Stop this. Now. With big guns, if that's what it takes.*

"I only kissed you to get you off my back." She smirked at him. "I don't *want* you."

"Yes, you do. It's obvious," he said, but he flinched before he said it like maybe he wasn't sure, and it gave her just enough doubt to straighten her back, aim, and fire.

"If you touch me again, it will be *without* my permission," she said, every word precise and meaningful. "*Obvious* enough for you, Romeo?"

Recognizing her words for the warning and threat they were, he flinched again, his whole body stiffening, his eyes growing icy as he stared down at her, searching her face to ascertain the severity of her meaning, ugly words like *assault* and *rape* passing invisibly between them and souring the sweet night air.

Her conscience pinched a little, but she remained firm in her refusal of him, even as he raked his eyes down her body, stopping at the breast he'd caressed so intimately and eyeing it with disdain.

Finally, he eased his palm away from the phone, staring into her eyes and purring, "It was a slice of heaven, *petite*. I'll call you sometime."

Sarcasm was thick and mean in his tone, and he licked his lips provocatively, a premediated gesture meant to make her feel slutty and small. A debonair dismissal. A line he'd told a thousand women a thousand times, meant to remind Libitz that she was a tiny blip on the landscape of his conquests. And a kiss that had momentarily rocked her landscape was actually just . . . nothing. She knew that's what his words and gestures were trying to convey.

And yet . . . his eyes were intense, despite his efforts to relax them. With a man who had a modicum of respect for women, she might have wondered if it was a defensive move—if maybe a kiss that had been utterly intoxicating to her had unexpectedly been the same for him. But with a predator like J.C., who, according to people she trusted implicitly, cared about his own pleasure and nothing else?

These were words and gestures purely meant to one-up her refusal of him and make her feel dirty. It was a good strategy on his part. It worked.

"I hope not," she murmured, ignoring the flush of heat in her cheeks as she adjusted the bodice of her dress and took another step away from him. "I hope *never*."

His eyes flashed with anger.

"*Tu vas fermer ta putain de gueule*," he growled softly into the phone.

She'd learned enough French curse words at prep school to know that he'd just said, "Shut your fucking mouth," and she gasped softly at the lewdness of his language, wholly uncertain if he was talking to his sister or to her.

Only one thing *was* certain: J.C. Rousseau was a mine-field of a man—nothing about him was simple or genuine. He was complicated and ruthless, smart and devastatingly sexual. And yet Libitz was drawn to him, fascinated by him, her body still throbbing, her heart still fluttering. Even now, both of them having rejected each other and exchanged insults meant to sting, she felt more raw lust for him than she'd ever felt for anyone.

In all her life, Libitz had never run from anyone, yet she felt an overwhelming urge to flee from J.C. Rousseau—to get away from him and never look back. It took all her strength to stand her ground and wait for him to hang up his phone so they could settle their business and go their separate ways.

"I'll be there in five," he spoke into the phone, still staring at Libitz with cold, narrow eyes. "You owe me."

Without looking away from Libitz, he tapped on the phone and put it in his pocket. He was angry. She knew he was angry, yet his eyes seemed to soften a little as he tilted his head to the side and looked at her like he couldn't quite figure her out.

"So that's it?"

"That's it. One kiss."

"But it was good, *n'est-ce pas*?"

Her lips parted in surprise.

The unexpected gentleness in his voice caught her off guard, confused her, moved her even, but she'd already decided, long before this moment on a terrace in the moonlight, that J.C. Rousseau was off limits for her, and she had no interest in rethinking that conviction now.

She shrugged with ennui, hoping she looked much more dismissive than she felt inside. "I've had better."

He clenched his jaw, his quick temper flaring, his last vestiges of patience or gentleness gone. "You're a bitch."

"I've been called worse," she replied, refusing to let him see that his words stung.

"I feel sorry for the man that falls for you," he lashed out, clenching his fists by his sides.

And though she didn't take the time to dwell on it, somewhere deep in Libitz's mind, she marked the moment, because his reaction felt . . . off. It felt far more emotional than it *should* be.

"That's your prerogative."

He sniffed, his expression mean. "You're skinny, flat, hard, and cold. You're not my type anyway."

Her stomach fell, and she had to swallow forcibly over the lump that rose up in her throat, but she raised her chin and narrowed her eyes. "And you're disgusting, egomaniacal, and think you're God's gift to women, but volume doesn't equal skill."

"So we basically hate each other," he muttered.

"Pretty much," she whispered.

Feeling strangely and unaccountably miserable, she gulped, unable to look into his eyes anymore. She glanced over her shoulder at the happy couples dancing in the ball-room, blinking her eyes rapidly.

"That said, my best friend just married your . . ."

She turned back to finish what she was saying, but he was already gone, a lone figure striding across the dark lawn, farther and farther away with every second.

Libitz took a ragged breath, reaching up to wipe at her eyes. Wait. Tears? Tears for *him* when she almost never cried? Oh, no. No, no, no. That was *not* okay.

"Stop it," she hissed, closing her eyes and inhaling again, a smoother and deeper breath this time.

When she opened her eyes, he was gone from view. Her tears dried up quickly as she thought about the hateful words they'd exchanged, though surprisingly, they didn't bother her as much as they probably would another woman. They'd each said hurtful things, meant to prey on each other's insecurities with a practiced finesse on both sides. In a strange way, they canceled each other out, and she almost marveled at the skill it took to verbally spar so evenly with someone. In a grudging admission of respect, she had to recognize that part of her—a very sick and cerebral part of her—had even enjoyed it, up to and including the insults he thought would hurt the most.

She took a deep, even breath and exhaled into the night.

All that remained now was the fading taste of him in her mouth and the throbbing of her heart as she thought about their kiss. The way her body had reacted to him—blossoming, opening, arching closer, reaching for him like she was a sunflower and he was the sun. She couldn't remember *ever* responding to a man with such vulnerability, like they were plugged into each other in a way that was safe and real.

For just a moment, she wondered what it would have been like to give in . . . to sleep with him. And for that moment, her heart trembled with such unfulfilled longing, it almost flattened her, because . . .

You're a bitch . . . and . . . *we basically hate each other.*

Now she'd never know.

But at least she'd been strong, and their anger toward each other would eventually fade, wouldn't it? Of course it would. And in the meantime, she hadn't fucked her best friend's brand-new brother-in-law, which meant that she had no regrets.

At least that's what she told herself as she turned back to Kate's wedding, walking into a room of joyful revelry with an unexpectedly heavy heart.

Chapter 3

"I can't believe it's been almost a month since your wedding!" cried Libitz, jumping up to close the door of her office so that she could talk on the phone to KK without interruption. "How was the honeymoon?"

"Heaven," said Kate, her voice gooey, and Libitz could perfectly picture her best friend's dreamy expression.

"Mooréa. God, that's so romantic. I followed your pics on Facebook, but you have to tell me everything!"

"I will. I promise," she said. Kate paused, and when she spoke again, her voice had gotten very serious very quickly. "But, Lib . . . I have something else to tell you first."

Libitz had been straightening the orders and invoices on her desk, but now she froze, worried by the grave tone of KK's voice. "Wha—I mean . . . is everything okay?"

Kate sighed. "Are you sitting down?"

Libitz lowered her hands to the edge of her desk and sat down as a shot of adrenaline made her heart race into high gear. "Now I am. Kate, you're scarin—"

"I'm having a baby!" shrieked Kate, all pretense gone as joy warmed her voice. "I'm sixteen weeks pregnant!"

Libitz's eyes flew open as she slumped back into her chair and sighed loudly. "You scared the shit out of me!"

"Ha ha!" Kate giggled. "Sorry! I didn't want you to guess, and you're so freaky about always knowing exactly what I'm thinking, so I . . . oh, Lib, I'm sorry. Are you okay?"

Libitz laughed, nodding her head and sitting up. "Yeah. I'm okay. And you're . . . KK, you're pregs? Wait a second! Sixteen weeks? You were pregnant at your wedding!"

"Pays to be fuller-figured once in a while," said Kate. "No one knew. Étienne and I decided to keep it a secret until after the honeymoon."

"A baby," sighed Libitz. "Oh, my God, Kate. You're going to be a mom! Soon!"

"Uh-huh," said Kate. "Christmastime."

"Chanukah-time," corrected Libitz.

"The *best* time," said Kate. "And Lib, we just found out this morning . . . we're having a girl."

Libitz didn't expect the sob that escaped from her throat, but her eyes swelled with tears as she pictured her best friend holding a beautiful baby girl. "KK. That's amazing." She sniffled softly, sitting up in her chair and wiping her tears away. "But promise me you won't name her something seasonal like 'Holly' or 'Merry,' okay?"

"Too late!" Kate giggled, the sound so happy that Libitz chuckled too. "We already decided on Noelle."

Libitz groaned. "I should have guessed."

"We also decided something else . . ." Libitz took a deep breath, sensing the importance of whatever Kate was about to say. "We want you to be Noelle's godmother, Lib."

Her breath caught and she blinked back more tears. Though she would have insisted on being Noelle's surrogate auntie, she hadn't expected an honor this great.

"But Kate, I'm . . . *Jewish*."

"Same God," said Kate gently but firmly. "Besides, we checked. Since Jean-Christian is Catholic, you don't have to be."

The loud sound of tires screeching in her head made Libitz scowl.

"Wait. What? What does *he* have to do with it?"

"Oh," said Kate, giggling softly, "I forgot to mention. We want him to be Noelle's godfather. Étienne's talking to him tonight."

"But *why*?" blurted out Libitz, horrified at the idea of Kate's smarmy brother-in-law being allowed anywhere near her goddaughter. And God! She'd have to stand up next to him in a church again? Gah! No!

"Ummm"—Kate's voice was a mix of amused and bemused—"because he's her uncle? Who *else* would we choose?"

"Stratton?" demanded Libitz. "Barrett, Fitz, Alex, Wes?"

"I love them, but they're not—"

"Literally, *anyone else* on the face of the planet!"

"Lib, are you serious?"

"Yes! He's a . . . a reprobate. A letch. He's disgusting! You can't . . . I mean . . ." Libitz stopped talking, suddenly realizing what she was saying and to whom. "I just mean . . ."

"You don't know everything about him," said Kate with quiet conviction.

"I know all I need to know."

"I wish you'd tell me what went down between you two at the wedding," said Kate, some of the previous warmth missing from her voice.

Libitz bit her upper lip, considering Kate's words, but then decided against saying any more about the relentless way he'd pursued her only to end their beautiful kiss with a scathing shower of verbal abuse.

"Nothing, KK. Seriously. It was nothing."

"Did you two . . . ?"

"No! Absolutely not."

"Because I know that you both, you know . . ."

"We're both a little slutty?" supplied Libitz. "Fair enough. But no. We didn't fuck, Kate. I promised you we wouldn't."

More importantly, I promised myself. And thank God. How could I face him across the baptismal font if I'd banged him at KK's wedding?

"You know I don't judge . . . but it would make things awkward, Lib."

"I know that," said Libitz, "which is why we didn't. I promise. We just—we don't get along."

Kate was quiet for a few minutes before she spoke again. "Can you try harder? For Noelle's sake?"

Libitz's lips softened, turning up in a smile as she thought about her goddaughter, growing safely but surely within her best friend's body. She breathed deeply, thinking of how much she would love that little girl, taking her to Broadway shows and the American Girl store for tea. They'd get their toes painted together, and Aunt Libby would shower her with gifts. She'd be Noelle's auntie, a special friend . . . her godmother. Oh, God. Her heart ached with the goodness of it.

"Of course," she said. "I'll slay dragons for Noelle, and you know it." *I can certainly put up with Jean-Christian Rousseau.*

Kate laughed, all the warmth returning to her voice. "I know that. You were my only choice. Étienne said we could ask Stratton and Mad instead, but I insisted on you. I love Mad, but it *had* to be you, Lib. It just . . . it *had* to be."

For the third time in their conversation, Libitz's eyes welled with tears, and she sniffled again, clearing her throat. "Well then, it's settled. Now stop making me cry and tell me all about the jungle sex you and Ten had in Mooréa!"

"I paid over a million dollars for it," said J.C. evenly, sitting back in his desk chair and feeling annoyed. The office at his gallery was dark, and he was going to be late to Jax's if he didn't get a move on. "I expect it here on time."

"Rousseau-san," said Hiroto, his art dealer in Tokyo, "it isn't that simple. It was flagged in customs, and now—"

"Not my problem," said J.C., glancing at his watch. "Have it here in Philadelphia by tomorrow or keep it and return my million. Clear, Hiroto-san?"

"*Hai.* It will be done."

J.C. placed the receiver back in the cradle and shuffled the papers on his desk back into a file folder with an irritated sigh. He'd paid $1.2 million for the 1967 Kusama, and he had someone coming up from Washington, DC, to retrieve it on Monday. He wasn't about to lose the sale due to Hiroto's ineptitude.

His phone buzzed as he stood up from his desk, and he glanced down at the screen to find a group text his sister had sent to her siblings.

JACQUELINE ROUSSEAU: Dinner. 8:00pm. Don't be late.
JACQUELINE ROUSSEAU: And, J.C., I want to show you something. Remind me.

His little sister had gotten bossier since settling down last month with her new fiancé, Gardener Thibodeaux. All things considered, however, J.C. was happy to see her with someone who was so crazy about her. Fuck, Gard had actually pissed away most of his trust fund buying Le Chateau, their childhood home, for Jax. If that wasn't love, J.C. didn't know what was.

Not that he knew anything about love.

He didn't.

And that was the way he wanted it.

Except . . .

Since his brother's wedding last month, he'd felt a subtle shift in himself. Fucking Felicity had gotten stale, so he'd been making more excuses to get out of seeing her. He craved something different, something challenging and more exciting, something that didn't come so easy and feel so cheap. He just didn't know how, or where, to find it.

But tonight—the first time his entire family would be reunited at Le Chateau since the wedding? Tonight felt a little weird for him. Étienne was married to Kate. Jax was engaged to Gard. Even Mad, who returned this morning from a week in London with her new boyfriend, Cort Ambler, seemed to have her eye on settling down. That left J.C. still free as a bird, fucking whomever he wanted and committing to none. Is that what he wanted forever?

He was thirty-four years old, and he'd never—not in almost twenty years of adulthood—had a mature, loving, committed relationship. He hadn't allowed it. And at this point, he didn't even know if he'd be able to figure out how.

So fuck it. There was no point thinking about it.

He sighed, standing up from his desk and flicking off the light as he left his office and closed the door behind him. In the dim light of the gallery, he moved slowly, checking out the paintings and sculptures, allowing his guard to fall, allowing warmth and wonder to fill his heart. His eyes followed bold contours and sought out subtle shading in a Picasso original. He stopped under a mobile made from Swarovski crystals and let a rainbow of twinkle lights shower him like a blessing. Shifting his gaze to a colorful Kandinsky, he felt the joy of the childlike technicolor brushstrokes as he continued toward the door. But as he did every night, he stopped by the Andrew Atroshenko portrait of a ballerina he'd tucked securely into a dark nook by the door about a month ago and stared.

The angles of her body—of the arm raised over her head, of one leg flexed almost perfectly behind her, of the flat plane of her chest in a close-fitting, corseted, white satin bodice—made his body tighten and his eyes widen. She was exquisite. Sublime. She was nowhere near the most expensive piece in his gallery, but she was among the most precious to J.C., filling him with an almost painful melancholy as he bid adieu to her every night.

"You shouldn't have called her a bitch," he muttered to himself softly before turning quickly away, punching his code in the security pad and closing the front door behind him.

"Neil!" called Libitz, rising from her desk with a grin to embrace her boyfriend, whom she'd been dating for a little over three weeks.

Neil Leibowitz, to whom her mother had introduced her at a cocktail party almost a year ago, had gently pursued Libitz for months, calling her every four to six weeks to ask if she'd join him for dinner, a concert in the park, a Mets game, or a movie. Each time he made a different suggestion, and each time Libitz politely refused. But when he called her on the Sunday night she returned from Kate's wedding, she'd suddenly accepted his invitation, making them both stutter in surprise.

"W-wait! Did you just say yes?"

"I guess I did."

"Did you mean to?"

No. Not really. She had no idea where the word "yes" had come from, but she decided to roll with it. "Yes, I'd love to go to a winetasting with you, Neil."

"Libitz," he'd said, laughter thick in his Brooklyn-accented voice, "if I'd-a known a winetasting would make you say yes, I would've suggested it last October!"

She'd laughed politely, though if he'd asked her a moment before, she couldn't have actually told him what sort of date she'd finally accept. Something within her just felt desperate to do something, to go somewhere, to move on, to say yes to someone.

As he entered her office, kissed her cheek, and gathered her in his arms, Libitz closed her eyes and breathed deeply. Per usual, Neil smelled comfortingly of vanilla, which was, he claimed, part of his charm. His grandfather and father had started their family-run company, Baked Kosher of New York, back in the 1960s, and fifty years later, Neil and his brother, Aaron, who'd attended NYU's Stern School of Business together, were being groomed to take it over.

It was a successful business that supplied fresh-baked challah to bakeries all over New York, New Jersey, and Connecticut, in addition to temples and synagogues that ordered the loaves by the dozens for Shabbat fellowship dinners. And Neil's position as vice-president of operations afforded him an extremely comfortable lifestyle: a Crown Heights townhouse with four bedrooms and a private garden and a house in the Hamptons he co-owned with Aaron. He never arrived to pick her up without a huge bouquet of fresh flowers and, of course, loaves of freshly baked bread—one for her and one for her parents.

Her mother called Neil a *mensch*, which, translated from Yiddish, meant she thought he was a good man—a "catch" for her only daughter—and Libitz supposed he was. He was a grown-up (unlike some people from recent memory). He was also polite and earnest, serious and focused—the sort of man who'd be a good provider and loyal husband. He'd take their sons to see the Mets on summer Saturdays and take Libitz to Paris for their anniversaries. Life would be comfortable and safe with Neil.

And then, one day, after Mahjongg at his mother's house with the girls, you'll pick up a gun and blow your brains out from sheer boredom.

Wincing from the rawness of the thought, she swallowed, leaning away from him, careful to conceal the sharp disappointment she felt inside. The last thing she wanted to do was hurt Neil. She'd sooner drown puppies or pull the wings off butterflies.

"So?" she asked brightly, forcing a pleasant mood. "What are we up to tonight?"

He grinned at her, pushing his glasses back up to the bridge of his nose and reaching into the back pocket of his black slacks. He held up two tickets.

"I was thinking . . . Shakespeare in the Park."

"Neil!" she exclaimed, feeling genuinely excited and guilty for her previous thoughts. Neil *wasn't* boring. She'd mentioned on their previous date that she loved Shakespeare and here was Neil, *thoughtful* Neil, doing something chosen especially for her. He was solid and kind and dependable, and those were good things. Excellent things. "Which play?"

He waggled his eyebrows in a move that he probably thought was charming but made Libitz groan and sigh inside.

"*A Midsummer Night's Dream!*"

With startling speed, her mind segued back to Kate's wedding reception, to a deep, lightly accented French voice—*Though she be but little, she is fierce!*—J.C.'s lips on hers, his palm cupping the fullness of her breast, his fingers rolling her nipple, his erection straining against her drenched sex, his—

"Libitz?" questioned Neil, reaching out to touch her arm.

"What?" she whispered, reaching up to palm her cheeks and drop her gaze to the floor.

Today Kate had invited her to a housewarming party over the upcoming Labor Day weekend. She and Étienne were buying an estate not far from where Étienne grew up, and Libitz promised that she would go down to Philly for the weekend to help set up Noelle's nursery and spend some time with Kate.

After they'd hung up, for most of the afternoon, Libitz had been distracted by the idea that she'd be seeing J.C. again in a few short weeks. Moments of breathless anticipation and excitement would follow furious promises to herself not to go anywhere near J.C. unless it was absolutely beyond avoidance.

While perusing the first draft of her gallery's new catalog for fall, she lost herself in memories of his tongue sliding against hers, the way it felt to be trapped in the strength of his embrace, his heart beating wildly under her flattened palms. Then, just as she was about to search for him on Facebook, she'd jerked the computer plug out of the wall so she couldn't.

"Libitz? *A Midsummer Night's Dream*?"

"No," she answered softly, still distracted by a deluge of memories about a man she wanted to forget.

"No?"

She winced, lifting her eyes from her shoes and looking up at Neil as she lowered her hands. "I'm . . . sorry. I don't— I don't feel very well. My head aches . . ."

"You seemed fine a minute ago."

She took a deep breath and sighed, tilting her head to the side, searching his kind brown eyes. "You're too good for me, Neil."

He stared back at her for an unexpectedly intense moment before reaching for her hand. "Give me a chance, Lib. Don't cut me loose yet."

The simple sweetness of his words impacted her, and she tried to smile for him but found she couldn't. "But I should. I should cut you loose right now."

He shook his head. "Don't. Please don't."

Taking her other hand, he pulled her back against his chest, wrapping his arms around her and rubbing her back gently. "Forget the play. Let's go get a bowl of spaghetti, huh? A glass of Chianti? You don't even have to talk. I'll talk. You can ignore me if you want."

"What good would that be?" she asked, closing her eyes, finding herself calmed by the slow, even motion of his palm against her back.

"It'll be good for me," he said, "because you'll be sitting across from me."

She leaned back, looking into his hopeful face and feeling terrible that she was distracted by another man who was so woefully unequal to Neil.

"You're too—"

"—good for you?" he finished. "No."

Dropping his lips to hers, he kissed her gently for the first time. Lips to lips. No tongue. No demands. No passion. No control. Just a sweet touch of skin to skin to make her stop talking, to let her know that he wasn't ready to let go of her after only three weeks of dating. "I don't know if that's true, but I'm willing to take the risk. You?"

How could she say no? He was sweet and sturdy, selfless and simple, kind and thoughtful. He was everything that every woman could ever want, and fuck, but she wished it was enough.

She nodded. "Sounds nice."

He tore the tickets in half and placed the pieces on the edge of her desk. "Then let's get going."

J.C. had almost been late to dinner, but luckily the traffic had been leaner than usual, and he'd made it out of the city in good time. Pulling up to Le Chateau, he cut the engine and admired the flowers that someone had planted around the fountain in the center of the driveway. Looking up at the

front portico, he realized that the improvements in green-
ery didn't end there—large urns of flowers greeted him on
either side of the front door too.

He considered walking right in for a moment but thought
better of it. This wasn't his childhood home anymore. It
was Jax and Gard's home, and he needed to respect the new
owners by letting them welcome him.

He rang the bell and Jax swept open the double doors,
grinning from ear to ear at her eldest sibling. "*Bonsoir!*"

"*Bonsoir, doudou,*" he said, using a nickname that he'd
given the girls when they were little. He bussed each cheek
and inhaled deeply. "Gard's cooking?"

"Mm-hm. Gumbo."

"Thank fuck. The last time you cooked, I chipped a tooth
on the steak and lost a layer of skin, the corn was so hot."

He grinned at her to let her know he was teasing. As much
as J.C. and his siblings gave each other a hard time, they'd
die for each other too.

"I never claimed to be a chef," she said, relieving him of
the bottle of wine in his hands. "By the way, remind me to
show you something."

"What?" he asked, mildly curious, since this was the second time she'd mentioned it.

"Nothing. Just . . . a painting. I found it in the attic. It's
probably nothing, but . . ."

"But?"

"I don't know. There's something about it." She shrugged,
waving her free hand. "Later. For now, come and sit. Étienne
and Kate look like they're about to jump out of their skin. I
think they're moving, and they don't know how to tell us."

J.C. frowned, feeling unsettled, and followed Jax into the
game room, where J.C. had bested his little brother in every
Nintendo game known to man. This wasn't good news. He
liked having Ten, Jax, and Mad close. He'd go so far as to

admit he *needed* them close. He hated the idea of Ten and Kate moving away.

"Moving? Are you sure?"

"I don't know," said Jax in a singsong voice. "What *else* could it be? Étienne knows you'll freak if they move."

They entered through the double doors together, and Mad jumped up to hug her brother. "Hey, stranger."

"You look good, *petite*," said J.C., kissing her cheeks before looking into her eyes. "Had fun in London?"

Her complexion changed from pink to red, answering his question in a way that made him hope that Cort Ambler was serious about Mad and not just playing around. Because big fucking woe to Cort if he made Mad look like this and didn't follow through.

"Yes," she said. "Lots."

"When's he back?"

"Labor Day," she said, sighing with longing. "But he's coming home the weekend after next to see me."

"For how long?" asked J.C., nodding with approval.

"Long enough," said Mad cheekily. "I'm meeting him in New York from Friday to Sunday."

"If you need anything," said Kate from the couch, "I'll give you Lib's number."

"Thanks," said Mad, turning to smile at Kate. "How is Libitz? I barely got to talk to her at your wedding, but she seems so interesting!"

"She's great! I just talked to her this morning," said Kate, grinning meaningfully at Étienne before looking back at Mad, Jax, and J.C., who stood shoulder to shoulder before them. Kate giggled softly. "Do you want to tell them or should I?"

"My turn," said Étienne, kissing Kate's temple tenderly before standing up.

"So we wanted to tell you that—"

"You're moving!" cried Jax.

"No," said Ten, shaking his head, his face confused. "Well, actually, yes. We are. We're moving out of the city to a place we found here in Haverford, but—"

"We guessed it!" said Mad to her twin. "Well, we *knew* you were moving—"

"But we were afraid you were going farther away," said Jax, stepping forward to hug Étienne. "Thank God you're sticking around! We'll be neighbors!"

"Um," said Kate, standing up beside Étienne, "that isn't the only news."

"There's more?" asked J.C., who'd gotten momentarily distracted at the mention of Libitz, who was doing "great" and probably hadn't given him so much as a second thought since the wedding, while he'd been cursed with vibrant, all-too-frequent memories of her.

"What news?" Jax released her brother, stepping back to shift her eyes back and forth between Kate and Étienne. "Are you okay?"

"Oh, for heaven's sake!" growled Étienne. "Yes! I'm fine!"

"Then what is it?" asked Mad, concern written all over her face.

Kate took her husband's arm, grinning at her sisters and brother-in-law. "We're having a baby!"

Jax and Mad gasped in unison, and Étienne turned to look at his wife, caressing her face with his eyes before dropping a sweet kiss to her lips. "You stole my thunder, *chaton*."

"You were taking too long," she said, kissing him back.

Jax threw her arms around Étienne again, while Mad embraced Kate, and J.C., standing just behind his sisters, stared awkwardly at his celebrating siblings.

A baby.

His little brother was having a kid.

Over Jax's shoulder, Étienne looked up at him, and J.C. shook his head as though clearing it, then plastered a smile on his face, nodding at his brother with approval.

"*Félicitations*," he said, and Étienne reached for him, pulling him into the hug he was already sharing with Jax.

When Mad finally released her sister-in-law, J.C. hugged Kate gently, kissing her cheeks and wishing her congratulations, but inside he was reeling. This wasn't just Ten and Kate getting married or Jax and Mad finding serious boyfriends. This was a kid. A person. A new generation of Rousseaus. He was going to be someone's uncle. And it made his chest constrict with an uncomfortable, unfamiliar emotion that felt way too big for him to hold inside.

"Champagne!" exclaimed Mad, hurrying to the kitchen while Jax followed her to share the good news with Gard, leaving J.C. with the soon-to-be parents.

"I'm glad we have you alone for a second," said Étienne, sitting back down on the couch beside Kate and taking her hand in his. "There's something we wanted to ask you."

J.C. lowered himself onto the coffee table before them. "Anything you need."

"We need a godfather for Noelle," said Kate, her sweet lips smiling at him. "And we want it to be you."

"Who's Noelle?" he asked, staring back and forth between them, trying like fuck to process what was happening, what they were asking of him.

Étienne chuckled. "We didn't get to share that part yet. Kate's sixteen weeks along. We're having a girl."

J.C. gasped with surprise. "You already know?"

Kate nodded, placing her free hand over her belly. "We found out this morning."

"So Noelle is . . ."

"Our daughter," said Étienne, resting his hand gently over Kate's before looking back up at his brother. "Your niece."

"My . . ." *niece*. He couldn't even say it. It felt too strange. Too huge. One little word that expanded his heart, adding a little room next to Étienne's in his heart. "Wait. You're asking *me* to be your daughter's godfather? But . . ."

His heart started racing as he stared at them, their words, their request, taking shape in his mind. Not only his niece but his *goddaughter*. A little someone who would look up to him, look to him for protection and comfort, for guidance and direction, a little girl who would—

He flinched, sitting back from them.

No. Wait.

He thought about his track record with women, his penchant for screwing and leaving, his determination never to commit to anyone. What kind of a role model was he?

He looked up at his little brother gravely, panic making his lungs constrict. There was no way on God's green earth that he was the right man for the job.

"*Attends! Écoute, Étienne . . .*"

"*Non.*" Étienne reached out, putting his hand on his older brother's knee and locking eyes with him. "*Toi, Jean-Christian, seulement toi, mon frère.*"

You. Only you. My brother.

Étienne's eyes were severe—dark and strong and full of faith that Jean-Christian didn't feel he deserved.

"*Pourquoi? Pourquoi moi?*" asked J.C., thinking that there wasn't a worse person on earth to be the guardian of a little girl than him.

"Because you took care of me." Étienne sighed softly, still holding his older brother's eyes. "Because I never had to see what you saw. Because you always went with him into the city so he wouldn't take one of us instead, so we wouldn't have to see, so we wouldn't have to be the excuse he used."

J.C. inhaled sharply, sitting back from his brother, shock making goose bumps rise on his skin. "You knew?"

"I suspected," said Étienne sadly. "Now I know for sure."

J.C. dropped his younger brother's eyes, ashamed of the things he'd seen—the women his father would kiss and maul in the elevator of the Morris House Hotel as the electric doors closed—ashamed of the way his mother would search his face for answers he couldn't give.

"Hey," said Étienne softly. "You protected me. You'll protect Noelle too."

"*Oui*," said J.C., looking up at his brother with gratitude and conviction. "*Oui. Avec ma vie.*" *With my life.*

Étienne sat back on the couch, putting his arm around Kate and pulling her close. "So yes? You'll be her godfather?"

"It's an honor," said J.C., nodding at Kate. "*Merci*, Kate. I won't let you down. I won't let *her* down."

"You're not out of the woods yet," said Kate, a minxy smile tipping up her lips as Jax and Mad returned with champagne and glasses. "Lib is going to be her godmother."

Fuck. Of course she was.

Prickly, skinny, angry Libitz who hated him.

Smart-mouthed, foul-mouthed Libitz who kissed like a Siren and wanted nothing to do with him.

He would be bound to her for life now, watching over a child who belonged to both of them equally.

Great. Fantastic. Aces. What a fucking mess.

And yet the baby growing in Kate's belly was *his* blood, *his* flesh, part of *his* family, and already safely housed within *his* heart. The second he'd heard her name, he'd included that child under the umbrella of profound love and unswerving protection reserved for his siblings only. Noelle Rousseau was *his* niece and *his* goddaughter. Fuck Libitz Feingold if she didn't like it. She'd have to learn to live with it. He wasn't going anywhere, goddamnit.

He smiled at Kate, certain that he'd never had to work harder to appear pleased. "Wonderful."

Kate snickered. "That's what I thought."

"J.C.!" said Jax, placing the ice bucket on the coffee table. "Let me show you the painting before dinner. Mad? Pour the wine? We'll be back in a sec to toast our new niece!"

Grateful to be able to leave the room for a moment, J.C. followed Jax up the twisting staircase of Le Chateau, mostly ignoring her chattering about what she'd found in the attic since the ownership of the mansion had been turned over to her and Gard.

What would Libitz think of the fact that they'd be sharing such important roles in Noelle's life? Would she co-godparent with class, or would he need to be on his guard, waiting for her to poison his little niece's head with whisperings of her evil *Parrain Jean-Christian*? Well, screw that. No one was getting between him and his goddaughter. He'd make damn sure of that.

". . . I thought about taking it to an appraiser, but I know nothing about where to go or who to ask. Plus I'm not really sure it's my style anyway. I guess it's been up here for ages. It's signed by Pierre Montferrat, who must be one of Maman's cousins? I don't know. Anyway . . ."

J.C. plodded up the attic stairs behind Jax, thinking about the kind of godparents his niece deserved—the kind of godparents he wanted her to have. He couldn't be in an active fight with Noelle's godmother. No. That wasn't okay. It wouldn't be okay for *her*. Noelle deserved the best of everything. She needed a safe and secure circle of adults who loved her, not two lunatics who fought every time they were in the same room.

So, fine. The next time he saw Libitz, he'd apologize for calling her a "bitch." He'd explain that he was a little drunk and she'd wounded his pride, but he'd had no right to say such a thing to her. An hour earlier, he would have as soon rotted in hell than apologize to that shrew, but this wasn't just about him and Libitz now. It was about Noelle. And just as he'd loved her father enough to protect him from ugliness, he'd do the same for his niece.

". . . seriously, I can't figure it out because she's *so* familiar, it's driving me crazy. It's like I've seen her before, but . . . well, you'll see. Anyway, it's probably not worth much, but here it is."

J.C. finally focused on what Jax was saying, looking up as she flicked on a light and pulled a large canvas into the center of the dusty attic. He looked up at the back of the old canvas.

"See here? It says *Les Bijoux Jolis*. I'm guessing that's the title?"

He nodded distractedly. "Probably."

So it was settled. The next time he came face-to-face with Libitz Feingold, he'd apologize.

Jax reached for the top corners of the large canvas to turn the portrait around, and J.C.'s jaw dropped as he stared at the painting. His breath caught. His blood raced cold. He blinked, wondering if he was hallucinating, then stepped forward to take a closer look at the woman in the portrait. She wasn't stunning, but she was memorable, her body naked but for an emerald necklace she wore around her neck, her jet-black hair and wide eyes achingly familiar.

The murmured words "I'm sorry" left his lips on the very tail of a released breath.

The thing is, he hadn't expected to come face-to-face with her again quite so soon.

Chapter 4

"I can juggle things, Lib," said Neil from the easy chair in her bedroom, watching as she packed her suitcase. "If you want me there, I can make it. I really want to meet Kate."

Libitz looked up from folding a pair of jeans and shook her head. "Rosh Hashanah's in two weeks. I know how busy you are."

"So what? Aaron can handle it."

Libitz stopped what she was doing and put her hands on her hips. "No. I can't let you do that."

Neil gave her a pointed look. "Or maybe you're not ready to introduce us yet?"

"No!" Libitz dropped his eyes, turning her back to him as she pulled a crisp white button-down blouse from her closet and removed the hanger. "You know that's not the reason."

"Do I?"

She glanced up at him, wishing her cheeks weren't flushing, though she could feel the heat rising in them. "Yes. You do."

"Lib . . . we've been dating for over two months now, and . . ."

His voice trailed off as Libitz continued arranging her clothes in the suitcase. She knew what he was getting at, and she'd been dreading this conversation. They'd been dating for two months, but they really weren't moving forward.

Though they saw each other twice a week and Neil was a regular at her parents' house for dinner, he'd never met any of her friends. Nor had he ever spent the night at her place or had her overnight at his. He'd invited her to stay over, his eyes suggesting how much he'd like to be more intimate with her, but Libitz had explained to Neil that she wanted to take things slowly between them. Except by now, eight weeks after their first date, "slowly" had turned into "glacial" somewhere along the way. Aside from some kissing, they hadn't done much of anything else, and Neil's patience was waning.

It wasn't that Neil wasn't attractive—he was. At five foot five, he was wiry but fit from morning jogs around his Brooklyn neighborhood. He had a thick head of reddish-blond hair, a sprinkling of charming freckles across his nose, and eyes so big and blue, they made his whole face appear angelic behind stylish glasses.

Libitz sighed. Tall, dark, and stunning had always been more her taste, but that wasn't Neil's problem. She *wanted* to be attracted to him. She hoped that a little more time together would do the trick.

"And what?" she asked, hoping to truncate the conversation by appearing annoyed.

Sure enough, Neil dropped her eyes, shrugging apologetically. "I just wish . . ."

"Neil—" she started.

His voice returned with more confidence and resolution when he interrupted her. "I just wish I felt like you liked me as much as I like you."

"I *do* like you," she said, the words coming naturally.

"I don't just *like* you. I *want* you, Lib." He searched her eyes with frustration, his voice dropping when he continued. "I want you to want me too."

Her eyes widened at his unexpected boldness.

"Be patient," she whispered, guilt making her breath catch and hold, because honestly, she wasn't sure that patience would help.

"I am," he said simply, sitting back in the chair and sighing. "I don't mean to put pressure on you, but I'm thirty-four and I want a family, Libitz. I want a wife and a couple of kids. I can't afford to waste time in a relationship that's not going anywhere."

Terribly uncomfortable with his words, Libitz opened her mouth to say something but couldn't think of a single thing to say. She couldn't reassure him because she didn't know where their relationship was headed. She couldn't promise him anything because, as yet, she didn't feel the sort of attraction for him that would move them forward. And yet she cared for Neil. She really and truly liked him, saw the goodness in him, recognized how good he could be for her.

"Say something," he begged her. "Say anything."

She released the breath she'd been holding and tried smiling at him.

"Don't cut me loose yet," she said, repeating words he'd said to her a few weeks ago. "Give me a little more time?"

Recognizing her plea, he laughed softly, nodding his head, a sweet smile slowly spreading across his face. "Fair enough." Taking a deep breath, he sighed as he stood up, crossing the room to stand beside her. "I think I'll head out."

She turned to him. "You're a good man, Neil Leibowitz."

"So you tell me."

Putting her arms around his neck, she pulled him close, closing her eyes as she pressed her lips to the warm skin of his neck, leaning into him as he gathered her close.

"You are," she whispered, wishing that the ridge of his erection pushing against her didn't make her feel like backing away.

He leaned back to look at her, then drew forward, pressing his lips to hers. But just as his tongue swiped along the seam of their mouths, Libitz pulled away.

"Got to finish packing. See you soon?"

Disappointment clouded his eyes, but he nodded at her. "Sure. Call me when you get home."

"I will," she said, stepping out of his embrace and smiling. "Have a good weekend, okay?"

He nodded, backing out of her bedroom. "You too, Lib."

J.C.'s car idled at the Haverford train station.

He was fifteen minutes early, but it was a beautiful evening, and with the top down on his vintage red Citroën DS convertible, he figured he'd soak up some rays while he waited.

When he'd arrived at Kate and Étienne's new place, an estate they'd named Toujours, Kate had opened the front door and looked at him in surprise before leaning forward to kiss his cheeks.

"J.C.! You weren't supposed to be here until five."

He had glanced at his watch. "It's five fifteen."

"What? No! It can't be!"

"I promise it is."

"The whole day got away from me! Lib gets here in twenty minutes! I have to go ask Étienne to pick her up . . ."

He pointed a thumb over his shoulder. "Étienne's in the backyard having a lively argument with the garden hose."

Kate giggled. "He wants to set up a sprinkler for Caroline for tomorrow."

"Fitz and Daisy's daughter? Is she old enough to enjoy a sprinkler yet?"

Kate nodded vigorously. "She turned one in June, and she's toddling all over the place. She'll love it!" Then she sighed, looking tired. "I guess *I'll* go get Lib."

"Let me go," he said.

"You?" Kate, whose belly had just started showing in earnest, looked up at her brother-in-law suspiciously. "Why?"

"Well," he said, grabbing his keys from his pocket, "I figure it'll give us a chance to bury the hatchet now that we're godparents-to-be. We need to figure out how to get along, right? For Noelle's sake?"

Kate covered her bump lovingly, nodding at him with a cautious smile. "I guess that's true . . ."

"So there it is," he said, his body humming at the thought of seeing Libitz again so soon. He knew there was a good chance she'd be spending Labor Day at Toujours, but he wasn't positive until now. "I'll go."

Kate had leaned forward, kissing J.C.'s cheek again. "Be nice?"

"Of course," he promised, turning back to his car.

And now here he was, with fifteen minutes to kill, waiting for a woman he hadn't seen in two months—a woman he hadn't stopped thinking about since they'd kissed at his younger brother's wedding, a woman about whom he'd become quietly obsessed with since the night Jax had shown him *Les Bijoux Jolis*.

The chance of it happening in his life—an intersection between art and reality—was so unlikely, J.C. had never actually prepared himself for it. Art was his love, his most extreme passion. For the face of Libitz, a woman with whom he'd shared unparalleled physical chemistry in the form of one stupendous kiss, to suddenly appear in a portrait almost eighty years old wasn't just unnerving; it felt strangely like . . . fate. Like something bigger and wider and more profoundly unexplainable than mere coincidence. And J.C. wasn't about to leave it unexamined. He *couldn't*, even if he'd wanted to.

He'd asked Jax for the portrait that evening, and she'd happily given it to him, asking if he recognized the model. He did, of course, but told her he didn't, because he wasn't interested in sharing his connection to the art, even with Jax, whom he loved and trusted. It felt too visceral to off-handedly comment that the model looked exactly like Kate's best friend, like it would somehow minimize the devastating effect the portrait had on him.

Returning to Jax's house the following Saturday, J.C. had stared at the likeness for well over an hour in the dusty quiet of Le Chateau's attic, tracing the contours of the woman's face with his eyes, touching the curve of her shoulder with the pad of his forefinger, resting the back of his hand lightly over her exposed breast, the pert nipple reminding him of the one he'd rolled between his fingers so many weeks ago.

He'd packaged up the portrait carefully and removed it to his gallery, where he'd carefully examined it before asking Jessica English's favorite and most trusted art restorer from New York to inspect it. Graves Fairleigh had commented on the flaking and scratching, tsking over a rip in the upper left quadrant and discolored varnish, but promised he could have the portrait restored to its former glory.

When Graves suggested that they package the canvas, however, J.C. found himself unable to let the artwork out of his sight. Instead, he paid the acclaimed restorer thrice his normal wages to work on *Les Bijoux Jolis* in a small workspace in the back of J.C.'s gallery.

Once it was fully restored, J.C. had considered placing it in the alcove where Atroshenko's ballerina bid farewell to him every evening, but reluctant to share her, he'd decided on *une place de choix* across from his desk, over his guest sofa instead, where he could glance up at her a thousand times a day.

Undoubtedly the focal point of the portrait was supposed to be the emerald necklace, which sparkled against the girl's skin like an unlikely trophy. But, J.C. barely noted it. All he saw was the model as though blinded by her.

He had become intimately familiar with model's body—the graceful way her feet crossed each other, the olive-ivory color of her shapely legs and soft belly against the dark velvet of the settee. Following the very slight flare of her trim hips and tight waist, he wondered what the artist, whom J.C. had figured out was his great-uncle, had felt as he painted the pinkish-brown areolas of her breasts and the distended pink nipples that glistened with the summer heat. Her neck was delicate, her shoulders angular, and her hands, like her feet, crossed, one over the other, on the seat of the divan. But it was her elfin face that most arrested him—the berry pink bow of her lips, the flushed peaches of her cheeks, the jet-black of her eyebrows and lashes, and the enormous brown eyes that seemed to see the entire world with an innocence he feared and coveted.

To anyone looking in from the outside, J.C. was a man quietly obsessed, or he would be, if anyone knew about the painting and his intense feelings for it.

An announcement from the train platform alerted him that the local train from Philadelphia would be arriving in three minutes, and J.C. cut the engine of his car, swinging his body from the low seat of his convertible and pushing the door shut behind him. Stepping up to the platform, he leaned against a metal bar by the stairs, peeking down the tracks. Per usual, he felt eyes on him—women waiting for the train, wives waiting for their husbands, college girls heading into the city for the weekend. But instead of making eye contact with any of them, he let their hungry eyes roam over his body and tried to quiet the fierce thumping of his heart.

Rationally he knew that there was no connection between the Libitz Feingold from present-day and the model with whom J.C. had become infatuated over the past several weeks, yet his anticipation grew as the tracks began to vibrate and shudder. Suddenly the train whooshed past him with a fiery blast of wind, the brakes shrieking as it slowed down, the silver bullet coming to a stop in the station. His body tensed, straightening away from the bar behind him as he scanned the doors that suddenly jerked open and the waves of people that emptied onto the platform.

Wives embraced their husbands, mothers opened their arms to returning children, and businessmen walked hurriedly to their cars, eager to begin the last long weekend of the summer. And for a moment, J.C. despaired that she wasn't on the train platform as the swell of humanity thinned to a conductor talking to a station agent. Still scanning the open doors of the train, he was pulling his phone from his back pocket to call Kate when the pointy toe of an ultrasexy black sling-back heel stepped out onto the platform.

His eyes widened as they trailed up denim-clad legs, artfully frayed at the knees and near the pussy, and sailed past a tiny waist to a loose black scoop-neck tank top embellished with a collection of gold chains around her neck. Her lips were a fierce fire-engine red, and oversized Jackie O. sunglasses completed her ensemble. From one bent elbow, she carried a large black leather purse, and several gold bangles on her wrist clanked together as she pulled her black rolling suitcase behind her.

Fuck.

Fuck. Fuck. Fuck. Fuck. Fuck.

I am in so much fucking trouble, thought J.C., stepping forward as she scanned the platform, and he raised his hand in greeting.

Fuck.

Fuck. Fuck. Fuck. Fuck. Fuck.

Thanks, Kate. Thanks a lot.

Though she'd firmly instructed herself on the train ride not to react to him, the second she saw Jean-Christian Rousseau standing alone on the Haverford train platform, her entire body surged with electricity like she'd touched a live wire. Her mouth watered, goose bumps rose up on her skin, her nipples tightened into hard points, and her clit throbbed for the first time in months, starting a chain reaction in her pelvis. Liquid and hot, she felt her body ready for him like he was about to drop trou in the middle of a public train station and she was going to mount him like a stud for hire.

She hissed a held breath through her lips, furious with herself.

It was a chemical fucking reaction over which she had zero control, yes, but it pissed her off mightily nonetheless. Narrowing her eyes and setting her jaw to irritated, she stood completely still as the conductor yelled an old-fashioned "All aboard!" before the double doors closed behind her. The train lumbered away from the station, and she and J.C. Rousseau were left staring at each other from a distance of about fifty feet away.

Taking a deep breath, Libitz walked toward him.

You can do this. You can do this. Be polite. Don't let him get under your skin. Think of Noelle.

He stood still, facing her, waiting for her to make her way to him, looking as delicious as ever. Worn jeans fit him perfectly, molded to his body like a comfortable second skin, and on top he wore a blue-and-white gingham long-sleeved shirt rolled up to his muscular midforearms. His sunglasses hid his eyes, but the lips she had dreamed about for months were still as sensual as fuck, tilted up into a small grin that made her insides clench with longing. His hair had grown a little since the wedding—it was wavy and dark, tamed into submission with some sort of gel, but a thick lock had escaped and hung over his forehead. Libitz rolled her eyes behind her glasses. Beside the word "sexy" in the dictionary, no doubt there was a picture of J.C. Rousseau.

"Hi," he said as she approached. "How was your trip?"

"Fine," she answered, stopping about five feet away from him. "Almost missed my connection in Philly but managed to run for it."

"Good." He nodded. "Can I help you with your bag?"

"It rolls."

"Okay," he said, reaching for it.

She jerked the handle back. "It *rolls*. I don't need help with it."

He raised his hands, palms up. "I wasn't going to *steal* it, Elsa. I was just going to put it in my trunk for you, but suit yourself."

Elsa. The ice princess.

It was bad luck that HBO Family had been showing *Frozen* for most of July and August this summer, and while flipping channels, Libitz had caught it at least twenty-eight (million) times. And of course, every time she saw it, her mind would return swiftly to thoughts of Jean-Christian.

The thing was, she liked the character of Elsa. She related to her. Because Elsa had special control over water, able to turn it to snow and ice, she felt different—knew she was different from everyone else around her . . . much like dark-haired, brown-eyed, Jewish Libitz, who had attended prep schools mostly populated by blonde-haired, blue-eyed Christian girls like Kate English. Being a little different had often made Libitz feel separate from her peers, the same way Elsa felt separate from her people in the movie.

Feeling different was one thing, but it had been a long time since Libitz had felt inferior to someone else just because of her ethnicity. She refused to let anyone make her feel less-than when she was actually quite proud to be of European-Jewish descent. Not many of her direct ancestors had survived the brutality of World War II. Casting his comment in this light made her feel stronger, and she raised her chin, eyeballing him.

"You can call me Elsa all you want," she said. "I don't mind it. In fact, I take it as a compliment."

"Is that right? Chilly appeals to you, does it?"

She shrugged. "I'm not chilly. But I'm different, and I won't be ashamed of that."

"Different from what?"

"From you and all your WASPy friends."

"WASPy?" he scoffed. "I'm not Anglo-Saxon or Protestant, ice princess. More like Norman and Catholic."

"Oh," she said, lowering her glasses just a touch. "Okay. That makes you a W-N-C. A WaNC. Do you call yourselves 'wankers' for fun?"

"You know what?" He lowered his glasses just as she had, staring into her eyes as his danced with something that looked a little like amusement mixed with admiration. Finally, with a bit of gravel in his tone, he said, "It's good to see you again, Libitz."

The unexpected emotion she heard in his voice set her a little off kilter when she was primed for a quarrel. And the way his dark-green eyes searched her face as though caressing it, remembering it, and finding pleasure in its recovery made her want to sigh.

"Oh. Well, okay then," she mumbled.

He chuckled softly, reaching for her suitcase again, and this time she yielded it to him, but not before his fingers brushed hers, sending a jolt of awareness throughout her body. For a moment, they both froze, his fingers mingling with hers, barely moving, warm and welcome against her skin. When she pulled her hand away and turned toward the steps behind him, she damned the heat that was flushing her cheeks.

"So, um, how far is it to Kate's?"

"Not very," he answered from behind her. "Their new house is in the same general neighborhood as Blueberry Lane."

She stepped down the stairs before him, careful to hold onto the railing so she wouldn't totter in her five-inch Louboutins. At the bottom, he passed her, walking over to a darling red vintage convertible.

"A Citroën!" she exclaimed with a gasp.

"You know them?" he asked, looking up from the trunk, where he'd placed her suitcase.

"Of course! My dad's a car nut."

"What does he drive?"

"He *drives* a Mercedes S-Class, but his true love is a fully restored 1955 Jaguar XK-140 in racing green," she said, caressing the hood of J.C.'s gorgeous car with both palms. "He'd approve of this baby."

She smiled down at the pristine paint job before raising her glance to find J.C. staring at her with barely restrained lust from the other side of the car.

"If I say something, can you try not to take it the wrong way?"

She tilted her head to the side and nodded once.

"I could listen to you talk about cars for hours."

"Really?"

He nodded slowly. "It's the hottest fucking thing I've heard in months."

"What was the hottest thing before that?" she asked in a breathy voice, trapped in the intensity of his stare.

He shook his head like something was funny.

"You," he said simply, "telling me I was a 'disgusting egomaniac.'"

She bit her bottom lip and dropped his eyes.

"Lib," he said, his voice rough, and it occurred to her that it was the first time he'd ever shortened her name like that . . . and she liked it. She liked it so fucking much.

Raising her chin, she looked up at him.

"I'm sorry for calling you a bitch," he said. "You're not. And even if you were, I was totally out of line to say that."

He couldn't have surprised her more if he'd pulled out a ukulele and started strumming "Blue Moon" while doing a soft shoe. She stared at him, so undone by his sincere apology, she was speechless.

"That's all I wanted to say," he added. Then, "No, there's more. We're going to be Noelle's godparents, and I still don't know why Kate and Ten would choose me for the job, but they did. And I just . . . I mean, it's important to me. I don't want us to hate each other and be fighting and . . . fuck. I'm not doing this very well."

"No. You're doing great," said Libitz softly. "I feel the same way."

"You do?"

She nodded. "We don't have to like each other, but we can be civil. For her sake."

He flinched as she spoke, his lips tightening as he opened his door and plunked down in the driver's seat. His voice had lost all its previous warmth when he muttered, "Yeah. We *definitely* don't have to like each other."

She sighed, realizing where she'd gone wrong. Sitting down in the passenger seat beside him, she put her bag on her lap and touched his arm.

"Hey . . . I didn't mean it like that. I was trying to say I agree with you. I want us to be really awesome godparents for Noelle. No matter what."

He stared straight ahead, nodding distractedly like he was thinking about something or trying to figure out something that was troubling him. His profile was devastating, and she took some pleasure in openly gazing at him as they sat in silence with her hand on his arm and a tentative truce blooming between them.

Finally, he turned to her, pushing his sunglasses on top of his head so he could look her in the eyes.

"Hi. I'm Étienne's brother, Jean-Christian. It's nice to meet you," he said, offering her his hand.

She took off her glasses too, folding them and placing them in her purse before reaching out to take his hand in hers. "Hi. I'm Libitz Feingold, Kate's best friend."

She knew that they were both remembering the way she'd capped off the introduction the first time they'd met— by telling him it wasn't cold enough in hell for her to fall for him.

As they clasped hands, he raised an eyebrow in challenge. "Anything else?"

No matter how much of a jerk he'd been at Kate and Étienne's wedding, he seemed different now. Mellowed out. Matured. More careful. Less smarmy. She assumed it was because of the responsibility they'd share for Noelle, and she respected that he was trying to turn over a new leaf with her. Plus, he was making it so much easier for her, since she'd promised herself to do the same, and he was doing most of the work. It made her feel grateful. It made her want to give him a chance.

"Yes." She cocked her head to the side, offering him a small, warm smile as she pumped his hand. "It's nice to finally meet you."

Chapter 5

"Lib!"

"KK!"

Kate, who was waiting outside the front door, put her arm around Libitz's shoulders, ushering her inside the enormous brick house. "I see you survived the drive from the station." She glanced over her shoulder at J.C., who was getting Lib's suitcase out of the trunk. "And J.C. appears to have both eyeballs still in place."

Libitz raised an eyebrow in question.

Kate shrugged. "You didn't scratch them out."

She chuckled softly and raised her hands. "Nails sheathed . . . for now."

"Good to hear it," said Kate, squeezing her shoulder with approval. "Do you want to freshen up before cocktails?"

"No way I'm delaying alcohol," said Lib, grinning up at her friend.

"Where should I put Lib's bags, Kate?"

Kate gave Libitz a look and mouthed *Lib?* before turning to her brother-in-law. "Would you be a darling and put them in the gray guest room at the end of the upstairs hallway to the right?"

"Sure," he said, holding out his hand for Libitz's black purse.

Looking into his eyes, she let it slip from her shoulder and handed it to him. "Thank you."

"No problem," he answered, winking at her as he took the bags upstairs.

Kate put her arm around Lib's waist, guiding her into a grand dining room and through swinging doors that led to the kitchen.

"Ummm . . . is it just me? Or did he have a brain transplant?" said Libitz, marveling over the changes in J.C. since the wedding in June.

Kate opened the fridge, took out a bottle of chilled Chardonnay, and poured Libitz a glass, gesturing to a round table for eight that sat in a nook off to the side of the cooking area. Floor-to-ceiling windows looked out onto a patio, pool, and expansive bright-green lawn.

"What do you mean?" asked Kate, setting the wine in front of her friend, then turning back to the counter for a prepared platter of grapes, cheese, and crackers.

"I mean . . ." said Libitz, taking a sip of her wine as she sat down, "the level of smarm has been halved since last we met."

Kate sat down across from her, tearing a sprig of grapes from a larger vine. "Are you sure you gave him a chance?"

"KK . . . believe me, he was disgusting."

"Oh, come on. He couldn't have been *that* bad."

You're a bitch.

"He was."

"Maybe he was drunk at the wedding? Everyone gets drunk at weddings, and guys act like asses when they've had too much."

Maybe, thought Libitz.

But giving a moment of thought to their interactions that weekend, she quickly dismissed the idea that his behavior at the wedding was merely the result of drinking. It had been consistently smarmy all weekend. Nor did she believe that she'd misjudged him two months ago—he had acted like a predator and an asshole.

And that said, the J.C. she met today wasn't a completely new person. He'd still called her "Elsa" earlier at the train station. He'd still bantered with her in the car as cleverly as he had at the wedding. The difference was in the delivery. It felt more playful now and less dirty. In the simplest possible terms, she felt less like a piece of ass and more like a person.

She sighed, annoyed to be spending so much time thinking about him. "Let's talk about you instead. How are you feeling?"

"Changing the subject, huh? Okay. But when I've got you good and drunk, I'll make you talk," warned Kate. "And how do I feel? Fat. Well, fatter than I did before. And gassy. They never mention the gas."

"You *look* beautiful," said Libitz. "Pregnancy suits you."

"I felt her kick last week," said Kate, her smile dreamy and soft. "Can you believe I'll be a mom by Christmas?"

"Chanukah. And yes, of course I believe it. I'm thrilled for you."

Kate reached for Libitz's hands. "The party's on Sunday, which means lots of prep work tomorrow. How about we spend Monday shopping? Baby clothes, a bassinette—"

"Booties! Some soft blankets!"

"A little bathtub?"

"Yes! And fluffy towels."

"You don't mind?"

"Mind?" exclaimed Lib. "Are you kidding? I get to go shopping for my goddaughter! And you better let me spoil her, KK!"

Kate nodded solemnly as she made herself a cracker-and-cheese sandwich. "But of course."

Libitz caught some activity on the lawn out of the corner of her eye and looked out the windows to see Étienne and J.C. scramble away from a sprinkler that suddenly shot a blast of water into the air. She turned to Kate and they giggled at the men, who were trying to sprint toward the sprinkler but were getting caught in showers every time.

"What in the world are they doing?"

"I mentioned something to Étienne about having a sprinkler set up for Caroline English, Fitz's daughter, and he's been at it all afternoon." Her shoulders trembled. "I don't think he's ever set up a sprinkler before."

"Why don't you call Jax's boyfriend to come over and give him a hand? Isn't he a gardener?"

Kate gave Libitz a look as she stuffed another cracker sandwich in her mouth and stood up to look out the window. "What's the fun of that?"

Libitz cackled as J.C. reached down to hold the sprinkler in place while Étienne leaned down to fiddle with the controls, which rewarded the brothers with a sudden stream of water that drenched them both.

"P-p-points for t-trying?" stuttered Kate through giggles, swiping at her eyes.

J.C. sprang up, gesticulating with his hands while yelling something that looked suspiciously like "*Merde! Merde! Merde!*" and Étienne kicked the sprinkler across the lawn while shaking his hair free of droplets.

A moment later, they heard the sound of water being turned off, and a few seconds after that, both men stood in the kitchen doorway with wet hair and soaked shirts, looking thoroughly disgruntled.

"*Pourquoi ne pas le tenir?*" Étienne demanded of his brother.

J.C. screwed up his face in annoyance. "*Est-ce que tu me le reproches?*"

"English, *s'il-vous-plaît*," said Kate, heading for the door and leaning forward to peck her husband on the lips. "Don't drip on everything. I'll grab some towels."

Libitz smiled at the men, holding up her wine in cheers. "Well done!"

"Why don't *you* try it?" asked Étienne, putting his hands on his hips and looking pissy.

"No, thanks," she said, taking a sip and trying not to notice the way the Rousseau brothers looked with droplets in their dark hair and their shirts molded to their cut chests like second skins. "I'm a city girl."

"The fucking thing is slippery, and there are no goddamn instructions!" said Étienne. "What if the water comes shooting out like that at Caroline on Sunday? She could lose an eye!"

"How 'bout pouring two more glasses of wine, Elsa?" asked J.C., still standing behind Étienne on the kitchen mat, looking wet and delicious.

"*Qui est Elsa?*" asked Étienne over his shoulder.

Libitz grinned at J.C., placing her wine on the table and fetching two more glasses from the chrome rack hanging from the cabinets near the sink.

"*Ne t'en fait pas.*" *Don't worry about it.*

"So, Lib," said Étienne as she approached them with the wine glasses. "How's Ned?"

Why she flicked a guilty glance to J.C. was a mystery for the ages, but she did, and his eyes narrowed, searching hers, as he raised the glass to his lips.

"Who's Ned?" asked J.C. after a sip, his tone chilly.

She cleared her throat, swapping J.C.'s intense gaze for Étienne's more cordial one. "Do you mean Neil?"

"Yeah! Neil," said Étienne, nodding. "Kate says he's great."

"Kate says *who's* great?" asked Kate, returning with two towels, which she handed to her husband and brother-in-law, taking their wine glasses and setting them on the table.

"Neil," said J.C., the way someone else might say "dog shit."

Libitz sat back down at the table, wondering about the clenching feeling in her gut, the way her heart clamored as though in denial of something she'd never admitted. She gulped anxiously, finishing her glass of wine.

"From what you've told me, he sounds super, Lib," said Kate, sitting across from her friend. "What's it been now? A couple of months?"

Careful not to look up at J.C., Libitz nodded. "Yeah. About, um, five weeks."

"Five weeks?" asked J.C. "Did you start dating him the day after Kate and Ten's wedding?"

Libitz raised her chin, looking straight into his eyes. "Yes."

J.C. nodded, his expression frosty as he took the glass back from Kate and sat down in the chair beside Libitz, though there were six others to choose from. "Interesting."

"Kate says he runs a bakery," said Étienne, grabbing a piece of cheese as he took a seat beside his wife.

"A bakery," said J.C., his voice thick with sarcasm. "How glamorous."

"It *is*," insisted Kate. "It's the largest kosher bakery on the East Coast."

Libitz gave J.C. a sidelong glance, raising her eyebrows in challenge.

Game on. He grinned at her. "Does he do a great *short*bread?"

"Nope. He's known for his *long* baguettes," Libitz shot back.

"Kosher bakery, right?" asked J.C., sipping his wine as he stared at Libitz over the rim.

She nodded, unable to keep her lips from trembling, because, truth told, at some point she had started to look forward to his quick retorts and whip-fast wit.

"So no pork in the pie, huh?"

Without being able to help herself, she snorted with laughter, grateful that she hadn't risked a sip of wine before his comment, because J.C. and his brother would have had a second shower.

He was quick. Goddamn, but he was quick. And fuck, but she enjoyed it.

Staring up at him, she watched the last of his iciness thaw to warmth as his shoulders shook with laughter. "Good one, huh?"

She nodded through giggles. "Good one."

Finally able to take a deep breath, she turned away from J.C. to look at Kate, only to find her best friend staring at her with wide, worried eyes and parted lips.

"KK?" prompted Lib.

"What is going on here?"

Libitz sobered. "Huh? What do you—"

"Mean? You just giggled, Lib. *Giggled*. You do not giggle. You occasionally chuckle like it hurts. What the—what the *hell* is going on between you two?"

"*Chaton*—"

"No, Étienne! I need to say this!" Kate looked back and forth between Libitz and J.C., and Lib had known Kate long enough to know that her friend was truly upset. "You two are *not* allowed to have a fling! Do you hear me? You can't! Because it won't work out, and you'll end up hating each other, and then Noelle won't have—I mean . . . sh-she won't . . ." She stood up from the table, knocking the chair down behind her as she rushed from the kitchen.

Libitz bolted up to chase after Kate, but Étienne blocked her way. "Let me go."

"I didn't mean to upset her!"

"I know." Étienne reached for Libitz's shoulder and squeezed it gently. "Nothing's going on between you two, right?"

"Right!" said Libitz. "Nothing! We barely tolerate each other!"

"He gets it," said J.C. quietly from behind her.

"She's just"—Étienne shrugged—"pregnant. Super-emotional. Worried about the party on Sunday. Still trying to get the house the way she wants it before then. And in about ten minutes when she stops crying, she's going to be so embarrassed . . . Please, just—"

"We'll act like nothing happened," said J.C., who stood up behind Libitz. "Tell her not to worry."

"Thanks," said Étienne, giving them a grimace before heading for the door. "It's not you. It's her."

Libitz watched the door swing back in Étienne's wake, then reached up to press her hands against her hot cheeks. It had been a long time since she'd seen Kate so upset, but it was a good reminder that no matter how handsome or charming she found Jean-Christian Rousseau, nothing was allowed to happen between them. Absolutely nothing.

She turned to face him, uncertain of what to say in the wake of Kate's exit.

"I feel terrible."

"We didn't actually do anything."

"I know," said Libitz. "But she's pregnant."

He cringed, shrugging his shoulders before sitting back down in his chair. "I didn't see that coming."

Nor had she. "It was a good reminder."

"Of what?"

"That nothing's changed since the wedding. You and I are not a good idea."

J.C. scowled as he reached for his glass, raised it to his lips, and took a long sip. "Not that it matters. You're with Neil. Neil the baker with a long baguette."

"He's nice," she said, hating how weak the words sounded in her ears but unable to think of anything more compelling to say about Neil.

"*Nice.*" He looked up at her, nailing her with his dark-green eyes. "Does Nice Neil make you feel the way I make you feel?"

Her cheeks flared with heat and she dropped her eyes, suddenly fascinated with Kate's kitchen table. "I don't know what you—"

"I know I affect you, Lib. The same way you affect me. There's no use in denying it."

"Actually, there's a lot of use in denying it," she said softly, tracing her finger over the wood grain of the table. "Denying it is for the best."

"You really believe that?" he asked, his voice low and careful.

She looked up at him and nodded. "I do."

"Why? We're obviously attracted to each other. Why not . . . ?"

"Because Kate's right. We're family." She sighed. "Or we may as well be. We're going to be Noelle's godparents, J.C.—"

"Jean-Christian."

"What?"

He leaned forward. "Call me Jean-Christian, not J.C."

"Fine. We're going to be Noelle's godparents, *Jean-Christian*. That needs to be our priority, not some fling with zero chance of lasting and a great chance of making things really awkward between us."

He flinched as she spoke, leaning back in his chair as he stared at her like she'd just hurt him. "Okay, Elsa. Have it your way."

Her phone buzzed in her back pocket, and she reached for it, grateful for the distraction.

"Nice Neil the baker?" asked J.C., reaching for the bottle of wine and adding the remainder to his glass.

"No," she said, reading the text. "A client . . . looking for a Kandinsky."

Libitz hit "Reply," hating that she had to say no, because Mrs. Carnegie was a client Libitz had been trying to land for three full years. To have Mrs. Carnegie at her gallery showings, for other dealers to know that she was a client, would be a huge boost for the L. Feingold Gallery. But the sad reality was that Libitz didn't have a Kandinsky to sell—he wasn't an artist whom she collected. She could direct Mrs. Carnegie to a different gallery in New York that might have one, or she could offer to try to obtain one, but that would take time, and surely Mrs. Carnegie wasn't accustomed to waiting for—

"You have one?" asked J.C., *er*, Jean-Christian.

"No," she said, shaking her head, "but my friend Camilla might."

"What if you did?" he asked.

She looked up at him. "If I had a Kandinsky? I'd sell it to her, of course."

"Would you make a good commission?"

"Of course. Money's no object for Georgiana Newland Carnegie."

"But I think there's more to it," he said intuitively.

"She'd be an amazing client. Just having her as a patron would vault my gallery to the next level." She sighed. "That said, I can't procure an available Kandinsky out of thin air. When I get back to New York, I'll have to look around and see what I can find. Maybe she'll be willing to wait."

He searched her eyes gently, as though trying to make a decision about something, and her heart throbbed with longing as she stared back at him, the moment strangely intimate and yet without a hint of innuendo—just two passionate art lovers discussing their trade.

"I have one," he finally said.

"A Kandinsky?" She leaned forward. "For sale?"

"It wasn't." He shrugged. "Now it is."

"Are you serious?"

He nodded. "It's yours if you want it."

"Not *mine*. But I'll broker it."

"And I'll pay you well for that service."

"You weren't even going to sell it, J.—*Jean-Christian*. I can't take—"

"Either you make something on this deal or you forget it, Lib."

She wet her lips, catching the bottom one between her teeth for a moment. "Which Kandinsky is it?"

"*Composition Seven*," he answered.

Her breath caught. She knew the exact piece—its bright colors and bold brushstrokes were exactly what Mrs. Carnegie was looking for. "God, that's perfect."

"Glad to hear it."

"Do you really mean it?"

"Yes."

"But . . . why would you do that?"

He took a deep breath and another sip of wine, staring at her in a way that made her feel hot from the lobes of her ears to the tips of her toes and everywhere in between.

"Because I want to." He shrugged. "Because I can."

He placed his glass back on the table, staring at it intently, running his index finger around the rim until it hummed. "Come and see it tomorrow. At my gallery."

"I will. Thank you."

"I'll come and get you at nine."

She nodded. "Sounds good."

He looked up at her. "What'll we tell Kate?"

"The truth," she said simply.

"And that'll be okay?"

"It'll have to be," said Libitz, folding her hands on the table. "It's just business."

He nodded at her slowly, staring at her with an inscrutable expression. "Just business."

"No one is upset with you, *chaton*," said Étienne's voice from the dining room. "I promise. Come back and sit with us."

"Jean-Christian?" Libitz whispered, her hand darting out to clasp his, her heart swelling with emotion as he looked up from his humming glass in surprise. "Thank you."

His eyes widened as his fingers squeezed around hers for only a moment. "It's my pleasure."

The door opened, and they looked up to see a chagrined Kate standing beside Étienne. "I'm the worst," she said, sniffling pitifully. "I'm just so hormonal! I had no right to accuse you two of anything. I'm so sorry, Lib."

"KK," said Libitz, standing up from the table and crossing the kitchen to gather her best friend into her arms, "stop! We all love you. We understand."

"Forgive me, J.C.," Kate said over Lib's shoulder.

"Kate," said Jean-Christian from behind Libitz, his voice warm and kind, "there is nothing to forgive. Everything, *chérie*, is perfect now."

Chapter 6

As J.C. pulled into the driveway of Toujours the next morning, he considered what an unexpectedly excellent time he'd had last night at dinner. Kate and Étienne had flanked the table, leaving Jax and Gard on one side and J.C. and Libitz on the other, and J.C. was struck by how naturally Libitz blended in with the Rousseau siblings and their partners, the six of them making a merry party as Kate told the story of "Étienne and the Rogue Sprinkler." Thankfully, this prompted Gard to insist on coming over today to help set it up perfectly, with the addition of something called a Slip 'N Slide that Gard insisted Caroline English would love.

He'd watched Libitz—subtly, of course—as she grinned at Kate's anecdote or answered Jax's questions about her gallery in New York. Occasionally, her elbow would brush against his as she lifted her wineglass, and he felt those touches soul deep, enduring an under-the-table boner for most of the evening, which made him yearn for more from the enigmatic Lib.

Back at Princeton, he'd dated a visual arts major who had a freakish obsession with time travel books and movies. She'd talked nonstop about a Scottish romance novel that she insisted should be made into a movie and made him sit through a dreadful film with the dead guy from *Superman* and the chick from *Dr. Quinn, Medicine Woman*. The best thing about the movie was the music: notably *Rhapsody on a Theme of Paganini* by Rachmaninoff, which was seductive enough that they'd ended up fucking hard on her dorm bed halfway through the movie.

Suddenly the plot of that movie came back to him as he parked his car in his brother's driveway. The dead guy from *Superman* had become obsessed with a seventy-year-old portrait of Dr. Quinn, even though she was long dead by the time he'd actually seen the painting at a historic hotel. Because of his fixation on the woman in the portrait, he worked tirelessly to travel back through time to find her. For no good reason that could be explained, he felt a connection to the model he could neither forget nor deny.

Yesterday Libitz had said that there was "a lot of use in denying" their attraction to each other, but J.C.'s feelings for her weren't just about attraction anymore: they were all twisted and tangled with their mutual love of art, their delectable verbal sparring, and an ongoing sexy battle of the wills. Lately those feelings had been anchored by the fact that they'd be sharing the godparenting of Noelle and imbued with the magic of the Montferrat painting and Lib's uncanny likeness to its model.

Before the Kandinsky opportunity had presented itself yesterday, he didn't know how he was going to introduce Libitz to *Les Bijoux Jolis*, yet he was desperate that she see it. He needed to know if he was alone in the mysterious spell it had woven over him, because he suspected that he wasn't . . . or *wouldn't be* once she saw it. With no true and solid basis for his hunch, he felt certain that she would be as affected by the painting as he.

And with all these thoughts swirling like soup in his head, he hopped up the steps of his brother's house and raised his finger to ring the doorbell. But before he could actually make finger-to-bell contact, the door opened an inch, and Libitz slipped out.

"C'mon! Hurry!" she whispered, grabbing his jacket sleeve and speed-walking down the steps to his car. "She thinks you're a taxi!"

Deprived of the chance to open her door for her, he rounded the car and jumped into his seat, starting the engine quickly. "What happened to honesty?"

"It's overrated," muttered Lib, pulling down the sunglasses that had been perched on top of her head.

J.C. flicked a glance to the house as he put the car in drive, relieved that neither Kate nor his brother was darting from the house in a flurry to stop their now-illicit getaway.

Once they were down the driveway and through the gates of Toujours, he turned to Libitz. "What changed?"

"When I woke up this morning, she was sitting on my bed, all weepy, sorry for what she'd said last night, but not for the intentions behind it. She's really scared that we're going to hook up, break up, and hate each other for life."

"Huh."

"She kept saying it would be high stakes for a meaningless fuck."

Just as it had bothered him last night when she'd referred to today as "just business," it rankled him again now when she used the word "meaningless." Whatever Lib was to him, "meaningless" wasn't part of the equation.

He hazarded a glance at her, noting for the first time that she was wearing emerald earrings that sparkled and shined like the necklace in the painting. For a moment, he stared at her ear, almost hypnotized while they waited to merge onto a main road. A sharp pang of longing twisted his guts even though he reminded himself that it was a coincidence and nothing more.

"So, um . . . what did you say? To Kate?"

"I told her not to worry. We're *not* happening."

He flinched. "You're so sure about that?"

"Yes."

"No hint of doubt."

"None."

They were both quiet for a few minutes of stormy silence before Libitz's spoke up again. "One, I'm sure you have a piece of ass stashed away somewhere."

A mental picture of Felicity flashed through his head, and he scowled.

"Two, I'm with Neil."

His lips curled at the idea of Nice Neil's floury hands anywhere near Libitz.

"And three, somewhere along the way . . ." Her voice, which had been firm and decisive with her first two reasons, had changed now. It was softer and more tender, almost wistful. ". . . I decided that I don't want meaningless anymore . . . and you're, well . . . you're *you*."

"And all I do is meaningless?" he asked dryly.

She shrugged. "If the shoe fits . . ."

She was right, of course, but the word felt hollow and bitter in a way it had never felt before. "Meaningless" had always felt right. Safe. Comforting, even. But here and now? Sitting next to Libitz, speeding toward his gallery to show her something so beautiful, it had attached itself unerringly to his heart? They didn't feel right, safe, or comfortable. For the very first time in his life, they felt . . . wrong. All wrong.

He stopped at a red light, turning to her. She lowered her glasses to the bridge of her nose and nailed him with a look. "Tell me I'm wrong."

He couldn't.

"Meaningless" was the right word. For all his life, he'd been meticulous in keeping every potentially romantic relationship purposely shallow, ditching his partner at the merest hint of her wanting more.

And yet he couldn't stop thinking about Libitz—hadn't been able to shake her from his mind since the night he'd kissed her in the moonlight—and his feelings for her didn't show any signs of slowing down or retreating. If anything, they were growing, they were strengthening—he had the strangest premonition that they might even be here to stay. *There's an exception to every rule*, he thought, staring at her profile: at the severity of her bobbed black hair and the gleaming emerald stud that glistened in the lobe of her ear like some sort of cosmic sign.

He huffed out a breath of annoyance and looked away from her. He could say nothing that would prove to her that he was changing, wildly, every day. There was no evidence, no obvious change of behavior, no solid example to prove that a brain he'd wired one way at age eleven was suddenly rewiring itself more than two decades later. If he wanted her to see that he was becoming a different person, he'd have to show her.

Challenge accepted, he thought as the red light changed to green. He pressed down on the gas and zoomed toward the city.

Half an hour later, Libitz found herself standing in the middle of a small but very posh gallery in downtown Philadelphia. The walls had been painted dark-gray and the floors were made of black marble with tiny bits of embedded crystal that twinkled in the dim light. Over her head was an original Anthony Primo blown glass chandelier, suspended like an aquamarine medusa, and the eclectic art on the walls ranged in movement from impressionism to neo-minimalism.

Jean-Christian disappeared down a back hallway for a second, telling her to look around, and Libitz closed her eyes, breathing in the scent of his gallery. There was a hint of fresh paint, the slight, pleasing odor of old canvas, the heat of the lights, glass cleaner, and shipping boxes or crates. As she breathed deeply, she heard music playing—low, sexy jazz—from hidden speakers, and she opened her eyes to find Jean-Christian standing no more than a foot away, staring at her.

Her lips parted, and she released the breath she'd been holding.

"Your eyes were closed," he murmured, the way one would whisper in a sacred place, like a chapel or shrine.

"I was breathing it in."

"Do you always do that?"

Her bottom lip slipped between her teeth. She was so *aware* of him, standing so close to her. She imagined she could feel the heat of his body, smell the leftover scent of the leather jacket he'd been wearing in the car and a faint hint of mint, maybe from brushing his teeth. He didn't smell like vanilla, she realized as a weight lifted temporarily from her chest.

"Yes," she said, still looking up at him.

His eyes traced her face, and she wondered if he was keeping himself from dropping them to the green silk blouse she was wearing with dark-blue jeans and nude patent-leather sling-back pumps. Her nipples tightened, the memory of his hand cupping her bare breast making her cheeks flush with heat.

"Why?"

She gulped, feeling her flesh bead against her bra, no doubt pushing against the flimsy fabric of her top. "It gives me a sense of place."

"And . . . ?"

Standing in his gallery, surrounded by pieces he'd carefully curated, was turning out to be more erotic than Libitz
would have ever guessed. She cleared her throat, damning
her fierce attraction to him and wishing it away. "You have
excellent taste, but I suspected that before walking in. I
think you—I think you *love* this gallery."

"That surprises you?"

"Very much."

"You didn't think I was capable of love?"

Tough question.

She knew that he was capable of loving his siblings—she'd
seen it in his eyes at Étienne and Kate's wedding and last night
at dinner with his brother and sister. But familial love was the
easiest kind, wasn't it? Loving other people and things that
didn't organically belong to you was much harder.

"I don't know you well enough to answer you," she hedged.
"But from what I *do* know, *romantic* love has certainly never
been a priority."

She didn't mean it as a dig, so she didn't like it that he
looked wounded, that she'd inadvertently hurt him. She slid
her eyes away from his face and looked at the careful lighting
over a Jackson Pollock, the near-perfect matte and frame,
the artful way he displayed a modern sculpture on a pedestal
beside a famous Van Gogh.

"You love art, Jean-Christian. I can see that."

His face had cooled, however, and this assessment didn't
warm it.

"Come on, Elsa," he said, giving her his back as he stepped
away. "You're here to see a Kandinsky."

She followed him, stopping before *Composition Seven*,
which hung without noise or competition on its own wall a
few yards away.

"Mrs. Carnegie will be thrilled," she said, stepping closer
to the painting. There was no doubt about its authenticity,

and her lips tilted up in an easy smile of wonder as she admired it. "It's stunning."

"I can arrange to have it packaged and sent on Tuesday. Right after the holiday weekend. I assume you prefer private courier?"

"Yes, thanks," she said. "I'll have my assistant—"

"No need. I've already called the company I work with here in Philly and had it reinsured for eleven million. I have the address of your gallery, or I'm happy to send it directly to Mrs. Carnegie. Your call."

"I'd like to be there for the installation," said Libitz, breathless from his efficiency and trying not to find it a tremendous turn-on.

"Of course. I'll arrange for it to arrive at your gallery by Tuesday evening and leave any remaining details to you."

"I'll wire the—"

"We can worry about that later."

"Jean-Christian."

"Fine," he said with a sigh. He caught her eyes and held them intensely, clenching his jaw as he searched them for the answer to a question that he hadn't asked.

"What?"

"Why don't you—come into my office. I can type up an invoice."

She nodded. "Thank you. This is a big transaction, and I know we're . . ." She was about to say "family," but that didn't sound right at all. Nor did "friends." Nor did "enemies," much to her surprise. "Business associates" sounded way too impersonal for people about to pledge their love and guidance to the same baby, and "acquaintances" would be ridiculous, seeing as how she could still feel the imprint of his hand on her breast almost two months later.

"*What* are we?" he asked her, taking a step closer.

She gulped, opting for honesty. "I don't know."

His face—his beautiful, chiseled face, which had looked so stormy a moment before—softened. "I don't either."

"Can we let that be okay for now?"

He grinned at her, nodding slowly. "Yes."

Why her answer had made him feel so happy, he wasn't sure. Maybe because for the first time in his own life, J.C. was also in unchartered waters. He didn't have a tidy little box for Lib's keeping. He didn't know what to call her. He only knew that the longer he knew her, the more his feelings for her swelled in proportion to his attraction, which was quickly becoming all-consuming.

Never in his life had he seen anything as fucking beautiful as Libitz standing under his Anthony Primo, eyes closed, surrounded by art he'd handpicked, breathing in the *je ne sais quoi* of his gallery the way other people sipped fine wine or appreciated music. He understood what she was doing, he had done it himself more times than he could count, and it was insanely erotic to catch her in the act of inhaling his most sacred space. It did wild things to his heart that he'd never seen coming.

As her heels clacked over the marble just behind him, he tensed in excitement and anticipation. The best was yet to come. *Les Bijoux Jolis* hung on the wall of his office across from his desk, and he intended to watch her carefully as she first laid eyes on it, to see if he was alone in his fascination or if she felt the sort of kinship to it.

They stepped into his office, but when Libitz reached for one of the chairs in front of his desk, he gestured behind her to the couch.

"It's more comfortable there."

She looked over her shoulder at the couch, and from where Jean-Christian strategically stood, he could see the exact moment her eyes slid up to the portrait, and he watched intently as she turned her entire body, slowly, slowly, to face the painting.

Gasping softly, she stepped closer, her eyes glued to the model's face on the far-left side of the portrait, her hand reaching up as if to touch the canvas before suddenly stopping herself and lowering her arm to her side.

"Who—what . . . what is this?"

"It's called *Les Bijoux Jolis*," murmured Jean-Christian, moving to stand beside her, his eyes flicking quickly to the bejeweled model, then back to Libitz.

"My God . . ." she hissed, taking another step closer.

"It's uncanny, isn't it?"

She darted a quick glance at him, her eyes wide and troubled. "At first glance, I thought maybe you'd had it commissioned. I couldn't understand . . ."

"Why I'd have a portrait of you in my office?"

She nodded slowly. "Yes."

"It was painted in 1939."

"By whom?"

"Pierre Montferrat."

"I've never heard of him."

"He was a French painter in Marseille . . . and my great-uncle."

Her neck jerked to the left, and those huge, wide brown eyes were suddenly trained on his. "Your uncle?"

"Mm-hm. My sister Jax found the portrait in her attic."

"In 1939," murmured Libitz. "O'Keefe and Dalí were popular. Modernism ruled. No one was doing this."

"*Someone* was."

"I mean to say it wasn't popular," she said, still staring up at the portrait. "Etty painted the Titian copy . . . when?"

"Um . . . 1823, I think," said J.C., "though Manet painted *Olympia* in 1863."

"Still," said Libitz, "this was painted seventy-six years later."

"People have been copying *Venus* forever," commented J.C., realizing that his arm was brushing hers, though she didn't seem to notice.

"This is no copy," she protested. "It's . . . I don't know. It's haunting. Her, um . . . her expression is—what is it?"

She looked up at J.C., searching his face for guidance. His gaze slipped momentarily to her lips before sliding back up to her eyes.

"Young. Hopeful. Lovely."

"Yes," she murmured.

He stared deeply into her eyes, transfixed by the nearness of her, the clean fragrance of her perfume heady, the naked intensity of her eyes alluring. "Too young for emeralds. Too hopeful for a country on the brink of war. Too lovely for . . ."

"For what?" she asked, leaning closer to him, her breath choppy and shallow between them.

". . . me," he whispered, dropping his mouth to hers.

The last time Jean-Christian had kissed Lib, it had been via coercion and with an intense hostility sizzling like static between them. This time was completely different. This time her lips were pliant and willing, and her body molded effortlessly into his. She looped her arms around his neck to pull him closer, and when he slid his hands down her back to her ass, she let him pick her up, locking her ankles around his waist with a low moan of approval. Holding her firmly against him, her sex flush against his through two layers of denim, he had no doubt she could feel the throb of his erection, swelling to full, almost-painful, rock-hard size between them.

Backing up to his desk, he leaned against it with Libitz still entwined around his body, adjusting her so that his cock pressed up into the hollow between her legs, and she moaned. He felt the slight pinch of her fingernails against the skin on the back of his neck as she arched her back to rub her breasts against his chest.

Sliding his lips from her mouth to her neck, he groaned, "You're so fucking hot" as she twisted her neck to give him her ear, which he bit hard enough for her to whimper before demanding his lips again. He sealed his mouth over hers, plunging his tongue into her mouth, and she met it with hers, tangling with abandon, her breath choppy and shallow. She tasted like coffee and sugar, like good coffee and real sugar, bitter and sweet, and he reveled in the taste that so accurately represented the woman in his arms. Sharp, but unexpectedly tender.

He wanted her.

Dear God, how he wanted her.

But his phone, on the desk beside them, was buzzing and banging loud enough that it couldn't be ignored. Libitz drew away from him, her eyes glazed, her lips slick and red.

"Answer it."

With a sneer of frustration for whoever was calling, he picked up the phone, still holding her tightly against him with one hand, their noses an inch apart, their panted breath mingling.

"What?"

"*C'est Étienne.*"

"*Oui.*"

"Are you busy today?"

Lib's heart beat wildly against his chest, but her forehead rested on his shoulder. She didn't fight to leave his arms—her ankles were still locked around his waist and her hands still linked behind his neck. It was challenging, trying to hold her with one hand, but he tensed his grip around her—if she wasn't going anywhere, he sure as hell wasn't going to let her go.

"*Peut-être.*" *Maybe.* It all depended on the woman in his arms.

"Jax found a cradle in the attic, and she wants us to have it for Noelle. Can you pick it up for me? Kate's still trying to get everything organized for tomorrow, and I think she'll cut off my balls if I leave."

"For Noelle." One of the only names on earth that could have cut through his fog of lust.

"Yeah. Can you help me out?"

"Of course."

"Oh! And Kate said that Libitz had a meeting downtown this morning. Maybe you could call her and give her a ride back to Haverford? Kate feels bad that she had to take a taxi this morning. As long as you're coming here anyway? You don't mind, do you? I'll give you her number and you can text her. 212-555-3232. You two have to learn how to get along."

"Mmm," he hummed as Lib's lips scorched the skin of his throat with a kiss. "I feel confident we will."

"Yeah, but don't take it too far, okay? Kate's serious about you two not hooking up. She'd be a mess over it. Keep your dick in your pants . . . or in Felicity, okay?"

He heard Lib's short gasp of breath in his other ear and winced. Fuck. She was so close to him, she'd heard his brother loud and clear and froze in his arms. When she released the breath in a hiss, her hands unlocked from behind his head, and she untangled her legs, slipping down the front of his body and taking a step away from him as he released his arm from around her tiny waist. He stared at her—at her hurt, increasingly angry eyes.

"I have to go," murmured Jean-Christian to his brother, clenching his jaw with frustration.

"See you later. And be nice."

The line went dead, and J.C. shoved the phone back into his pocket.

"Who's Felicity?" Libitz asked.

"Just a distraction. Like Neil."

"I'm not *fucking* Neil," she said softly, then dropped his eyes, flinching like she'd given too much away.

Juxtaposed against the rush of awesome he felt at this admission was the reality that she stood before him looking angry, hurt, and yes, God, still gorgeously fucking aroused.

He reached for her. "Lib . . ."

"That was good advice." She pulled her arm out of his reach, lifted her eyes, and nailed him with a hard look. "Keep your dick in Felicity, J.C. You can send me an invoice for the Kandinsky. Let's go get the cradle, and then you can leave me alone."

"Not possible," he said, surprised by how fervently he meant it. He wasn't going to be able to leave her alone, and the sooner they both accepted it, the better.

"Then I'll go back to New York this afternoon."

"Libitz, come on . . ."

"No," she said softly, shaking her head, her face colored with deep regret. "I shouldn't have let that happen."

"You say that like it's an option to ignore what's between us. You can't, Lib. I certainly can't. It's magnetic. It's chemistry. I haven't been able to get you out of my head for weeks."

She inhaled sharply, whispering, "We're not good for each other."

She was wrong. She *was* good for him. She was the only woman he'd ever met who'd made him even consider love and commitment and forever. That *had* to be good.

"Please . . ."

"Back off or I leave today, J.C. I mean it."

Her voice was low and sharp, and there was no doubt in his mind that she was serious. Thinking of Kate's disappointment and fury, he put his palms up in surrender, unable to keep the frustration from his narrowed eyes as he whispered, "You win."

She gave *Les Bijoux Jolis* one last longing look, then turned and walked out of his office.

Chapter 7

Libitz stared out the window as Jean-Christian drove them out of Philadelphia, her stomach in knots, a lump in her throat, and adrenaline making her jumpy even though the car was silent and her seat was comfortable.

Not possible . . . You say that like it's an option to ignore what's between us . . . It's magnetic . . . It's chemistry . . . I haven't been able to get you out of my head for weeks . . .

His confession, which mirrored the feelings in her own heart, had started a process she'd desperately hoped to avoid: Libitz was falling, head over heels, for Jean-Christian Rousseau, and it scared the ever-loving shit out of her.

She'd been on the brink at Kate's wedding, of course, quietly swept away by his dark good looks, sexual energy, and focused attention. Frankly, she'd only avoided sleeping with him out of sheer willpower and her loyalty to Kate.

But this?

This was much worse.

Before, she'd lusted after his body. Now she was feeling an indelible unwanted attraction to his head and maybe even to his heart.

And fuck, but she'd worked hard against this happening—shooting him down at the wedding and dating Neil as soon as she got home as a way to distract herself from memories of Jean-Christian but also to focus herself more intently on a mature, meaningful relationship.

She winced because all of it was for naught: she couldn't ignore what was between them. She was trapped with him in a maelstrom of desire, attraction, and fast-growing feelings, and Noelle's impending arrival only served to solidify the feelings she so desperately wished to avoid.

She felt it in the way she'd pulled him to her when they kissed, how much she wanted his hard body pressed against hers. She felt it in her kinship to his beautiful gallery and in the way he'd described *Les Bijoux Jolis*, a portrait so hauntingly beautiful, so thrillingly erotic, so unaccountably personal, she couldn't stop picturing it.

Goddamn it.

She was falling. And she was falling hard.

So what now? she asked herself.

Fuck him to get him out of my system?

That was a terrible idea, chiefly because the possibility of getting Jean-Christian out of her system was long gone. Fucking him would only serve to heighten her longing—she'd know the bliss of his body sliding into hers, the hard rod of his cock moving against the tender, throbbing flesh of her sex. She'd know the look on his face when he came inside of her, know the sounds he made when he climaxed and the way his skin smelled after sex. She would never be able to forget the way it felt to be held in his arms as she reached her own peak, his heart thundering beneath her ear as she rode out the surges and spasms of promised pleasure.

No. There would be no getting rid of him once she'd had him. There would only be a lifetime of wanting more. A lifetime of wanting something she couldn't have. A lifetime of temptation and yearning, seeing him at every major life event of the child they would share.

So what now? her heart demanded again.

You're falling for him . . . but you can't fuck him.

You want him . . . but you can't have him.

You can't ignore him . . . but you can't forget him.

Taking a deep breath that sounded jerky in her ears, she closed her eyes, searching desperately for a solution, and as if God heard her plea, a sudden vision of Neil appeared in her mind.

Neil. She sighed, some tiny measure of peace taking the edge off her panic. *Call Neil*.

She opened her eyes and turned to Jean-Christian. "Do you mind if I make a call?"

"Be my guest."

She took her phone from her purse and dialed Neil's number, praying he'd pick up quickly.

"Y'ello?" he greeted her, 100 percent a born-and-bred New Yorker.

"Neil," she sighed. "Hi."

"Lib!" he cried, and she knew he was smiling. She could hear it in his voice, and it made her smile too. "How's Philly?"

"Good," she said. Out of the corner of her eye, she saw Jean-Christian's fingers tighten on the steering wheel, his knuckles an angry white. She shifted her body away from him, looking out the window. "I miss you."

"You do?" He chuckled happily. "I miss you too."

"Pick me up at Penn Station on Monday night?"

"Of course I will."

"And"—she cleared her throat and lowered her voice a touch—"plan to stay over at my place?"

Neil was quiet for a moment before speaking, but when he did, his voice was huskier than it had been before. "Are you sure, honey?"

He'd never called her "honey" before, and she wished she liked it more than she did. She clenched her jaw and gulped. "Mm-hm. I want you to."

"I'd love that, Lib."

"Okay then."

"I didn't"—he paused before starting again—"I didn't expect this. It makes me really happy."

She winced. "You're such a good man."

"I just know what I want," he said. "I knew it the first moment I laid eyes on you, Lib."

Her heart stuttered at his admission, and the panicky feeling she'd been trying to assuage a few moments before came rushing back, much worse than before.

"I'll text you my train info," she squeaked.

"I'll look out for it. I can't wait."

"Bye, Neil."

"Bye, Lib."

Pursing her lips, she pressed "End" on her phone and dropped it back into her bag. She didn't dare look at Jean-Christian, but she could feel the tension, the fury, the frustration being thrown from his body like heat.

"How'd *that* feel?" he snarled.

"Fine," she answered, wishing her voice had more conviction.

"Bullshit. You feel like shit now, and we both know it, Elsa." She ground her jaw, refusing to look at him. "You're going to fuck someone you don't want to try to forget someone you do." He let that thought sit for a minute before adding, "It doesn't work. I've tried it. It just makes everything worse and hurts someone who doesn't deserve to be hurt."

"You don't know—"

"Don't kid yourself, sweetheart. I've had a lifetime of meaningless sex . . . which is exactly what you just offered to Neil." His words, like jagged glass, cut her. "Poor trusting bastard."

"Fuck you!" raged Libitz, hating him for wanting her and making her want him when he had nothing else to offer but smirky grins and no-strings-attached screwing. "Just because you like cheap and shallow doesn't mean you get to criticize me for wanting something real!"

"Get off your high-fucking-horse. You're not being *real*. Whatever you've got going on with Nice Neil is the antithesis of real. You started dating him about five minutes after we kissed at Ten's wedding. You're just using him."

"And you're just a whore with a big cock!"

"And wouldn't you love to know exactly how big," he growled.

Yes. Wait. No!

"You're a pig," she spat.

The sound of brakes screeching would have made her lurch forward even if he hadn't suddenly come to a stop on a dime by the side of the road. He snapped the gearshift into "Park" and turned to her.

"Listen up, Libitz," he said, his eyes boring into hers as his chest rose and fell rapidly. "Any way you slice it, you're using him to get away from me. You know it, and I know it."

"So *what*?" she demanded, blinking her burning, confused eyes at him. "Why is that wrong?"

"Because it just is!" He reached for her head, cupping the back of her skull with his hand as he yanked her closer. "Because this . . . *us* . . . is *right*."

She didn't fight him when he kissed her, his tongue invading her mouth to mate with hers the moment their lips connected. Whatever was wrong between them, their physical connection was so undeniably strong, she couldn't force herself to push him away. She didn't want to. She didn't know how. And she was so tired of fighting her attraction to him, shutting down her thoughts of him, and pushing away her growing feelings for him. Falling for him wasn't something she'd planned; it was just something that had happened . . . and she'd never felt so helpless about anything else in her entire fucking life.

"It scares me too," he murmured, his lips hot on her neck, his teeth biting her earlobe and making her gasp, then whimper. "I can't stop thinking about you, Lib. I've tried, but I can't . . ."

She reached for his face, cradling his cheeks and demanding his lips once again. His free hand groped at her shirt, slipping inside the thin silk, under the lace of her bra to cover her breast with his hand as he had when they'd kissed in the moonlight at Kate's wedding. She didn't push him away. She arched her back, filling his hand with the small mound of flesh and moaning when he rolled her erect nipple between his fingers.

Hot tears, uncharacteristic and unwelcome, burned her eyes as he ravaged her mouth, as he explored hidden depths, plundering hot, wet crevasses that felt branded by the intimacy of his touch, almost like she didn't belong to herself anymore. Almost like she belonged to him.

"Lib . . . Lib . . . Lib . . ." he whispered. "We were made for this . . ."

She inhaled his breath, nipping at his bottom lip as he smoothed his hand back up from under her bra, leaving the taut points of her breasts longing for more of his touch.

Opening her eyes, she found his black and wide, fixed on hers, as hot as she'd expect, but surprisingly vulnerable.

"I'm not fucking you by the roadside," he said between panted breaths. "The first time we fuck, it's going to mean something."

She gulped, the muscles at the crux of her thighs contracting with lust, the ice around her heart thawing as he said "mean something," words she doubted he'd ever said to another woman.

"This is messy, Jean-Christian," she murmured, using her fingers to clear away the moisture that had gathered at the edges of her eyes. "Really fucking messy."

"It doesn't have to be." He rubbed at her cheek with his thumb, the touch tender, almost reverent.

"We can't be reckless." She reached for his hand and pulled it away. "There's too much at stake here."

"I know," he whispered, leaning back in his seat, his eyes still holding hers, pleading with hers. "Don't sleep with Neil."

She winced, shifting away from him as she straightened her bra and blouse. Taking a deep breath, she backhanded her slick lips before looking at him. Honestly, she had no idea what to say. She exhaled slowly as she gazed at him.

"Let's just . . . see what happens." How she managed to muster a small smile wasn't totally clear to her. Maybe it was just because she was staring into his eyes, and in their depths—deep, deep in the forest-green wilds of them—she saw something that felt a little bit like hope. "Deal?"

"Deal."

But he felt unsettled. The idea of her fucking Neil on Monday night was going to eat him up inside.

And yet . . . the way she was looking at him right now? Like maybe, through the almost-insurmountable terrain of his father's legacy of betrayal and his mother's pain, he could someway, somehow, find his way to her? It made his heart swell with hope and wonder in a way he'd never experienced before. And though he didn't feel it coming, suddenly he was smiling back at her like she hung the moon and all the stars, and to save his life, he couldn't stop the rush of endorphins that made him feel like anything—*anything*—was possible if this woman wouldn't give up on him.

He'd realized, in the days following Étienne's wedding, that the emotion he'd felt watching Libitz with her prep-school friends at the reception had been jealousy. Before that moment, he'd never felt that sort of true, primal jealousy over a woman—never known it, never wanted a woman to *belong* to him the way he wanted Libitz. Without that feeling of possession, jealousy had never kicked in. But he'd felt it then, and he felt it now as he considered her phone conversation with Nice Neil. And it fucking killed him to think of her choosing Neil because he, Jean-Christian, was unable to best his rival for her heart.

Confident that he was at least as wealthy and well educated as Neil, he had an edge physically, because he already knew that Lib's attraction to him was stronger than her attraction to her so-called boyfriend. Where he lost—where he would *always* lose—was that she was looking for a "meaningful forever," which no doubt Neil could offer, while the concepts of both "meaningful" and "forever" still scared the shit out of Jean-Christian. They scared him so much, he almost doubted he could change into a person who would consider either "meaningful" or "forever." Was it even possible for a thirty-something man who'd lived most of his life in the shadow of his father's blatant and abusive infidelity to figure out how to offer a woman something real?

He sighed with frustration, turning away from her and shifting the car into "Drive." "We have a cradle to pick up."

She nodded. "Sounds good."

"No matter who I am or what I've done," he said, almost more to himself than to her, "I'll always be there for Noelle. She's . . . I mean, I'll never let her down. Never. I want you to know that."

"You already love her."

He did. He had from the moment Étienne and Kate had told him about her. That was a fact.

She chuckled softly, as though pleased. "You know what? Being a godparent looks good on you, Jean-Christian Rousseau."

"And on you, Mademoiselle Feingold," he responded, grinning at her as the complex thoughts in his head were whisked away by the sound of her husky laughter. "Hey . . . you know the way you just said my name? Your accent isn't half bad."

"My genes thank you."

He raised an eyebrow. "Come again?"

"I'm French," she answered. "A quarter, I think. My mother's mother, my bubbe, is French."

"A hundred percent?" he asked, merging back onto the highway.

"I . . . hmm . . . you know? I think so, but I'm not sure." She twitched her lips in thought. "I never met my great-grandparents, and my bubbe doesn't speak French. She's a proud American, and my grandfather was born and raised in Brooklyn by fourth-generation Russian Jews. But every year, at Chanukah, my grandmother makes 'madeleines.' They're these little—"

"—scalloped-shaped butter cakes."

Libitz nodded. "Uh-huh. You know them?" She scoffed at herself. "Of course you know them. You're *French* French."

Jean-Christian, like his siblings, had been born in Paris, and he had called it home for the first twelve years of his life. Even now, twenty-two years later, he still retained French citizenship, spoke the language perfectly, watched Les Bleus kick ass on the soccer field religiously, and preferred reading books in his native language whenever possible. So something about the possibility that Libitz was also ethnically French felt like a puzzle piece fitting perfectly into place, and he shamelessly reveled in it the same way flowers bathed in sunshine. It just felt . . . good.

"I had no idea you were French," he said.

She shrugged. "I'm also Russian, Polish . . . and I'm sure there's some other stuff in there."

"But your grandmother makes madeleines at Chanukah?" he asked, eager to focus on what they had in common.

"Yes. It's tradition. When I was a kid, I was surprised when I realized that none of the other kids had madeleines at Chanukah. Just us. When I asked my bubbe about it, she didn't know *why* she made them every year, just that her mother had done the same. In Israel, they make donuts called *sufganiyot* at Chanukah. She guessed that maybe madeleines were the French version." She shrugged.

"We have them year-round, but my mother puts candied orange peel into the batter at Christmastime," said J.C., "then dips them in chocolate."

Libitz gasped, then turned to face him. "I think I just had an orgasm."

"*Merde.*"

"They sound *amazing.*"

"They are," he said, wondering if Jax had his mother's recipe tucked into some drawer at Le Chateau. Maybe he could find out and try making them for Lib as a surprise. "Do you know where your great-grandmother was from?"

"No clue," said Libitz. "I really don't know very much about her."

"And you never knew her?"

Libitz shook her head. "She died when I was a baby."

J.C. nodded, turning onto Blueberry Lane and stopping at the gate in front of Le Chateau to enter a code into the security pad. "We're here."

"You know, I just thought of something," she said. "You mentioned that your sister found *Les Bijoux Jolis* in the attic, right?"

"*Oui.*"

"Well . . . do you think there could be anything else up there? Letters? A journal? Something to tell us a little bit more about the painting? I'd love to know more about it."

J.C. wanted to kick himself that he hadn't thought of it before now. "I'm sure Jax wouldn't mind if we took a look around."

She raised her eyebrows and nodded with approval as he parked the car and cut the engine. "A treasure hunt. I can't wait."

Half an hour later, after Gard had helped move the heavy cradle to the back seat of Jean-Christian's convertible and Libitz had exchanged pleasantries with Jax over coffee, Jax led them up four flights of stairs to the attic of Le Chateau, telling them to behave themselves as she headed back downstairs for a conference call with some TV executives in New York.

"Behave ourselves?" scoffed Libitz, batting at a creepy cobweb hanging from the low, raftered ceiling. "What exactly does she think we're going to do up here?"

Jean-Christian chuckled softly from behind her, but his laughter stopped as his arms wrapped around her waist and the heat of his lips pressed against the back of her neck. "This?"

A shiver rushed down Libitz's spine as she leaned her head back against his chest and closed her eyes. Damn him, but he knew how to make her wet in an instant.

"Or this," he purred, sliding one hand under her blouse and resting it flat on the warm skin of her stomach as he bit her earlobe.

"Or this," he said, scoring her neck with his teeth as he raised his hand to her breast and gently squeezed it through her bra.

Libitz whimpered softly, turning in his arms and looking up into his dark and dilated eyes.

"What does Neil have that I don't?"

She gulped over the lump that instantly formed in her throat. "Did you know I'll be thirty on December 17?" She nodded. "I will. I'll be thirty years old."

"Okay . . ." he said slowly, searching her face like he wasn't sure where she was going. "I'll be thirty-five on April 11."

She took a deep breath, forcing herself to hold his eyes as she shared her truth. "I want kids, Jean-Christian. I want a home. I want to spend my life with someone I love, someone who loves me back."

He nodded almost imperceptibly, his expression darkening.

"I . . . God, it would have been so much easier if I'd met you a year ago," she said. "Before Kate and Étienne reconnected. Before thirty started looming on the horizon. I would have slept with you, no problem. And I would've been able to walk away with a wave and a smile."

His brows furrowed, and she tried to back out of his arms, surprised when he tightened them around her.

"I've had a lot of fantastic sex," she said. "Like you, I've had a lot of fun. I don't regret it. I wouldn't trade it." She pursed her lips, dropping his eyes. "But it's time for something else now."

"Does Neil want what you want? A wife and kids? Forever?"

She thought of Neil—of his strawberry-blond hair and the freckles on his arms. She pictured his eyes, soft and tender, when he looked at her, his arms bearing gifts: flowers, Challah, kindness, goodness, stability . . .

She looked up at Jean-Christian's handsome face and nodded. "Yes."

"Does Neil want *you*?"

If she wasn't certain of Neil's intentions, Jean-Christian's question might have hurt her, might have stung. But she was certain. Neil had fallen for her over a year ago—his persistence in pursuing her told her so. His voice when she asked him to stay over on Monday night told her all she needed to know.

"Yes," she said. "Neil wants me. *Only* me."

She didn't mean it as a dig against Jean-Christian, only as a truthful answer to his question. But his countenance cooled immediately, and he released her, reaching up to rub his chin with his thumb and forefinger, looking over her head at the boxes, trunks, and furniture behind her. He must have been holding his breath, because he released it with a huff, avoiding her eyes.

"Well, then. That's that."

It doesn't have to be! a voice inside of her bellowed. *It could be you and me, if you wanted me . . . if you wanted what I want from life.*

She swallowed, blinking her eyes and blaming the attic dust for their sudden burn. "Yes. I suppose it is."

He looked back at her, his face turning thunderous as the silence between them grew thick and heavy. Finally, he half-shouted at her: "I don't want it! I never did. I don't want to be someone's husband. I don't want to hurt someone I'm supposed to love, to let someone down who I promised to—I mean, fuck! How do I even know I'd be a good father? I don't. I'd probably be shit just like my . . ." He scoffed, rubbing his chin again, his eyes furious. "And forever? Forever is for chumps who think it exists."

"Chumps like me?" she asked.

"Sure! You. And Neil. And Kate and my brother. And even Jax and Gard, buying Le Chateau and playing house like a couple of kids."

He had his fists clenched at his sides, and though she'd thought to spar with him when she'd asked, "Chumps like me?" his answer had unexpectedly disarmed her. His words were so naked, so desperate. It only took a second for her to realize that he wasn't trying to be a dick; he was scared. Someone had done a number on him. And it was a doozy.

"And none of us will work out?" she asked in a low, even voice, trying to understand.

"How the fuck should I know? Maybe you will. Maybe you won't. But there are no guarantees, are there? Any of you could change . . . could become selfish fucks who . . . who . . ."

"Who what?"

His head fell forward, and he stared at the grimy floor, all bunched muscles and coiled anger, barely restrained fury emanating from his body like heat.

She reached out gently and touched one of his fists, little by little covering it with the palm of her hand, her thumb working itself into the tight spiral formed by his fingers curled into his thumb. And slowly—so very slowly—his fingers loosened and unfurled until she was holding them, until she could lace her fingers through his and clasp their palms together.

Looking up, she found him staring down at her, his lips parted, his face set as though in pain. Raising their hands to her lips, she kissed the back of his, rubbing it tenderly against her cheek. When she lowered them, she offered him a small smile.

"It's okay," she whispered.

"It's not," he answered. "I'm . . . I'm not capable of—"

She raised her free hand and clapped it over his lips, frowning up at him. "Of course you are. We *all* are."

He clenched his jaw so tightly under her palm, she wondered if the hinge would pop. Withdrawing her hand slowly, she looked deeply into his troubled eyes.

"Listen . . . you're right, Jean-Christian. There are no guarantees. And yes, any of us could change at any time." She raised her chin, thinking of her parents and grandparents. All still married. All still working hard to build *l'chaim tovim*, a good life. "But forever exists. I promise you it does.

And no, it's not for chumps or punks or hacks. Because forever takes work." He stared down at her, his face angry but not, she realized, closed off. It made her wonder if he was listening to her. It made her continue. "That's how I know that you're capable—that anyone is capable. It's not a predetermined thing like your blood type or eye color. It's a choice. It's a choice to love someone and be faithful to them and do the work. We're *all* capable of that."

He didn't say anything. Not a word.

As the oppressiveness of his silence grew, she loosened her fingers from his, taking a step back and looking around the attic.

"Well, um . . . I didn't mean to lecture you. I just . . . um, so, where did Jax find the painting?" She let her eyes rove around the dim, dusty space, feeling self-conscious about such a hypercharged conversation and wishing that she hadn't suggested they look for more clues about the painting.

"Lib," he said softly.

She jerked her head around to look at him, thankful for the sound of his voice and eager to hear something—anything—from him.

"Yes?"

"You really believe all that?"

"My grandparents have been married for sixty-one years. My other grandparents for fifty-seven. My parents for thirty-six." She inhaled deeply through her nose and exhaled through her mouth, nodding confidently. "Yeah. I believe it."

He stared at her long and hard, as though absorbing everything, mulling it over and trying to find a place for it. Finally he nodded curtly and gestured to an area behind her.

"She found it over there."

J.C. watched her slip around an old steamer trunk and disappear behind a five-foot-high ornate armoire, still reeling from the force and certainty of her words.

It's not a predetermined thing like your blood type or eye color. It's a choice. It's a choice to love someone and be faithful to them and do the work. We're all *capable of that.*

He had seen happy marriages, of course . . . or rather marriages that *looked* happy. But his cynicism always got the better of him as he wondered if it was a facade—if the smiles of "happy" couples were faked to conceal a world of pain behind them. *One of them is cheating and the other just doesn't know,* he'd reason. Or he'd think, *They're still in the "in love" stage,* as his parents had been for a long time, but one day it would all change. When he felt a longing for "happily ever after" surge up inside of him, which pretty much happened whenever he was with his siblings, he shoved it down, reminding himself that someone would have to be "the strong one" when all their relationships went to shit and they came crying to him. He didn't believe in true love . . . or at least he didn't want to.

But Libitz's fervent convictions had been seared instantly into his brain, leaving him uncertain of his course for the first time in a long time. It was better not to commit to anyone, wasn't it? It was better not to risk hurting someone. It was better to play the field and love no one. Wasn't it?

If that's what he believed, why hadn't he said as much to her? Why hadn't he shared his truth with her? Why had he listened in rapt silence, his heart beating out of his chest, hanging on every word like they were lifelines instead of the thoughts of one delectable little New Yorker?

Was it possible that everything he'd conditioned himself to believe, to *want,* wasn't actually what he believed or wanted at all?

"I think I might have found something amazing!" she cried, suddenly appearing beside the armoire, holding several dusty relics in her arms.

He grinned at her, surprised the gesture came so easily.

Yeah, he thought, hope spreading through his chest like a balm, like something he'd lost so long ago, he almost didn't recognize it inside of him. *I think I might have found something amazing too.*

Chapter 8

"Show me what you found."

Behind the well-preserved Louis XIV armoire, she'd found a roll-top desk. Opening the bottom drawer, she found what appeared to be a mangy journal, a stack of yellowed letters, and an old-fashioned men's shaving case in a rolled leather pouch with two dull brass buckles.

Holding her treasures in her arms, she made her way around the armoire to Jean-Christian, looking for a table on which to place them. Finding none, she lowered herself to a squat and placed them gently on the dusty floor. Then she sat down cross-legged beside them and looked up at him.

"Don't you want to see?"

"We're just going to sit on the floor?"

"Hell yes!" she exclaimed.

He gave her a look before joining her on the weathered wooden boards, sitting across from her. "Well . . . ?"

She handed him the leather shaving case. "Was this his?"

J.C. used his hand to dust off the side of the pouch and found initials burned into the leather. "PVM. Pierre Victor Montferrat. Yep. Must have been."

"Open it! I'll look in this," she said, reaching for the journal.

The art historian in her said that she shouldn't be looking at these antique things here—that they should take them to his gallery where they could spread them out on a table under white lights and handle them with gloved hands. But she couldn't resist learning more about Pierre Montferrat and, hopefully, the beautiful model in the painting.

Pushing the letters gently to the side, she placed the journal on a flat board and opened it gingerly, the old leather giving with a creak as she used a touch more force to smooth the front page.

Pierre Montferrat
47 Rue de Petit Puits
Marseille

A rush of anticipation coursed through Libitz as she reached down to turn the page, but she was interrupted by her partner in crime.

"Wow. Look at this stuff!" said Jean-Christian, who had opened the brass buckles and unfurled the leather case to reveal an ivory-handled razor, a small rectangular ivory box to hold soap, an ivory-handled brush that still had most of its bristles intact, and a mirror with a geometric design carved into the ivory.

"Classic art deco," whispered Libitz, reaching out to finger the black spots of missing silver on the antique mirror.

"Hmm," said Jean-Christian, noting a zipper on the back of the case. "I wonder what's . . ." His sharp intake of breath stole her attention from the mirror, and she looked over to see his fingers pull an emerald necklace from the pouch, the tarnished setting and glittering jewels spilling into his hands.

"The necklace!" she gasped. "Is it—"

"Yes," he said. "I'm positive. It's the one from the portrait!"

Cupped in his hands, he offered it to her like a gift, and Libitz removed it carefully, searching for the ends before holding it up between them.

"My God," she said. "It's like holding history in my hands."

"It's not *like* holding history . . . you *are* holding history."

She gulped, raising her eyes to meet his. "She *wore* this."

He nodded, his smile as broad as a little kid's on Christmas morning. "Can you imagine?"

"You need to have it cleaned and appraised," she said, the gallery owner in her taking over. "This is an antique, and it's . . . silver. I'd never have guessed."

"Probably sterling covered with twenty-four-karat gold."

"Almost all gone now." She nodded sadly. "But still beautiful." Reaching for her purse, she took out her eyeglass case and put her sunglasses on her head. "This'll have to do." Slowly she laid the glistening gems on the black felt lining and shut the case, handing it to Jean-Christian.

He shook his head. "You keep it for me."

She nodded, a warm feeling inside making her smile at him. "Of course."

"How about that?" he asked, gesturing to the flattened journal with his chin and scooting around their small pile of booty to sit beside her.

"Cover page has his name and address. A ledger?" she asked, slipping the eyeglass case back into her purse and looking back at the book on the floor. "A journal?"

His fingers traced the faded name, but his eyes skimmed to the small stack of letters beside the book, bound with a yellowed ribbon. "What about these?"

"Letters," she said, looking at the vintage airmail envelopes.

"To my great-grandmother, I bet." He picked up the pile and scooted backward to sit against the steamer trunk. "Let's read them first."

She grinned at him and nodded, sliding back on the floor to sit beside him. "Okay."

As he untied the ribbon, part of the old fabric disintegrated to fragments, and he winced. "So damn old."

He reached for the letter on top and looked at the address and postmark. "From Pierre Montferrat in Marseille, France, to Amelie Montferrat Roche. So that's, um . . . my great-uncle writing to my great-grandmother, his sister."

Libitz's heart sped up with excitement as she slid slightly closer to him, shoulder to shoulder, so she could see better. "Sent in December 1939."

Jean-Christian gently squeezed the envelope that had been sliced open over seven decades ago and pulled the letter, written on thin airmail paper, from its home. He unfolded it and, after a moment, began reading snippets in English.

"Um . . . let's see here . . . *There is talk of . . .* um, *rationing. En Angleterre*, um, *in England, it has already started. Can you imagine a France in which you cannot have butter with your bread, dear Amelie? Today I shall try to find . . .*"

Libitz stared straight ahead at the dust that floated around the attic in a beam of sunlight as Jean-Christian haltingly translated letter after letter from Pierre Montferrat to his sister, switching back and forth from murmured French to carefully chosen English. Though Amelie repeatedly begged her brother to join her and her family in Montreal, he was unable to due to poor health and an increasingly tumultuous France under Nazi occupation. The letters were vivid and descriptive, and her heart ached for a brother who waited too long to leave, hoping the France of his youth might be restored before the end of his life. But alas, it was still under German occupation when he died, and he would never see his sister again.

". . . *my trusted friend, Jules Vichy, has promised to keep my things safe until they can be shipped to you.*" Jean-Christian cleared his throat, his voice breaking at times, clearly moved by the tone of farewell in Pierre's final letter. "Um, let's see here . . . *There will be no more letters after this one, dear sister. I beg that you remember me always during our sunny days at the Vallon des Auffes when the fish practically jumped into our little boat. Do you remember collecting them into a bucket and running home barefoot to mother? I can still feel your small hand clasped in mine and the hot sun on our backs. Forever I will be your older brother* . . . um, *Pierre, watching out for you until we meet again in God's glory, my little—*" He sniffled. "*My darling little sister.*"

Jean-Christian folded the final letter and carefully tucked it back inside the envelope as Libitz took a shaky breath beside him and wiped the tears from her cheeks.

"He didn't make it to the end of the war," murmured Libitz, whose head had dropped to his shoulder over an hour ago. "He never saw her again."

J.C. turned from the pile of letters in his lap, his lips grazing the top of her head. He pressed them against her sleek black hair, closing his eyes and picturing *Les Bijoux Jolis*, which had been his great-uncle's final painting in free France. Pierre's friend, Jules, must have shipped it, along with his desk and other belongings, to J.C.'s great-grandmother in Montreal at the end of the war.

"It's so sad," said Libitz, her usually strong voice thready with emotion.

J.C. adjusted slightly to put his arm around her and draw her against him, kissing her head again. He nodded, thinking of Étienne, Jax, and Mad and how desperate he would feel to be separated from them during a war that would end up severing any chance to see one another again.

"But no word about the paintings or the model," said J.C.

"Maybe in the journal?" asked Libitz, reaching for it.

"Jean-Christian! Étienne just called wondering where you are."

Jax's voice sailed up the stairs, and Libitz straightened, wiggling out from under his arm as if caught doing something they oughtn't.

"We should go," she whispered, fishing her phone from her back pocket. "Oh, my God! It's almost two!"

He picked up the letters and stuffed them gently into the journal. He called down to Jax, "Coming. Tell him we'll be there in ten minutes."

The sound of Jax's laughter faded as she walked away from the base of the attic stairs, telling her brother that J.C. and Lib would be back soon.

"We lost track of time," said Libitz, standing up and brushing off her jeans.

He immediately missed the warmth of her body pressed against his, the weight of her head resting on his shoulder. Looking up at her, he cocked his head to the side. "This was . . . fun. Is that weird?"

She seemed to weigh the question for a minute before rolling her eyes. "He thinks reading heartbreaking letters is fun."

He stood up. "Admit it. You loved it."

Without much coercion, she nodded. "I can't lie. I'm fascinated by stuff like this."

"How about I look through the journal and see if I can find anything about the model? And we can talk tomorrow at the BBQ?"

"Sounds like a plan. And maybe"—she shrugged—"maybe I'll e-mail a couple of galleries in Marseille and see if I can find any information about Pierre. Perhaps some of his work is still available for sale?"

J.C. nodded. "Definitely worth a shot."

She pulled her bottom lip between her teeth and held it for a second before letting it go. J.C. had a feeling she was waiting for him to do something or say something in particular, but he didn't know what. Suddenly, without warning, she stepped onto his shoes on tiptoe and touched her lips to his, once, twice, gently, without expectation or promise. When she drew away, she looked up into his eyes.

"I wish I could figure you out," she murmured, as though giving sound to a thought.

He searched her face, tracing the strong angle of her jaw, the softness in her cheeks and lips, the way her dark eyelashes framed her wide brown eyes.

"I'm not complicated."

She flinched, but just barely, backing away from him. "Don't kid yourself."

Then she turned and walked away, disappearing down the stairs and leaving him alone with relics of the past in the dim, dark attic.

When Libitz woke up in Kate's guest room the next morning, she opened her eyes with a start, her dreams from last night still so vivid, and it took her a few seconds of deep breathing on her back to convince herself they weren't real.

Her mind had conjured sharp, realistic images of her lying naked on Monsieur Montferrat's chaise, but instead of the older French gentleman painting her, his grand-nephew had wielded the brush. It was intensely erotic holding Jean-Christian's gaze as he stared at her over the top of the canvas, his eyes dilated and hot as he caressed the lines of her body with his eyes and brush.

Slipping her fingers into her sleeping shorts, she slid her middle finger over the carefully groomed triangular landing strip at the top of her clit. Inside the tender folds, she was soaked and slippery, her finger sliding easily over the erect nub of hidden flesh. She gasped as an image of Jean-Christian flitted through her mind, the sensory memory of his tongue in her mouth making her writhe with longing as she inserted two fingers into her sex, hooking them back to massage her G-spot. She whimpered, her hips lifting from the mattress in a shattering climax as she heard his words, *The first time we fuck, it's going to mean something*, in her head. Panting as her body jerked and convulsed, she rolled onto her side and tucked her knees to her chest, trying to savor the shivers of pleasure.

Her phone buzzed beside her on the bedside table, and Libitz reached for it, frowning when she realized it was a series of texts from Neil asking about her trip. She sat up in bed, sighing as she cataloged this new development in her so-called boyfriend. Neil hadn't been much for watchdogging her before now, but inviting him to sleep over seemed to have opened a floodgate of some kind. He asked questions about her trip and shared the mundane minutiae of his day. Neil was a good, solid man, but she really didn't want to hear about the number of Challah orders that were placed this year for Yom Kippur. And knowing that his mother had reached out to her parents to join them for dinner on Friday night added a pressure to the situation she suddenly resented.

Libitz groaned, placing the phone back on the bedside table and scooching under the covers.

What had changed?

"Oh, God," she mumbled.

Monday night. Asking him to sleep over on Monday night. That's what had changed things.

Apparently, sleeping together—or even the *promise* of sleeping together—was as good as a de facto engagement for

Neil. Libitz's breathing hitched uncomfortably as she picked up her phone and scrolled through the messages again.

No doubt. Neil's whole tone had changed, and she grimaced darkly.

For Libitz, having sex would have been about testing the waters (and Neil's goods). But for Neil, it was a lot more serious. In fact, she sensed that it would likely be the last step before he proposed marriage. Which meant that by asking him to stay over on Monday night, she'd inadvertently sent him the message that she was almost ready for . . . matrimony.

She groaned, furious with herself for not being more in touch with the situation and acting so impulsively when she called Neil from Jean-Christian's car yesterday. Because she suddenly realized—with startling clarity—that she wasn't interested in getting more serious with Neil.

Which meant that . . .

"Fuck," she muttered.

. . . Jean-Christian, *damn him*, was right. She was only using Neil to push the man she wanted out of her heart and mind. And in fact, that's what she'd been doing all along.

As soon as possible, she needed to end things with Neil before they got any more serious. She didn't want to hurt him, but she feared that was inevitable now. She'd raised his expectations to a level she'd never intended, and it was entirely her own selfish fault.

Blowing out an exasperated breath as she picked up her phone to call Neil, it buzzed in her hands, and she checked out the screen.

JC: Elsa . . . you up?

As a rush of adrenaline made her skin prickle with excitement and awareness, she typed back, "Yes. Just." Her heart practically beat out of her chest with anticipation.

JC: So I read through the journal, and I figured out something.
MYPHONE: Tell me!
JC: First . . . I bet you're hot in the AM.

Yes, she was superhot with her hair sticking up everywhere and her frayed cotton sleeping shorts halfway down her legs.

MYPHONE: Quit it. Tell me what you learned.
JC: Second . . . I dreamed about you last night.

Libitz sucked in a gasp of breath, her inner muscles convulsing one last time just from reading his text.

MYPHONE: You did?
JC: Third . . . the dream was crazy hot.

She lay back on the pillows, her fingers finding her still-sensitive clit and brushing it gingerly.

MYPHONE: It was?
JC: You were the model, and I was the painter.

She whipped her hand back and scrambled to sit up, staring at the phone, goose bumps rising over her flesh. She'd had the exact same dream.

"Oh, my God." She bit her lip, trying to figure out what to say. She couldn't very well say, "Me too!" Taking a shaky breath, she ran her fingers over the words before responding.

MYPHONE: You were painting me?
JC: Every inch of you.

Her whole body blushed, and she grinned, thinking of how tiny she'd felt sitting beside him in the attic yesterday.

MYPHONE: Must not have taken very long.
JC: I took my time.

As delicious as it was to flirt with him . . . one, she owed it to Neil to break off things first, and two, she needed to keep her wits. Jean-Christian was a minefield of a man. She needed to be very careful not to get swept away if she wanted any sort of real future with him; he was capable of breaking her heart in half.

MYPHONE: Are you going to tell me about the journal or what?
JC: Ok. Ok. He paid out 290 Fr. to a C.T. on Aug 30, 1939. It's in his notes on the side of his ledger where he itemizes the expenses for the portrait. I'm thinking that has to be the model. All the other costs are associated with an art store.
MYPHONE. C.T.?
JC: Her initials?

"C.T.," she whispered, nodding her head. "Who are you?"

MYPHONE: I'll e-mail some galleries now and see if they have any of Montferrat's work on display. Maybe she appears in another portrait and we can figure out her name.
JC: Sounds good.
MYPHONE: See you later?
JC: Can't wait. Wear something hot.
MYPHONE: Pig.
JC: There's my Elsa.

She grinned, placing her phone back on the bedside table as she hopped out of bed to take a shower.

J.C. chuckled at her text, then placed his phone back on the bedside table.

Under the sheets, his cock strained, tentpoling the fabric over his pelvis. He groaned, sliding his hands over the ripples of his muscular chest to flatten the thick erection against his stomach, rubbing up and down with the palm of his hand. Pre-cum lubricated his skin, and his fingers circled the throbbing head of his cock, pumping harder as his hips pushed upward and the back of his head smashed into his pillow.

He thought of Libitz . . . of her angles and softness . . . of the sounds she made when he kissed her . . . of the way her nipples hardened between his fingers. He saw her eyes flash with fire, saw her tongue lick her lips, and—

"Ahhhhh," he cried out, coming in hot spurts on his chest as he pictured her head thrown back in ecstasy, her small body convulsing around his cock as he came inside of her.

"Fuck," he groaned, whipping the wet sheet off his bed and throwing an arm over his eyes.

He had it so. Fucking. Bad. for this woman. He could barely remember what life looked like before wanting her.

When his phone buzzed beside him, he jumped like Pavlov's dog, grabbing it with a pathetic hope that it was her, calling to talk to him.

"Hello?"

"J.C.?" purred a cultured voice he knew too well.

His heart plummeted. "Felicity."

"Well, that doesn't sound like a happy voice."

He didn't know what to say. Covered with cum from an imaginary fuckfest with Libitz, he definitely didn't feel like talking to Felicity.

"Just busy. What's up?"

"Are we still on for today? Noon at the Morris House?"

Noon? Fuck. Had he made plans with her?

"I don't—"

"It wasn't in stone," she said quickly, "but you mentioned it the last time we got together."

No doubt he had, and actually, the timing was fine. Étienne and Kate's BBQ wasn't until five o'clock. Except . . .

Except he had zero—no, less than zero—interest in fucking Felicity. Frankly, much to his surprise, he had zero interest in fucking anyone who wasn't Libitz.

"Sorry, Felicity," he said. "I can't make it."

"Big plans?" she asked.

"Housewarming at Kate and Ten's new place."

"Étienne bought a house? I haven't seen him in ages! What fun!"

He groaned inwardly.

This wasn't something Felicity normally tried with him; they fucked and they occasionally socialized when one of them needed a date to an event, but he'd been careful to curb her expectations. He wasn't her boyfriend or anything resembling it; he certainly wasn't inviting her to his brother's house.

"I'll send your regards."

"I'd love to give them myself," she pushed. She followed this up with a nervous chuckle. "I know we've been keeping things casual, but . . . well, I wanted to tell you in person, but my divorce was finalized on Friday, and I thought . . . if you were interested . . ."

J.C. Rousseau didn't believe in leading a woman on. Never had. He believed in ripping off the Band-Aid when called for.

"I'm not," he said simply. "I'm not interested."

"Oh," she gasped.

"I don't want to hurt you, Felicity, but we're both adults. We knew what this was."

"I just thought that maybe . . ."

"No," he said firmly.

She was quiet for a moment before responding. "I misread the situation. I thought—well, I thought you might want—"

"No. I'm sorry. I think we both need to move on now," he said evenly. "I wish you all the best, Felicity."

Expecting her to say something similarly civil, he waited a moment to hear her say, "It won't last."

"What?"

She scoffed. "You think this is my first rodeo, J.C.? No, no, no, darling. Whoever she is? It won't last."

"I don't know what you're talking about," he said, though his heart rate quickened uncomfortably.

"Yes, you do. You've found someone else." She paused. "How do I know? I just do. I recognize it in your voice. But it has no legs, darling. It can't because the only appendage you have dangling below the waist is your cock." She chuckled softly. "Can't move forward without legs."

"You're speaking in riddles, Felicity, and it's—"

"I'll put it plainly, then: you're not the kind who commits, J.C. You're a whore, and you like it that way."

"I guess it takes one to know one," he said, civil good-byes forgotten.

"Fair enough," she said, "which is why it won't surprise you when I say that my arms will be wide open to welcome you back to my bed once this little flirtation bores you. Your cock is . . . epic. I enjoy you. So give me a call when you're ready."

He took a deep breath and sighed, wondering how Felicity-fucking-Atwell had somehow managed to get into his head. It made him angry, made his heart throb in protest at her words, made him hate that she saw through him so easily, made him doubt that he'd ever find himself in the sort of safe, committed relationship his brother and sisters had managed to find.

He tightened his jaw, focusing on his anger, his voice sharp and cold. "Sorry to disappoint you, *chérie*, but that day isn't coming."

She chuckled again, the sound brittle. "Well, then, best of luck, darling. You'll need it."

"*Au revoir*, Felicity," he said.

"Good-bye, darling."

He sat up in bed, frowning down at his phone as he pressed "End." Felicity's words circled in his head, juxtaposed against Libitz's little speech in the attic yesterday. *It's a choice . . . It's a choice to love someone and be faithful to them and do the work. We're* all *capable of that.* With a heretofore unparalleled longing, he realized how desperately he wanted her words to be true. He wanted them to come true with her. And for that, he needed more time with her—more time he couldn't have, since she was heading home to Nice Neil tomorrow.

But then again . . . he thought, his eyes narrowing as his lips turned up, *Why couldn't he have it?*

Turning back to his phone, he scrolled through his list of contacts, finding the New York City number he was looking for and dialing it quickly.

Chapter 9

"Jean-Christian!" exclaimed Mad as he pulled up in front of her building and she came bounding out of the lobby.

"Someone's in a good mood!" he said, smiling at his little sister from his car by the curb.

She grinned, jumping in beside him. "It's a beautiful day, we're going to a BBQ, Ten's having a baby, and . . ."

"And?"

Her eyes sparkled with excitement. "Cort's coming home early! He and Vic were offered a record deal in New York, and they start laying tracks the week after next."

"Hey!" he said. "That's great."

"I know. I could barely sleep after talking to him last night."

"So I'm guessing you'll be in New York a lot this fall."

"Some." She nodded as she buckled her seat belt. "There's more . . ."

Her face was filled with such happiness, such profound tenderness, it made his heart ache. "Tell me."

"We set a date, Jean-Christian. April 28."

"For your wedding," he said softly.

"For our wedding," she confirmed.

"You're really going through with it."

"Are you kidding? I can't wait to *go through* with it!" she said as he pulled away from the curb and waited at an intersection for a group of tourists to cross. "We want to have the reception at Greens Farms. The apple blossoms will be in full bloom."

"Sounds beautiful, Mad."

"It will be! And Jean-Christian," she said, her eyes watering, "I want you to give me away."

"Mad . . ." he breathed, the honor of her request taking his breath away.

"You're my oldest brother. You always looked after me. Looked after all of us. Will you?"

He took a deep breath and nodded, not quite able to trust his voice as he stepped on the gas.

"Thank you," she said, leaning over the bolster to kiss his cheek. "I'm putting my place on the market next week. We're going to live in his house. It's bigger, plus it has a recording studio. And there's a courtyard for Chevy."

Chevy was the mutt his sister and Cort had adopted a couple of weeks ago.

"So you'll keep a place in Philly?" he asked.

"Of course! Cort has a pied-à-terre in New York when he needs it for recording or playing concerts, but Philly's home for us. Always will be."

J.C. nodded, swallowing over the lump in his throat. "I'm happy for you, *doudou*."

"I wish . . ." her voice tapered off.

"What do you wish?"

"I wish you had someone too."

It's a choice to love someone and be faithful to them and do the work. We're all *capable of that.*

He slid a glance to her before looking back at the road. "I'm working on it."

"*What?*" Her head whipped around so fast, her ponytail hit her in the face. "Wait a minute! What did you say?"

He took a deep breath and huffed softly, trying to organize his thoughts. "I just . . . I don't know. Maybe I've been . . . maybe I might want something—I don't know—more?"

She was gaping at him. He could feel her eyes on him and see her open mouth out of the corner of his eye.

"You're going to catch flies," he advised.

She closed her lips, then opened them again, then closed them.

"Say something, Mad."

"I'm sorry, but . . . this is a lot to digest."

"Man, if you're going to give me this hard a time, I can't imagine what Jax and Ten will say."

"I don't mean to give you a hard time. I'm just . . . surprised."

"I'm teasing, *doudou*," he said, reaching over to pat her arm. "My track record doesn't exactly scream 'marriage material.'"

"But that's what you want? Marriage?"

No. Hearing it said like that? "Marriage," all bold and bewildering? No, it felt terrifying. He definitely didn't want that . . . did he?

A vision of Lib passed through his mind, her angles somehow soothing, her softness beckoning. He didn't know if he wanted "marriage" per se. He only knew he wanted her.

He shrugged. "I'm trying to be open to more. That's all."

"Well, wonders never cease," murmured Mad. "So tell me . . . has anyone in particular been the genesis to this remarkable change?"

"Can you keep a secret?" he asked her.

She leaned closer. "Of course!"

"So can I," he said, chuckling at her instant frown.

"You're a rat."

He straightened in his seat as they stopped at a red light. "Can I ask you a question?"

"Anything."

"*Maman et Père* . . . you know that . . ."

"What?"

"Well, they weren't very happy."

Her face clouded over a little and she nodded. "That's putting it mildly."

"How do you let go of that? How did you trust Cort? I mean—Christ, Mad! Jax told me that Thatcher was cheating on you, and yet here you are! Talking about moving in with Cort and setting a wedding date. How did you . . . I mean, how can you be so trusting? How do you know it won't all go to shit?"

"I love him," she said simply. "And he loves me. If I love someone and I'm sure he loves me in return, I have to trust him. I have faith in him."

"But what if he lets you down?"

She took a deep breath. "I suppose we could fall out of love someday. I hope not, but life is long, and I'm not such a dreamer that I would tell you it's impossible. But, Jean-Christian, I have some control over that. Even if we do fall out of love, I can work to find it again. I choose *him*. I choose *us*. Forever."

Work and *choice*. Two words that Libitz had also used. Was it truly that easy? Was loving someone a choice? Was marriage work? And with love and work, could he have something that had eluded his parents?

"You know I'm going to find out who she is," said Mad in a singsong voice, grinning at him.

J.C. chuckled at her minxy smile. "How about you tell me more about your wedding plans instead?"

Libitz had spent all morning and most of the early afternoon helping Kate direct caterers, choose music, and arrange centerpieces of mums for the round tables she'd had set up in her backyard. Luckily the weather had complied, and it was a gorgeous afternoon for a BBQ, complete with blue skies, sunshine, a light breeze, and the promise of a clear evening.

As the guests arrived, including Kate's cousins, the English brothers, and their significant others, the backyard took on a festive atmosphere. They watched Caroline English frolic through the sprinkler with delight, her mother, Daisy English, giggling every time her soaked toddler rushed back into her arms.

Jessica Winslow English and Emily Edwards English, both expecting, sat at a table with Jessica's sisters-in-law and new moms, Skye, Elise, and Margaret Winslow, cooing over the three baby cousins with delight. Christopher Winslow, who'd just won his first congressional seat in Washington last fall, had just proposed to his girlfriend, Julianne, while vacationing with the secretary of state on Cape Cod. Libitz waved at Julianne, who was speaking to Molly English, the new bride of the youngest English brother, Weston.

The only unmarried English brother was Stratton, who had his arm tightly around the waist of his girlfriend, Valeria, as they talked to his parents, Tom and Eleanora. But he was 100 percent off the market—it was just a matter of time until he popped the question and they started making *bambinos* of their own.

At a table off to the side were Alice Story and Bree Ambler, whom Libitz had met briefly at Kate's wedding and liked instantly. Both were strong, savvy, single businesswomen. *My peeps*, thought unmarried business-owner Libitz, crossing the lawn to sit with them.

"Is this seat taken?" she asked.

"Nope," said Bree, a striking platinum blonde with icy blue eyes. "It's all yours."

"Thanks," she said, placing her glass of Chardonnay on the table and joining them. "We met in the receiving line at Kate and Étienne's wedding, but I'm—"

"Libitz." Bree shook her hand. "Bree Ambler. I recognize you. You were the maid of honor."

Libitz nodded. "Kate's best friend."

"From New York?" asked Alice, shaking Lib's proffered hand with a strong grip and a warm smile.

"I own a gallery there."

"I work on Wall Street," said Bree. "We should have lunch sometime."

"I'd love it," said Libitz with a grin. "In the market for any art?"

Bree shrugged. "My sister's more the creative type."

"I'm not sure I've met her."

Bree and Alice shared a look.

"You'd know if you did," said Bree with a sigh. "She's . . . unforgettable."

"Speaking of unforgettable, I think I see Priscilla," said Alice, sitting back in her chair and rolling her eyes.

"What is she wearing? Is that a fucking muumuu?" asked Bree.

"Probably. She's *so* embarrassing." She turned to Libitz. "We both have what you'd call . . . 'black sheep' sisters."

"Pains in the ass," corrected Bree.

"On the topic of pains in the . . . backside," said Alice, who was definitely the more prim and proper of the two women, "look who just showed up!"

Bree and Libitz strained their necks to see Jean-Christian and Mad Rousseau walk through the French doors of Toujours and onto the brick patio. Libitz's heart fluttered with happiness to see him, to be near him, to know that within minutes, she'd hear his voice again.

"What an asshole," muttered Bree, lifting her wine.

"*D'accord,*" agreed Alice in French, clinking her friend's glass.

Both downed the contents and placed their glasses back on the table in unison.

"A note of warning," said Bree, turning her glance to Libitz. "See that hot piece of dark-haired, green-eyed ass over there?"

"J.C. Rousseau," said Libitz, keeping her face carefully neutral.

"Oh, of course," said Bree darkly. "You were in Ten's wedding, so you've already met him."

"Stay. Away," said Alice dramatically, shuddering as she placed her palm over her heart. "He's beautiful, but disgusting."

"What she said," added Bree with a knowing look. "Times a million. And he's dirtier than a Manhattan port-o-john."

Alice giggled but also nodded in agreement.

An unexpected rush of protectiveness stole Libitz's breath as she turned to look at him again. "Maybe he's just misunderstood."

"No," said Alice firmly. "Surprisingly, no. To his credit, he's very upfront about what he wants."

"And what he wants is cheap and dirty," offered Bree acidly, "if I recall correctly."

"You do!" said Alice with a knowing nod.

"He didn't seem that bad to me," said Libitz, turning to frown at the duo.

"Holy shit," said Bree, reaching for Lib's forearm and wrapping her fingers around it tightly. She leaned across the table, searching Libitz's eyes urgently. "Has he already gotten his hooks in you?"

"Honey," said Alice, her face concerned as she also leaned closer to Libitz, "You can't drink that Kool-Aid. It's spiked."

"It's lethal!" cried Bree.

"Don't be distracted by the hotness," warned Alice. "Just remind yourself that underneath is the devil."

Bree nodded in agreement. "Scorching hot with a stone-cold heart."

"Oh, God," moaned Alice, her eyes widening. "Is he coming over here? Why is he coming over here?"

"Fuck," muttered Bree, releasing Libitz's arm like it was hot. "Are you involved with him?"

"I'm . . ." Libitz gulped. "Not officially . . ."

"Oh, Christ!" said Alice, standing up with her wineglass. "I'm not staying to watch this. I need a refill."

"It's your funeral," said Bree to Libitz before standing shoulder to shoulder with her friend.

"Ladies!" greeted Jean-Christian, his eyes twinkling wickedly as he stopped at the table. "Hello."

Alice turned up her nose like he'd just taken a mastiff-sized shit at her feet. "J.C.," she said, nodding curtly. She looked down at Libitz. "Nice to meet you. Remember what we said."

"I . . ." said Libitz to her back as she hurried away.

"Hey, Bree," said Jean-Christian.

Bree's eyes were arctic as she stared at him.

"You're looking good," he said.

"Fuck you," she bit out.

"You've met Libitz," he said congenially, gesturing to her with his palm, as though Bree *hadn't* just cursed at him.

Libitz stared down at the table. The tension between them was so palpable, so awkward, she almost wished she could excuse herself, but she thought that would make things worse.

Suddenly Bree's voice was intimately close to Libitz's ear. She spoke in a passionate whisper: "We warned you. Run away while you still can."

Libitz looked up to respond to her, but she was already walking away, her fire-engine-red sundress a slash of angry crimson in the sunshine.

She shifted her eyes to Jean-Christian. "Friends of yours?"

He shook his head, his expression sobering. "Apparently not."

"Exes?"

"I knew Alice at Princeton. We went out a few times, but she was a little too prissy for me."

"By 'went out,' just to clarify, you mean 'screwed,' right?"

"No, actually," he said, taking a seat beside her. "We had dinner a couple of times. Caught a movie or two. Made out, yes . . . but we never actually fucked."

"You definitely fucked Bree," said Libitz, hating the mental image of them together—Bree's shock of blonde hair next to Jean Christian's almost-black. They would have been a striking couple.

He nodded. "Yes. I did."

"In more ways than one, I'd say," deadpanned Libitz.

He shrugged, but his eyes weren't as nonchalant as the gesture. "I'm not denying it, Elsa. I've fucked many."

She took a deep breath. No woman liked hearing these words from a man for whom she was falling, but the only response circling in her head was, *Me too.*

Like J.C., although probably not to the same extent, Libitz had engaged in a lot of gratuitous sex since high school. She didn't shit where she ate, which made anonymous one-night stands her favorite, unlike J.C. who had hunted on home ground . . . but she certainly had no room to judge him.

That said, however, deep inside she had an almost-painful longing to know that he was finished with that sort of serial polyamory. She had no right to ask it of him or expect it of him, of course. They were many things to each other—co-godparents-to-be, bound through a strong and beloved family connection, business associates, fellow art lovers, and co-conspirators in researching *Les Bijoux Jolis*. And sure, they'd kissed a few times, and he'd felt her up. But when she combined all that together, what did it make? Friends? No, that didn't feel right. But they weren't in a relationship either. She had no claim to him, regardless of the whisperings and yearnings of her heart.

They sat in uncomfortable silence for a few seconds before he nudged her in the side. "I brought the ledger. I left it inside."

Grateful for a more welcome topic of conversation, she turned to him and smiled. "Great! We can go take a look at it if you—"

Her phone started buzzing on the table, and she turned from him to find Neil's name and number lighting up the screen.

"Nice Neil?" he asked, looking pissed.

She nodded. "I have to take it."

"Fantastic," he muttered, sitting back in his seat.

Apparently, he wasn't going to give her any privacy. Okay. Fine. She pressed "Talk" and raised the phone to her ear.

"Hello?"

"Hey, honey. I saw you called."

Sometime between this morning, when she'd called Neil determined to break up with him, and now, several hours later, she'd decided that it was downright cold-blooded to break up with him over the phone. But she'd definitely hoped that she wouldn't have to talk to him again until she saw him on Monday.

"I, um . . . yeah. I got your texts. Not sure if I'm free for dinner on Friday."

"But it's Shabbat," he said.

"I know. I just . . . I have a meeting that might run late."

"Lib," he said, "I know your job's important to you, but Shabbat is sacred. I think you should make an effort."

Heretofore in their relationship, Neil hadn't made comments like this, and it annoyed her that he was being so heavy-handed. "We can talk about it on Monday."

"Yeah," he said, his voice flat. "About Monday . . . jeez, honey, I hate to do this."

"What's wrong?"

"I have to go up to the King Arthur campus in Norwich, Vermont, from Monday to Wednesday. My father was supposed to go, but he came down with the flu, and Aaron's running point on the Yom Kippur orders, but we need to renegotiate our flour prices with them, so I have to—"

"That's great!" exclaimed Libitz.

"But it means I can't pick you up," said Neil, his voice confused.

"Oh," she said, clearing her throat, trying not to sound as relieved as she felt. "Oh, right. Well, no worries. I'll just see you on Wednesday, okay?"

"Wait, wait, wait! Why don't you come with me?" asked Neil. "They're putting me up in this quaint little inn. It's beautiful, Lib. We'd have our own room. We could . . ."

His voice trailed off, hope and longing thick in its tone.

She scrambled, trying to think of an excuse for why she couldn't run off to Vermont for mediocre sex with Neil that would seal a dismal fate for her future. Looking up at Jean-Christian, she felt a smile spread across her face.

"I can't. I bought a Kandinsky for Mrs. Carnegie from a gallery in Philadelphia. I need to deliver it on Tuesday. In person."

Jean-Christian's dark-green eyes looked deeply into hers, soft with promise, brimming with the same relief she herself felt. He reached for her free hand and she let him take it, let him lace their fingers together.

"Aw," said Neil. "That's too bad, but I understand. Maybe you can switch things around to make Friday Shabbat work?"

"Um," she stalled, the feeling of Jean-Christian's flesh pressed flush against hers distracting her. "We can talk about it on—on . . ."

"Wednesday," said Neil. "I should be back in the city around six. I'll pick you up for dinner at seven?"

"Come in for a drink first," said Libitz, knowing that they'd never actually make it to dinner.

"Will do," he said. "Can't wait to see you, honey."

"Bye, Neil," she said, pressing "End" and lowering her phone as she stared deeply into Jean-Christian's eyes.

"Neil's got a business trip to Vermont," she murmured. "He can't pick me up on Monday."

"I broke things off with Felicity," he blurted out, leaning closer to her. "We're not—we're not getting together anymore. It's over."

She'd been holding her breath, but now she exhaled sharply in surprise, overwhelmed by his declaration and the implied meaning behind it. She sucked in a shallow breath, her fingers tightening around his, but that chaste contact wasn't nearly enough. She needed more. She wanted more.

"Can we—can we go somewhere?" she asked.

He nodded slowly, glancing back toward the house. "Your room?"

She tugged her hand from his. "Meet me there in five."

"You go in through the kitchen. I'll go around to the front," he said, giving her a hot look before standing up and striding away from her, toward the side of the house.

Libitz waited a few minutes, pretending to look at her phone while her heart pounded out of her chest. When she could wait no more, she stood up and slipped her phone in her back pocket, heading for the kitchen with her head down.

"Lib!" said Kate.

She looked up at her best friend, who was standing on the patio talking to Mad, Jax, and Gard.

"Lib, is everything okay? Your cheeks are flushed."

"I'm fine," said Libitz, smiling at them. "I was just sitting in the sun. In fact, I was going upstairs for some sunblock."

Kate grinned, looking at Lib's cream-colored satin tank top and sailor-front dark-blue linen pants. "I forgot to tell you how cute you look."

"Quit it," said Libitz. "You'll give me a big head."

"See you in a bit," said Kate, turning back to her in-laws.

Darting around the catering staff, Libitz hustled through the kitchen and into the dining room, her heeled sandals click-clacking over the slick parquet floor that led to the front vestibule. Glancing around the foyer to be sure that no one was around to put two and two together, she took the stairs two at a time, breathless by the time she reached the safety of the top. Racing down the hall, she stopped in front of her bedroom door, running a hand through her hair before opening it.

"Behind you, Elsa."

Turning around, her breasts brushed against Jean-Christian's chest as he backed her into the guest room and kicked the door shut behind them.

"You have cat skills," she said, "I never heard you coming!"

"Fair is fair, baby." Grabbing her around the waist, he jerked her against his hard body, his eyes onyx as he stared down at her. "I never saw you coming."

He leaned down, and his lips claimed hers with an intensity that stole her thoughts and her words and the ability to speak or think. Sliding his hands down her back, he smoothed them back up under her blouse, unlatching her bra so he could splay his hands over the skin of her shoulder blades as she reached for the hem of her top and pulled it, with her bra, over her head.

In the split second it took for her to bare her breasts to him, he reached behind his neck to tug his polo shirt over his head. Chest to chest, warm and wonderfully naked, they collided again.

Jean-Christian's hands skimmed down to her ass, pushing her firmly against his massive erection, and she gasped with pleasure, imagining how it would feel to have it lodged between her legs. She toed off her sandals and stepped on his shoes, letting him walk them back to the bed as he kissed her. When she felt the mattress behind her knees, she fell back, and he grinned down at her, lowering himself to his side, right next to her, where his view and access to her breasts was unimpeded.

As he dipped his head and took one dusky bud between his lips, she gasped, arching her back and saying, "The g-gallery in Marseille has five other, um, Montferrats."

One hand held the breast he was suckling while the other plumped its twin, caressing the stiff, straining skin of her nipple.

"Fuck, that's hot," he murmured, nuzzling the damp flesh with his nose before sucking it between his lips again. "Keep talking."

"Anh!" She whimpered, burying her head in the comforter as darts of pleasure unfurled all over her body, stealing her breath. "Di-different . . . models."

His lips skimmed from the breast he'd laved to the other, and his tongue circled her other nipple, playing with it like a cat stalking prey. "I called a friend at the Met."

"In . . . New York?" she asked, breathless as he dragged his teeth over her throbbing flesh.

"Is there another?"

"N-no," she panted, closing her eyes as he sucked the distended bud between his lips.

When she couldn't bear the sharpness of the sensation anymore, she plunged her hands into his hair and dragged his face to hers, demanding his lips, reveling in the feel of his chest pressed against hers as he rolled on top of her body and kissed her, bracing his weight on elbows planted by her head.

Reaching between them, she slipped her hand into his shorts, finding the velvet steel of his throbbing cock and wrapping her fingers around it as he groaned into her mouth, as his tongue tangled with hers.

Knock, knock, knock. "Lib?"

Through the haze of her lust-induced subconscious, Libitz started, breaking off their kiss and turning her head to look at the bedroom door with panic.

"Lib? It's Kate. Are you okay?"

"Fuck!" she hissed, unhanding Jean-Christian's cock and dragging her hands to his chest, pushing against the wall of muscle futilely.

"Uh . . . KK?" she squeaked.

"I was worried about you. Can I come in?"

"Uhhh . . ." Jerking her glance up, her eyes slammed into Jean-Christian's. "Gimme a sec, Kate?"

"Can I bring you anything, Lib? Aloe maybe? For the sunburn?"

"Yeah, uhhh . . ."

"Cold water," suggested Jean-Christian in a strained whisper.

"Maybe some cold water?" Libitz called. "And an aspirin?"

"Of course!" said Kate. "I'll be right back!"

Libitz looked back at Jean-Christian. "Get in the closet!"

He furrowed his brows at her. "What?"

"You have to hide!" she whisper-yelled, pushing at his chest.

"That's ridiculous. We're all adults. Why don't we just tell her?"

"Tell her what?" demanded Libitz. "We don't even know what this is!"

"Well, we could just say . . ."

"No! Get in the closet!"

She punched at his chest until he rolled off of her with a long-suffering groan. "This sucks."

"Get. In. The. Closet," she hissed, sitting up and grabbing her bra and shirt off the floor. "And don't come out until we're long gone!"

"We can be together if we want, Lib."

"We're not 'together,' Jean-Christian. Not yet anyway. When and if we ever *are* together, we'll figure out the right way to tell her," insisted Libitz. "But not like this."

She threw her shirt over her head and turned to find him sitting on the edge of the bed, hair mussed, muscular chest sculpted and beautiful, cock straining against his khaki shorts. Taking pity on him, she stepped between his legs and smiled down at him, bending to kiss his lips. "Please hide."

He sighed with annoyance, but his eyes were soft as he gazed up at her, placing his hands on her hips to draw her a little closer. "Let me drive you home tomorrow."

"Yes," she said, reaching to cup his cheek.

"Let me buy you dinner."

"Yes," she said.

"Come to the Met with me on Tuesday."

"Yes," she said again, bending to kiss his forehead and sweep an errant lock of hair back into the fold.

"I'm crazy about you, Libitz," he murmured, then flinched as though the words were a mistake, his eyes wide and worried.

She inhaled sharply, biting her bottom lip as she stared at him. Caressing his cheek before dropping her hand, she smiled and said sweetly, "Then get in the closet for me."

He smiled at her as though relieved and stood up. She reached down for his shirt and handed it to him, gesturing to the closet with one hand and straightening the bed once he was securely inside.

"Lib? I couldn't find aspirin. Just Motrin. Can I come in?"

Libitz grabbed a cardigan sweater from on top of the dresser and opened the door to find Kate in the hallway.

"Thanks, KK."

Kate handed her the vial of tablets and glass of water, then reached out to touch her friend's very flushed cheeks. "You *are* warm, Lib. No more sun for you today, okay?"

"You got it."

With a last longing glance at the closet, Libitz closed the bedroom door behind them and walked back to the party with her friend.

Chapter 10

Jean-Christian pulled into the driveway at Toujours at one o'clock on Monday afternoon, bounding up the front steps in the rain to ring the doorbell of his brother's house.

After exiting the fucking closet yesterday afternoon, he'd rubbed one out in the guest bathroom before returning to the BBQ, and he avoided Libitz for the rest of the night, uncertain he'd be able to keep from reaching for her if they found themselves together. It made for a frustrating and fairly miserable BBQ, half-listening to conversations as he zoned out, his eyes on a constant search for her, happy yet simultaneously jealous when he found her talking to someone else. The only voice he was interested in hearing was hers, and it sucked that she was so close and yet so off limits.

Finally, he'd decided to go home, but not before cornering Jessica English and asking her to take care of things at the gallery for a few days. She was on prematernity leave from her position as head docent at the Barnes Foundation but seemed excited to have a temporary job behind his desk at the gallery. After giving her a spare key and the security code, he'd left the party early, his balls still blue and his mood the same color.

But today was a new day—a new day in which he got to spend time with Lib, who wouldn't be sleeping with Nice

Neil tonight after all. He had a furtive hope that she might, in fact, be sleeping with him, as there would be no Kate English, er, *Rousseau*, interrupting them when they were about to—

"J.C.! Hello," said Kate, opening the door and leaning forward to kiss his cheeks. "It's very nice of you to take Lib to the train station. You've been her chauffeur all weekend."

"It's the least I can do for Noelle's godmother," he said.

"I appreciate that," said Kate. "It means so much to Étienne and me that you two are trying to get along." She cocked her head to the side. "How about some coffee?"

"No, uh, um . . ." His voice trailed off in a quiet sputter of distraction.

Over Kate's shoulder, Libitz was coming down the stairs. Wearing a simple denim shirtdress and knee-high brown boots with her short, black hair slicked back with gel, Libitz was effortlessly stylish and endlessly chic. Her brown eyes sparkled from where she stopped with one hand on the newel post, and the way she grinned at him made him feel like he was the only man in the world.

"Ready to go?" he asked.

She nodded and he forced himself to look away from her and back at Kate, who was staring at him with a pinched expression. Apparently he and Lib weren't very good at hiding their growing feelings for each other, because Kate seemed to have gotten up to speed over the course of about twenty seconds.

"*I* can drive her," said Kate, her tone curt.

Libitz stepped from the stairs and moved quickly to put an arm around her friend, turning Kate to face her. Her voice was gentle but firm. "No, Kate. Jean-Christian will drive me."

"Lib," said Kate, shaking her head back and forth slowly, her face pained. "You promised me."

"I haven't broken my promise," said Libitz, her voice soft and even.

"But I can *see* it," said Kate, a desperate edge to her voice. "I can tell that you two—"

". . . are attracted to each other?" she asked, flicking a quick glance at J.C. "We are. So what?"

Kate took a labored breath and placed both hands lovingly over her belly. "We *need* you both in Noelle's life. You understand that?"

Libitz looked up at J.C., her expression severe before turning back to Kate. "We do."

Looking back and forth between them uncertainly, Kate finally shrugged. "There's nothing I can do to stop you." She turned back to Libitz. "But I will not bounce back quickly if you two fuck this up. Got it?"

J.C. locked eyes with Libitz, nodding at her slowly, solemnly, silently promising her that she wasn't like the others, that whatever happened between them, it wasn't frivolous or cheap. He had no gift for predicting the future, but whatever was between him and Libitz, it *meant* something to him, and he wouldn't treat it lightly.

"We understand, Kate," he said gently.

Kate backed out of Libitz's arms, standing aside so she could look at them side by side. Her eyes were sad and terribly uncertain as she shrugged and mumbled, "You look good together."

Libitz took a step forward, "Kate . . ."

"Have a safe trip back to New York," said Kate, turning to rush up the stairs, the sound of soft crying accompanying her footsteps.

J.C. watched her go as Libitz called after her friend, "Kate, come back!"

"Give her some time."

She looked up at him. "I just made a pregnant lady cry. I'm the devil."

He shrugged. "If it's any consolation, *we* made her cry. It wasn't just you."

"I swear to God," said Libitz, poking him in the chest, "if this is just a game for you . . . if I'm just another conquest, a—a—"

J.C. reached for her, cupping her cheeks with his unworthy hands.

"It's not just a game to me," he promised.

"What is it then?" she whispered.

"I don't know," he answered honestly. "But it's not a game."

"Are you saying . . ." she said, averting her eyes from his for a moment before nailing him with a fresh and steady gaze, "that I *mean* something to you?"

He searched her eyes, waiting for a feeling of panic to rise up inside of him as he absorbed her words, but to his surprise, and delight, it didn't come. He didn't feel panic. He just felt . . . happy.

"Yes. You . . . this . . . us . . . yes. It means something to me." *Something big. Something amazing. Something that feels more life-changing every day.*

Her lips trembled as they tilted up into a surprised grin. "Is this the first time you've ever said that?"

"Fuck yes." He released a held breath in a whoosh. "First time I ever *felt* it."

She nodded slowly with approval. "It's a good start."

He leaned down and pressed his lips to hers, lovingly, softly, taking his time before pulling away. "Then let's keep going."

An hour into their two-hour drive, Libitz had learned quite a bit about Jean-Christian.

All his Sirius presets were jazz, with one rogue inclusion of bluegrass. He often spoke French under his breath—as he did when they missed a thruway exit or when the car ahead of them didn't use its signal to turn left—and she suspected, from his tone, that most of what he said was unfit for polite company. He nursed a large cup of Starbucks coffee during the ride that smelled suspiciously sweet. He told her it was a pumpkin spice latte when she asked, and his cheeks colored for a moment, like the admission embarrassed him. He shared with her that he had studied finance at Princeton, and for a while, he and his brother had managed an investment company together, but he hadn't enjoyed the business very much and was grateful when they were bought out and Jean-Christian could start his own gallery.

Two topics of conversation made him far more animated than any of the others—when he spoke of art or his family, his voice changed, softening with love or speeding up with excitement. And it occurred to her that it was very strange that someone so passionate about family and art would have such a difficult time with commitment. Though it didn't escape her notice that his fond memories of family never included mentions of his parents, only his siblings. It didn't take a human behavioral specialist to figure out that his parents had likely been unhappy, and their failed marriage was the genesis of his mistrust toward relationships in general.

It had touched her deeply at Toujours when he said, *You . . . this . . . us . . . yes. It means something to me.* But the sweetness of the moment was bitter when she reflected on Kate's face, her friend's expression of disappointment and the sound of her tears as she ran upstairs. Like many expecting mothers, Kate was hormonal and emotional, eager to have the very best of everything for her firstborn, but she wasn't being irrational. Her fears were sound: Jean-Christian was a wild bet at best. Still, Libitz couldn't seem to help making the wager.

It was an awkward situation to be sure . . . wanting Jean-Christian as she did, feeling the differences in him since their first meeting, yet owing her loyalty to Kate. Could she have them both? Was it possible?

"You've gotten quiet," he said.

She glanced over at him, at his impossibly handsome profile. "Just thinking."

"About . . . ?"

"Kate. Us."

"Us," he said softly. "Yesterday you said we weren't together."

"We're not . . . technically."

"Technically," he said, his jaw tightening, "you're still with Nice Neil."

"I'm breaking up with him on Wednesday."

Jean-Christian was silent for a moment before asking, "Because of me?"

"Because I can't let him think I'm his girlfriend when I'm spending time with you. It's not right. So yes. Because of you."

"So essentially," he said, "once you break up with Neil, we'll both be single because we want to spend time with each other. Isn't that the same as being together?"

"Maybe," she demurred. "We'll see on Wednesday." She turned to look at him, raising her eyebrows in challenge. "Isn't this the part where you go running for the hills?"

"Usually," he said. "But I left my running shoes at home today."

"What makes this time different?"

"You do. You make everything different, Elsa."

"Elsa." She gave him a sidelong glance. "Haven't I proven I'm not an ice princess?"

He laughed softly. "Yep. In spades. But the name suits you, so I'm keeping it. Any objections?"

"No," she said, grinning at him as butterflies pooled in her tummy.

Picking up her phone, which was charging in the console between them, she checked out her new messages, gasping with delight when she found one from Galerie des Fleurs in Marseille.

"The gallery wrote me back!" she said, clicking on the message.

"In English or French? I can pull over if you want me to translate."

"Hold on . . . um, English!"

"What do they say?"

Using her finger to scroll down the message, she read snippets aloud: "*Pleased to tell you we still have the five Montferrats from our website in stock . . . the models are not the same woman, but twins . . . if you look closely, you will see the sign of Gemini painted into Msr. Montferrat's signature whenever he worked with them . . . a personal folly. I once saw a Montferrat with a crescent moon and star in the signature . . . the model must have been Turkish.*"

Libitz looked up at Jean-Christian. "Did you notice anything about his signature in *Les Bijoux Jolis*?"

He shook his head. "No. But I'm dying to take another look now."

"Me too!"

She turned back to the message: "*Should you wish to buy one or all of the portraits, please contact me at . . .* and then it's just his info."

"Huh," Jean-Christian muttered. "I'd suggest we pull over and take a look at it now, but it's raining."

She glanced up at a green sign overhead. "We'll be in Manhattan in half an hour."

"You know?" he said, turning to her. "It occurs to me that I have no idea where I'm going."

"Upper West Side," she said. "West Seventieth and Central Park West."

"Tony neighborhood."

"I like it." She tucked her phone back in her bag. "Where are *you* staying?"

"West Seventieth and Central Park West?" he asked, glancing at her with a hopeful expression.

She shook her head. "Not until Neil's out of the picture."

His brows furrowed with annoyance. "Are you serious?"

"I am," she said.

"Then I guess I'll stay at the Mandarin," he said, referring to a hotel ten blocks south of her apartment building. He sighed, a slight growl accompanying his release of breath. "But fair warning: we're fucking hard on Wednesday night, Libitz."

Her breath hitched. "How hard?"

"So hard, it'll be morning when we're done. So hard, you'll be sore, but I'll be back between your legs the next night because you'll want me there. So hard, you'll swear there was never anyone else before me."

She whimpered softly, managing to murmur, "And then . . . ?"

"That's it. That's the long-term plan," he said. "You and me. Fucking. Indefinitely."

And because she couldn't think straight, let alone come up with a better plan than the one he proposed, she crossed her legs to quell her trembles and didn't argue.

After a stop for gas, some traffic, and a little trouble finding street parking, they finally arrived at Libitz's apartment around four o'clock, and J.C. insisted on pulling her suitcase and carrying *Les Bijoux Jolis* inside.

He was frustrated as hell that tonight wouldn't have a "happy ending," but in a strange way, he was a little relieved too. If they'd fucked tonight, while she was still technically dating Neil, it would have made her a cheater. And though, to the rest of the world, it might not seem that J.C. had lived his personal life with much of a moral code, its entire commitment-free structure ensured that he'd never be accused of cheating on anyone. He abhorred cheaters. He despised them. So as much as he hated waiting until Wednesday to have her, he was glad that she'd be finished with Neil when they finally slept together. He'd just as soon start their relationship on solid ground.

As that thought passed through his head, he gasped softly, shocked to his core that the words "start their relationship on solid ground" should issue so effortlessly from his brain when they'd never taken root there before.

Libitz turned to look at him after pressing the call button on the elevator.

"You look like my Sherpa," she said, grinning at him.

He placed the painting on the floor, resting it against his legs. "I'll be whatever you want me to be, baby."

"Do you have, like, a cache of suggestive lines that you've used all your life to seduce hapless women?"

"Hmm. I wonder if being a smartass comes as easy as, say"—he tapped his chin as though in thought—"your pussy under my tongue?" He shrugged. "Guess we'll find out on Wednesday."

"You're pretty full of yourself," she observed, putting her hands on her hips, which had the awesome side effect of making her little tits stick out.

"Until *you're* full of me," he volleyed back, "I'll have to pleasure myself."

"Oh, man." She chuckled. "I bet you were the guy in college who rated his fucks from one to ten."

He nodded at her. "And you were the girl who scared the shit out of every guy who secretly wanted to fuck your brains out."

"Ohhhh," she said, "is that why they all stopped calling? Out of fear?"

"Anyone who *stopped calling* was a monumental fucking jackass." As the elevator arrived, he picked up the painting, grabbed her suitcase handle, and stepped inside after her. "And they were all pussies."

She pressed the number fifteen, then turned to face him, cocking her head to the side. "So you're saying you're *not* afraid?"

"Oh, I'm terrified, Elsa," he said, smiling at her. "But not of you."

"Of what then?"

He'd been leaning against the brass railing at the back of the elevator, but now he stepped forward, closer to her, boxing her into the corner beside the control panel.

"Of wanting something new. Of who I am when I'm with you."

She reached up and palmed his cheek. "I like who you are when you're with me."

"Enough to place a bet on me?"

She nodded. "I'll be placing that bet on Wednesday night when I tell Neil to take a hike."

"But I can't promise you anything," said Jean-Christian, regretting the words when they left his mouth, even as he recognized their truth. "I wish I could, but I'm in unchartered waters, Elsa."

"I don't remember asking for promises."

"I might let you down."

"Probably."

"Or hurt you."

"Possibly."

"And you could end up hating me," he said, leaning into her touch as he closed his eyes.

She inhaled deeply, and when he opened his eyes, she was staring up at him, her eyes worried. "Is that what you want?"

"No!" he cried. "God, no!"

The elevator dinged to signal their arrival, and she dropped her hand. "Then make a choice to keep me safe and make me proud and make me adore you."

"It can't be that easy," he said, wincing as his mother's shattered face flitted through his mind and vowing never to be the cause of that pain for Libitz.

"Yes, Jean-Christian," she said confidently, ducking under his arm as the doors opened and leaving him to follow. "It is *exactly* that easy."

An hour later, they had cached a bottle of her favorite Sauvignon Blanc and stood side by side at her dining room table, staring at the portrait together as they waited for an order of Chinese to arrive.

"It's pi," he said for the umpteenth time.

"It's *l'chaim*," she argued, squinting at the tiny marking they'd found in Pierre's signature, cleverly hidden between the *t* and *f* in Montferrat.

"She was probably a math student."

"A math student by day and nude art model by night? Right!" Libitz scoffed.

"*L'chaim*?" asked Jean-Christian, bending over the painting. "Where in the world would he have met a young Jewish model? My uncle was Catholic!"

"And you think he went searching for his models at church?" she asked tartly. "Look closely. See this tiny slash to the left of the upside-down *U*? That's what makes it *l'chaim*. Believe me, I'm right. I was forced to go to Hebrew school from the cradle."

"And I was a finance major. That tiny slash is part of the *t*. Or an abrasion."

Libitz backed away from the dining room table where they'd unwrapped the painting and crossed her arms over her chest defensively. He was so deep in concentration, he didn't notice for a few seconds, but once he did, he looked up at her.

"What? Are you giving up the fight?"

"Do you have a problem with her being Jewish?"

"What? What are you—"

"Do. You. Have. A. Problem. With. Her. Being. Jewish?"

He recoiled like she'd hit him, standing up straight and putting his hands on his hips. "Are you serious?"

"Yes, I am."

His brows furrowed together, his lips an angry slash.

"Why aren't you answering?" she demanded, dropping her hands to her sides but keeping them in fists.

"I'm trying to decide whether or not to spank you," he spat, his eyes bright with anger. "Why the *fuck* would you ask me something like that?"

"Because you're . . . you're . . ."

She sputtered, all the wind promptly leaving her sails.

One look at his face told her the answer to her question. He was outraged that she'd even suggested that he was prejudiced, and she regretted making the assumption. It came from an old place of hurt and suspicion, and she hated that it still made her insecure from time to time.

She softened her voice, unfurling her fingers. "Because you were just fighting so hard to convince me it was pi."

"It *looks* like pi to me," he said, putting his hands on his hips, his face still furious. "Do I *look* like a bigot to you?"

She shook her head, taking her empty wine glass from the table and walking alone into her living room. Reaching into the wine fridge concealed under a wet bar, she took out another bottle of white wine and unscrewed the cap, pouring herself a healthy splash. When she looked up, Jean-Christian was standing in the doorway between the two rooms, staring at her, his expression guarded.

"You didn't answer me," he said.

"No," she said, taking a sip as she padded over to the sofa in bare feet. "You don't look like a bigot. *I* look like an idiot."

He turned around to grab his wineglass and followed her into the living room, pouring a refill before joining her on the couch. "So what was that?"

She sighed, meeting his eyes. "Insecurity."

"Yours."

"Mine. My Achilles' heel."

Jean-Christian took another sip of wine before placing his glass on the table and turning back to her. He reached out to run his fingers through her hair, and she closed her eyes, taking a deep, cleansing breath.

"I was one of four Jewish kids at a super WASPy prep school," she whispered without opening her eyes. She leaned into his touch, relinquishing her glass easily when he took it from her fingers and pulled her onto his lap, wrapping his arms around her. "I overlooked, even tolerated, the occasional under-the-breath comment about my religion and culture. But you have to understand . . . I was in the minority, and I was a kid. It was easier to try to blend in, even if that meant putting up with small-minded prejudice."

She could feel the heat from his neck on her lips and she leaned forward to nuzzle his skin as she continued. "But I'm an adult now . . . and I can't overlook or tolerate anti-Semitism anymore. I *won't*."

"You shouldn't," he said softly, gently cupping the back of her head as she dragged her lips over his throat.

"I know I'm oversensitive. I had no right to accuse you like that."

"It's important to you."

She nodded, pressing butterfly kisses along a blue vein. "Mm-hm. To be accepted for who I am. All of me."

"I don't care what your religion is, Libitz. I mean, I *care*, but it doesn't play any role in my regard for you."

She opened her eyes and leaned away to look up at him. "You're Catholic."

He nodded.

"I'm Jewish."

He nodded again. "So?"

"Is that going to be a problem for us, Jean-Christian Rousseau?"

"For my mother, yes."

"Yeah. For mine too," she said honestly.

"Now ask me what I'm prepared to do about it."

Her lips twitched with a smile that was bursting to make itself known. "What are you prepared to do about it?"

"Nothing," he said simply. "It's not her life; it's mine. And for now, I choose you. *All* of you." He bit her bottom lip, taking his time, letting it go with a soft pop. "But, Elsa, my darling, I will go to my fucking grave insisting that upside-down *U* is pi, not *l'chaim*."

Her smile turned into a snort, and she hid her face back in the warm curve of his neck. "You're a monumental jack-ass, you know."

"Yeah, yeah, yeah," he said, kissing the top of her head. "You and your sweet talk."

"I'm crazy about you," she said softly, whispering the words he'd said to her yesterday and feeling them deep in her soul, knowing that they were true.

"Then kiss me," he said, his voice husky with emotion and need.

And Libitz, who had truly started to understand the workings of his heart, was only too happy to comply.

Chapter 11

Jessica texted J.C. at ten the next morning to let him know that the Kandinsky had arrived safely at the Feingold Gallery and had been signed for by Libitz. Mrs. Carnegie was arriving at the gallery at four o'clock to collect the painting, after which J.C. and Libitz had an appointment to visit J.C.'s old college professor, Dr. Niles Harkin, at the Metropolitan Museum of Art. Dr. Harkin, who had a PhD in art history and taught twice-yearly courses at Princeton, was also the head of painting conservation at Manhattan's premiere art museum. He'd sent someone to the hotel concierge this morning to pick up *Les Bijoux Jolis* so that he'd have time to take a look at it before their meeting.

J.C. stared at Jessica's text, thinking back to last night. After Libitz had told him she was crazy about him, they'd made out on the couch like a couple of teenagers before their dinner had arrived, the doorbell interrupting them. Smiling at the memory, he scrubbed his hands over his face, remembering the disappointment in her eyes as she'd pulled her bra out from between two couch cushions and rebuttoned her dress while he'd answered the door.

He couldn't actually recall the last time he'd been physical with a woman when sex wasn't in the offering, and maybe it was the promise of more intimacy on Wednesday, but he didn't feel like any time spent with Libitz was wasted. In fact, he'd been in a ridiculous swoon since she'd told him how she felt about him . . . his heart throbbing like that of a sixteen-year-old girl who'd been asked to the prom by her crush.

By and large, J.C. had missed out on a lot of the conventional relationship milestones that most teenagers experienced. At age fourteen, he'd decided never to fall in love or let anyone fall in love with him. He'd get his rocks off, like his father, but he wouldn't hurt anyone like his father had hurt his mother. It had left him physically satisfied but emotionally stunted in some ways. A woman professing her affection for him in the past had left him, as Libitz had guessed yesterday, panicked and running for the hills.

Not so with her.

He'd been terribly infatuated with her at Ten's wedding, but now, as a thirty-four-year-old man with honorable intentions for the first time in his life, infatuation was giving way to a feeling altogether bigger and deeper—something that he still wasn't prepared to name or admit, something that still felt too fragile and too unlikely to ever belong to him.

Before he left her apartment last night, Libitz had given him the eyeglass case that held his uncle Pierre's emerald necklace, and with late morning and early afternoon to kill before picking her up, he made an appointment with a private jeweler in the Diamond District, where he could have it appraised.

Technically, it was Jax's necklace, since he'd found it in her attic, so J.C. figured he'd have it reset for his sister as a wedding gift, and she could wear it when he walked her down the aisle this February. Since he'd heard Gard refer to Jax's eyes as "emeralds" a time or two, it seemed especially fitting.

"You know a lot about emeralds?" asked the paunchy old gentleman behind a utilitarian counter in a nondescript jewelry store. He added a lens to his glasses to look more closely at the necklace.

J.C. shook his head. "No, sir."

"Ah-ha." The jeweler, Silas Greenbaum, an apt name for an emerald expert, checked out each gemstone carefully, holding the necklace up to the light before inspecting the stones again. "Yeah. It's good quality."

"How good?" asked J.C., resting his elbows on the scratched glass.

"Well, see . . . all emeralds have imperfections because they're naturally occurring beryl minerals. In fact, no imperfections would tell me it's a fake or synthetic."

"But it's not?"

"No. These are real. Filthy, but real." Silas removed the loupe from his eyeglasses and placed the necklace carefully on a bed of black velvet, straightening it until it was a perfect oval. "Setting's crap. Gold-painted sterling. You should have it reset."

"That's what I thought." J.C. didn't want to seem too eager, but he was curious as to its value. "How much do you think it's worth?"

"Hmm. Well, the color's good. You don't want to see yellow or brown, and these have a nice blue glow. Deep. Rich. That's a plus. See when I hold it up to the light? Look at this one in the middle. See how it sparkles like it's alive? Changes like it's still forming? Still growing? That's what makes it valuable. That's heirloom quality. This one emerald is over two carats for sure. All on its own, it's worth about fourteen thousand dollars. Just the stone."

"So . . . ?"

"The diamonds are chips. They're worth something, but they're not special. The emeralds are special, and there are fourteen of them. I'd give you a hundred and seventy for it."

"One hundred seventy thousand dollars?"

Silas nodded. "Yep. You could probably get a little more, but someone's going to have to clean it, take it apart, and reset it. That's work. That takes time."

"I don't want to sell it," said J.C., leaning away from the counter. "I want you to reset it. I'm giving it to my sister as a wedding gift."

"I guess you love your sister a lot," said Silas, showcasing four gold teeth when he smiled.

J.C. nodded. "I do."

"Well, you better. It'll cost you about eight thousand to do it in gold. Simple design. Goes up from there."

"I don't really care what it costs," said J.C., sliding his American Express card across the counter. "You'll find I'm good for it."

"My favorite kind of customer," said Silas, running the card to ascertain J.C.'s credit limit.

"But one thing," said J.C., unable to part with the *entire* necklace, even for Jax. "The emerald in the middle, the one you pointed out—"

"The anchor?"

He nodded. "The one that sparkles like it's changing and still growing . . . I want it."

"You want it?"

"Find one to replace it for the necklace and I'll buy it from you, but that one . . ."

"Mister . . . Rousseau," he said, staring down at the credit slip before handing J.C. his card back. "You want to spend fourteen thousand for another emerald when you've already got one?"

"Just do it," he muttered.

"Well, credit isn't a problem for you, but . . ." Silas shrugged. "Hey! You want me to make the solitaire into a ring?"

"No! Nothing like that!" J.C. scowled. "Can you just—just put it to the side, okay? I just want *it*, not a ring."

Silas held up his hands and took a step back. "Whatever you say. Let me just go in the back and grab an order slip. Take a seat, Mr. Rousseau. It'll take a little time to get everything in order, okay?"

J.C. nodded, stepping across a worn gray carpet to a small conference table that had seen better days. He sat down, frowning at the table as he traced a scratch with his finger. So far, nothing had spooked him where Libitz was concerned, but he couldn't deny a slight feeling of unease now.

Hey! You want me to make the solitaire into a ring?

A *ring*. The mention of a ring had completely unnerved him.

He swallowed, sitting back in the stiff chair and wishing his heart would stop racing. No, he didn't want a fucking ring. Frankly, he had no idea why he wanted the fucking emerald in the first place. But certainly not—*not*—for a ring.

Silas returned with the necklace and some triplicate forms. As he sat down across from J.C., he slid a small sealed Ziploc bag to him. Inside was the two-carat emerald, and J.C. stared at it like it might grow fangs and bite him any second.

"When you're ready to do something with it," said the jeweler, "give me a call."

J.C. slid it off the table and into the breast pocket of his suit jacket, the weight of the rock unreasonably heavy in his palm. He was grateful when it was securely tucked away, and he looked up at Silas with a neutral expression that took some effort.

"Shall we get started?"

"Miss Feingold," said Mrs. Carnegie, her eyes narrow as she inspected the painting, "well done. It's exactly what I wanted."

"I'm so glad," said Libitz, inclining her head in thanks.

With a subtle hand gesture, she advised her lead assistant, Duane, to move the painting from the table to an easel with gloved hands, so Mrs. Carnegie could see it upright.

Professionalism was paramount at the Feingold Gallery, and every one of her six employees knew it. Showing and selling paintings was managed with ballet-like grace and precision and with as few words as possible. She didn't want to impinge on her customers' experience with the art. She knew her place: she was their purveyor, not their friend.

"Yes. Yessss," sighed Mrs. Carnegie, moving closer to the Kandinsky to admire it. "It's so vibrant and naughty. Breathtaking."

From several feet away, Libitz nodded in agreement, giving Duane a look to tell him he was no longer needed. He slipped away without a sound, and Mrs. Carnegie was left almost alone with the art, Libitz's quiet presence neither a distraction nor an addition to her experience, only there should she be needed.

With her hands clasped behind her back, she must have looked the picture of serenity, and yet a swarm of bees whizzed and zoomed in her belly, and her eyes kept sliding without permission to the glass doors of the Fifth Avenue gallery. Jean-Christian had left her apartment at ten o'clock last night to check into his hotel, and she'd missed him every second since. All day she had imagined the moment he'd appear at the doors, walk through them seeking her eyes with his and, upon finding them, how he would—

". . . all right, Miss Feingold?"

She jerked her head to her client. "Ma'am?"

"I'm *so* sorry to interrupt your thoughts," said Mrs. Carnegie, lips pursing with annoyance as she took a step toward Libitz. "Am I *keeping* you from something?"

"Of course not," Libitz assured her, raising her chin and offering the older woman a small smile. "I'm so glad you're pleased with it."

Mrs. Carnegie's face clouded further. "Yes, yes. You've already said that. But can you have it installed *tomorrow*?"

"Tomorrow?"

"What have I been saying?" asked Mrs. Carnegie, becoming exasperated.

"Tomorrow is fine." Libitz touched a pager button hidden under the belt of her tailored black dress, and Duane appeared within twenty seconds, standing at attention behind Mrs. Carnegie. "Thank you, Duane. Please arrange delivery to Mrs. Carnegie's penthouse tomorrow. At what time?"

"Eight," said Mrs. Carnegie, turning back to the painting. "Bridge is at ten. It must be perfect by bridge so that Henrietta Goering can see it. She just *adores* Kandinsky."

"I'll see to every detail," said Duane in his low, cultured voice.

Libitz turned back to Mrs. Carnegie. "Will you have a seat, ma'am?" she asked, gesturing to a chic black lacquer table with four wingback chairs. "I'll get the paperwork and return in a moment."

"Yes. I don't have all day, you know," said Mrs. Carnegie, huffing softly as she sat down, her mood still soured by Libitz's slight distraction a few minutes ago.

"I'll be very quick," Libitz promised.

Sailing into her office on four-inch heels, she grabbed the file for the Kandinsky off her desk and the small Square reader for her iPad so that she could charge everything without returning to her office. But she couldn't resist taking a quick peek at herself in the mirror by the door before returning to the gallery floor. Her hair was gelled and styled today, slick and suave, and her dress, a clingy black Max

Mara sheath, looked professional enough for her day but would be sexy for her date to the Met with Jean-Christian. She had freshened her red lipstick before Mrs. Carnegie's arrival, and her Kohl-lined eyes were dramatic but not slutty. She looked sophisticated and urbane, and she nodded at her reflection, feeling satisfied.

Hurrying back to Mrs. Carnegie, she was surprised to hear girl-like laughter coming from the gallery floor. When she turned the corner from the back offices, she found Delilah Carnegie tittering with delight at Jean-Christian Rousseau, who sat across the table from her.

"Oh, you are simply wicked!" she said, patting Jean-Christian's arm.

"*Alors! Vous êtes méchante aussi, madame,*" he said, winking at her.

"Flirt!" she accused him, simpering behind two fingers.

He was . . . beautiful, and Libitz stole just a moment to admire him. His chiseled cheeks were high and perfect, his square jaw masculine, his green eyes dark and mysterious.

And he's mine, she thought, her heart swelling with the sort of emotion that could only be identified as love, no matter how inconvenient or risky. She was falling in love with him—wildly, madly—and she doubted very much there was anything she could do to stop it now.

"Here we are," she said, placing the contract on the table and taking a seat between Jean-Christian and Mrs. Carnegie.

"I'm not sure if you know," said Libitz, "but it was actually Mr. Rousseau who sold me the Kandin—"

"Oh, yes. *Jean-Christian* already told me."

"Delilah, you are a delight!" he said in a thicker-than-usual French accent. He finally slid his gaze to Libitz after he'd fawned sufficiently over the older woman. "*Bonsoir*, Mademoiselle Feingold."

"*Bonsoir*, Monsieur Rousseau," she answered, drinking him in with her eyes.

But he didn't hold her gaze as she'd become accustomed to. In fact, he dropped it rather quickly, turning back to Mrs. Carnegie. "I'm taking Libitz to the Met tonight."

"To the Met! How lovely! The opera?"

"The museum," he clarified. "We're on a bit of a treasure hunt."

"Is that right?"

He nodded. "*Oui*. We found an old painting, and we're both dying to know its history."

"*Que c'est excitant!*" exclaimed Mrs. Carnegie, leaning toward Jean-Christian conspiratorially. "Ah, to be young and in love again."

Libitz, who had been filling out the last of the paperwork, jerked her head up in surprise, her eyes slamming into Jean-Christian's at Mrs. Carnegie's inadvertently awkward mention of the *L* word. His face froze for only an instant before his eyes cooled to amusement, and he looked away from Libitz to smile at the older lady.

"Libitz and I share a love of art, not each other," he said smoothly.

Much to her dismay, Libitz gasped almost inaudibly at his comment, staring at his profile for a moment before returning her attention to the paperwork at hand. Though neither J.C. nor Mrs. Carnegie appeared to have noticed that her heart lay slain on the table, inside she ached.

Not each other.

Not each other.

Not each other.

The words circled in her head as she finished writing in Mrs. Carnegie's contact information, forcing herself to remain composed.

Why had he said such a thing? They'd so recently shared their feelings for each other, both using the words "crazy about you." *Why would he make such a bold point about there being no love between us?* Even if there wasn't, it seemed a very cold thing to say. *And why, dear God, does it hurt so goddamn much?* She blinked her eyes, horrified to realize that they were burning with unshed tears.

When she raised her head, she carefully avoided Jean-Christian's eyes, though she felt them boring into the side of her head.

"I need your signature here, please. And here," said Libitz, sliding the contract to her client. "And your card, please." Mrs. Carnegie handed her a credit card, and Libitz slid it through the Square reader.

Chancing a glance at Jean-Christian, she found him staring at the table, his face pinched, his lips pursed, his jaw clenched. He looked as upset as she felt, which was baffling, since he'd said the words so easily, as though they hadn't cost him a thing.

"Your signature once more, please," she murmured, handing Mrs. Carnegie a stylus and positioning the iPad before her. Subtly reaching for her belt, she pressed the button for Duane. It wasn't normal practice for her to let her assistant finalize details on a big sale unless there was another client waiting to see her, but she simply didn't trust herself right now. She blinked again, trying to swallow over the lump in her throat. She needed to get away from Jean-Christian before she embarrassed herself.

When Duane arrived, she nodded in thanks for his efficiency. "Please walk Mrs. Carnegie through the delivery process tomorrow. There's a call I must take." She held out her hand to the older lady. "Thank you very much. I hope you are very happy with the painting."

"I'm sure I will be," said Mrs. Carnegie, searching Libitz's face for a moment before turning to Duane. "Can we do this on the way to my car? I have somewhere I need to be."

Duane helped her with her chair, holding an umbrella as he held the door for her and walked her half a block to her waiting chauffeur.

Libitz pushed the signed papers into the file folder and picked up the iPad, clutching both to her breasts, unsure of what to say to J.C., who still sat motionless in his chair, staring down at the slick, black tabletop. She didn't want to go to the Met with him. She didn't want to go anywhere with him. The sweet but fragile connection they'd built suddenly felt flimsy and silly, and she felt embarrassed and foolish for trusting it.

"I don't feel very well," she said, reaching for the forgotten stylus. "If you'll forgive me, I think I'll just—"

His fingers shot up, wrapping around her wrist with an unyielding grip and forcing her to stay, though he didn't look up at her.

"Stop," he growled.

She didn't know what to say or do, so she stopped pulling away and stood still, waiting for him to say something else.

"I'm sorry," he finally muttered, his voice tight and gravelly.

"For what?" she asked, hating the way her voice broke. "We never promised each other anything."

Slowly, so slowly, he raised his head to look at her, and his eyes were shattered. Crushed. Panicked even. "Wait. What does *that* mean?"

"I get it. You're not into this anymore, so we can just—"

"I *am* into it," he said, standing up but still holding tightly to her wrist as though it was a lifeline, and he'd drift out to sea if he wasn't holding on for dear life.

"Then what?" she whispered, staring into his eyes as she lowered the file and iPad back to the table.

"I don't know how to do this," he said harshly, moving around the curve of the table to pull her closer. "I don't know how to feel comfortable with it."

"But you want it?" she asked, wishing she could quell the wild uncertainties in his eyes.

He nodded once, covering his heart with his free hand. "I want *you*."

She turned away from him, pulling him toward the back of the gallery where they could be alone. He followed her, sliding his fingers from her wrist to her hand.

In the dim, quiet light of the hallway, she turned to face him, backing him against the wall. "Are you freaking out? Is that what this is?"

The severe expression on his face softened and he nodded.

She exhaled, breathing a sigh of relief and cocking her head to the side as she glared up at him. "Are you sure that's all it is? Because I'm planning to make a *major* life change tomorrow, and if you're not into this—"

His lips crashed down on hers with a groan of gut-wrenching need, his hands landing on her hips to pull her between his legs as he leaned against the hallway wall, positioning her firmly against his body.

"I'm into it. I need you, Libitz. I want you. I'm crazy about you, baby," he murmured, his lips trailing down the column of her neck as he whispered his truth in a husky, emotional voice. "I'm sorry for saying that before. I didn't mean it."

She flattened her hands on his chest and leaned away to look up at him.

"Oh. So we *do* share a love of each other?" she asked, desperately trying to keep a straight face, since she suspected this question would make him extremely uncomfortable. She didn't care. After what he pulled back there, he deserved it. She raised her eyebrows and waited.

His eyes widened and he cleared his throat. "Well, um—I'm not sure that we need to, well, um—"

Her trembling shoulders gave her away, and he sighed, his whole body relaxing as he realized she was teasing him. She giggled softly, reaching up to cup his face. "There's no reason to freak out, Jean-Christian."

"*Though she be but little, she is fierce.*" He sighed, kissing her sweetly. "This is new for me. All of it."

I'm falling in love with you, she thought for the second time that afternoon, gazing up into his beautiful dark eyes.

"For me too."

Libitz rested her head on his shoulder on the cab ride up to the Met, and J.C. marveled over the fact that he had somehow sidestepped a meltdown. By her strength. By her grace. By her understanding and wisdom. In the space of a few hours, two of the most terrifying words in the world—"ring" and "love"—had been introduced into his life, and he hadn't spontaneously combusted or had an impromptu heart attack. In fact, he thought, resting his lips on the crown of her head, he was feeling . . . okay. Because of her. Because when he'd said that asinine comment about them not loving each other, her gasp of breath and the sudden flash of pain in her eyes were enough to make him want to die. He never, ever wanted to see that look on her face again. Never.

Leaning away from her just a bit, he tilted her chin up and kissed her. Though she didn't know it, it was a promise to her, and to himself, that he wouldn't hurt her again—that if she gave him her trust, he would prove himself worthy of it.

"What was that for?" she asked as the cab pulled up to the curb of the Met and he drew away.

"For being you," he answered, dragging his wallet out of his pocket and paying the cabbie.

"Little and fierce?" she asked.

He nodded. *Little and fierce . . . and mine.*

She was waiting for him on the sidewalk when he exited, and he took her hand as they walked up the grand steps together.

"Who are we meeting again?" she asked.

"Niles Harkin. Doctor. Professor. He taught at Princeton, and I audited some of his classes. We kept in touch."

"And he just happens to work at the Met?"

J.C. nodded. "He's the head of Painting Conservation."

"People in high places," she said.

"He had *Les Bijoux Jolis* picked up from my hotel earlier. We'll see what he has to say."

After receiving special passes at the front desk, a docent led them to the Sherman Fairchild Paintings Conservation Center, an eighteen-thousand-square-foot space where Dr. Harkin and his team worked to research, repair, and restore the paintings of the Metropolitan Museum of Art. The docent led them straight to Dr. Harkin's desk, where they found *Les Bijoux Jolis* propped up on a wooden easel, with Dr. Harkin sitting on a stool before it.

"J.C., ma boy!" he greeted his former student, his slight British accent welcome in J.C.'s ears.

"Professor Harkin," he said, shaking the older man's hand. "It's good to see you, sir. This is Libitz Feingold. She owns a gallery on Fifth."

"Miss Feingold," said Dr. Harkin, taking her hand. "Charmed." He narrowed his eyes at her, pulling his glasses from his forehead onto the bridge of his nose and looking at her face closely. "You bear an uncanny resemblance to the model in the portrait."

She smiled. "Yes, I know. We're hoping you can tell us more about her."

Dr. Harkin dropped her hand and turned back to the portrait, sighing deeply. "I can tell you a little, though Pierre Montferrat wasn't, I'm afraid, very well known, so there isn't much documentation about his works or models."

"What about the signature, Professor?" asked J.C. as they all stepped closer to the painting.

"It's the Hebrew word *l'chaim*," said Dr. Harkin, and Libitz's sharp elbow landed in his side.

"I thought it was pi," mumbled J.C.

"No, no. I'm quite sure it's *l'chaim*, because when I cut off this brown paper on the back . . ." They followed him around the canvas. "You see here? It says *Ayez une bonne vie*."

"Have a good life," translated J.C.

"*L'chaim tovim*," murmured Libitz.

Professor Harkin nodded. "Yes. I don't believe that inscription is a coincidence. 'Have a good life' on the back. *L'chaim* on the front." He looked from the painting to the couple. "I believe the model was Jewish . . . as you may have already figured out."

"*Some* of us have," said Libitz, giving J.C. a look.

"She's dark-haired and dark-eyed," continued Professor Harkin, squinting at the painting as he gestured to her features. "Judging from the portrait, even in its state of some disrepair, her skin appears olive-toned, not pink. Plus, as you may or may not know, in 1939 when this portrait was painted, the largest community of Eastern European Jews in Western Europe was living in Marseille. Aside from the portrait markings, time and place support her being Jewish."

"I knew it," said Libitz, looking up at J.C. in victory.

"However, history also supports the likelihood that she . . ." Professor Harkin cleared his throat, his voice taking on a somber tone. "A young Jewish woman living in Marseille in 1939 probably wouldn't have . . . I mean to say . . ."

"Survived," said Libitz quietly, taking a step back from the painting. "She wouldn't have survived."

J.C. put his arm around her, but her shoulders remained rigid under his touch.

Professor Harkin's eyes were sad as he looked up at Libitz and nodded. "Over thirty thousand Marseille Jews were killed in the Holocaust. Three-quarters of their community."

Libitz gasped, stepping away from J.C.'s touch to stand on her own, further distancing herself from the portrait. She looked back and forth from Professor Harkin to J.C., her expression horrified. "How can I find out . . . ?"

"I suppose you could see about art schools in operation at the time. Many young models were struggling art students." The professor sighed. "I'm sorry I can't be of more help."

Professor Harkin offered to have the painting rewrapped and sent back to J.C. at his hotel, and they shook hands, thanking him for his time, but Libitz was clearly upset as they left, and when J.C. suggested going out for a drink, she declined, asking for a rain check.

"I just . . . I can't," she said softly. "I think I'll just go home."

"Lib," said J.C., "we'll find out what happened to her. I promise."

"I don't know if I want to know," she answered, her eyes brightened by tears. "She was so beautiful, so young and hopeful. To find out she was tortured and died frightened in a camp . . . I just . . ." She reached up and swiped a tear from her cheek. "I don't know if I could bear it."

Whether she wanted his comfort or not, J.C. couldn't stand seeing her cry, and he pulled her into his arms, grateful when she didn't push him away. A light rain started to fall as they stood together on the sidewalk in front of the museum, and J.C. held her tighter, whispering close to her ear. "Let me take you home, okay? To be sure you get there safely?"

She looked up at him with watery eyes and nodded.

He flagged down a cab and kept his arm around her until they reached her apartment building.

"Do you want me to come up?" he asked.

"No, thanks," she said, gathering her things together. Just before opening her door, she turned back to him. "You know? I've heard the stories since I was a very little girl. Cousins and great-aunts who tried to get out and couldn't. My great-uncle Milo died in one of the camps. It's just . . . it's a part of my culture, my history . . . but it doesn't get easier. And she—she was so young and beautiful. Hopeful and trusting. I can't . . ."

J.C. winced at her pain, cupping her face and kissing her tenderly. "Will you be okay?"

She took a deep breath and nodded. "I will. I'll be fine by tomorrow. It just knocked the wind out of me."

He nodded as she scooted away from him and opened the door. "Lib! Text me if you need me, okay?"

She looked back at him, a very small, sad smile tilting her lips upward. "Jean-Christian," she said, "I still intend to talk to Neil tomorrow."

He hadn't wanted to ask, hadn't wanted to appear insensitive to her feelings about the model in the portrait. But he couldn't deny the rush of relief he felt at her words.

"Good," he said. "Call me after?"

She stood up, then turned around to nod at him. "See you tomorrow."

She slammed the door, and he watched as she entered her building, watched as she turned once to wave at him before heading for the elevator at the back of the lobby.

"Where to?" asked the cabbie.

"The Mandarin Oriental," said J.C. distractedly, taking out his phone.

If it turned out that C.T.'s end was brutal, he wouldn't tell Libitz, but what if she'd survived? What if she'd somehow made it out of Marseille?

He had an idea.

They hadn't asked Galerie des Fleurs about the other Montferrat models, but maybe if they could figure out who the Gemini models were, they could find out more information about the *Bijoux Jolis* model too.

Opening a fresh e-mail message, he started writing.

Chapter 12

Home early from her nondate with Jean-Christian, Libitz changed into pajamas and poured herself a glass of wine, thinking about C.T. and wondering what had happened to her.

"The War," as her parents and grandparents referred to World War II, was not just shorthand for the war itself but a catchall name for the catastrophic period of time that included the Holocaust, the genocide of millions of European Jews. The unfathomable notion that six million people of Jewish descent had been murdered for the sole crime of their religion was as painful and mind-boggling today as it had been seventy years ago. "The War" had always existed in her family's narrative and in the observation of days like Yom Hashoah, when she and her parents would attend services at their synagogue, light yellow candles, and recite the mourner's Kaddish together in remembrance of the lost. As Libitz had been reminded hundreds of times, the most important mission of future generations was to ensure that the world never, ever forgot what had happened to their people.

Perhaps because of this lifelong conditioning, Libitz felt a profoundly personal connection to the model in the painting in a way that resonated more deeply than old stories of relatives she'd never met. C.T. felt so *alive* to Libitz. The idea that this vibrant, beautiful girl had been led to the gas chambers, like so many other frightened, innocent European Jews, made her heart ache with sorrow in a way she couldn't explain to Jean-Christian.

Sipping her wine, she dialed her mother's number, needing to hear the familiar and beloved New York accent of her Brooklyn-born mother, who'd married up and now lived in a duplex not far from Libitz on Central Park West.

Ring, ring. Ring—

"Libitz? Sweetheart?"

"Hey, Mom," she said, reaching for a blanket on the back of her plush couch and covering herself as she snuggled against a throw pillow. "How are you?"

"I have a bad cold . . . but more important, how are you?"

"Aw, I'm . . . I'm okay."

"What's wrong, Libby? What happened? I can hear it in your voice. Myron," she called to Libitz's dad. "Libitz is upset!"

"I didn't do anything to upset her," said her father in the background. "Ask her what's wrong."

"What's wrong?" her mother asked into the phone.

"Nothing, really," said Libitz. "This painting I found . . . it just has me turned around."

"Go back to your program," said her mother to her father. "It's just about a painting." Her mother blew her nose before speaking again. "*Oy*, this cold."

"Have some chicken soup sent over from Artie's," said Libitz, referring to her mother's favorite delicatessen.

"Good idea," said her mother. "Tell me about the painting."

"It was painted in France in 1939, and the model was Jewish, and . . . I don't know. You know she probably didn't make it out, and it just . . . it's sad. I feel sad about it."

"Oh, Libby," said her mother. "These stories. Everyone has these stories."

"I know, Mom," she said, taking another sip of wine, exhaling a mournful sigh. "Hey . . . wasn't Bubbe's mother from France?"

"Mm-hm. My grandmother. *Ma grand-mère.*"

"You didn't call her Bubbe?"

"No. We called our other grandmother Bubbe. My mother's mother was *Grand-mère.*"

"I wish I'd known her."

"Not much to know," said her mother. "She was a quiet lady. But she loved art. Just like you, Libby."

"You never heard her speak it? French?"

"No," said her mother. "She didn't like to speak it. Learned English as soon as she got here and never spoke French again . . . well, until she was dying, poor thing."

"And then she did?" asked Libitz.

"Bubbe says she did. She'd get confused and speak French now and then, but my mother didn't understand a word of it."

"Do you know when she came over, Mom?"

"Late thirties, I guess. Before the war, but I'm not sure of the exact date."

Libitz sighed. She'd had a fleeting, ridiculous fantasy that maybe her great-grandmother had known the mystery model . . . whether she'd realized it or not, Libitz had hoped that maybe her mother could say something that would shed more light on the model's life.

"What was her name?" asked Libitz.

"Ummm. Camille."

C, thought Libitz, a rush of excitement making her fingers cold. "Camille what?"

"Lévy."

"No," said Libitz, rolling her eyes. "Her *maiden* name."

"All these questions! Libby, I have no idea. I doubt even your bubbe knows her birth name. You have to understand:

she turned her back on France—shut down whenever any of us asked her about it. I think it broke her heart."

"France? *France* broke her heart?"

"Mm-hm. It felt like that."

"But she came to New York *before* the war?"

"Yes, I think so."

Libitz sighed. The war started a few days after *Les Bijoux Jolis* was painted. She shook her head, annoyed with herself. She had an *emotional* connection to the painting, and it was making her fantasize about having a *personal* connection to the dead model.

"Are you all right, Libitz?"

"Mm-hm. Just wish I could figure out what happened to the model in the painting."

"Better not to know," said her mother, sneezing again three times in a row.

"Gesundheit," she murmured reflexively.

"Libby," said her mother, her tone changing from normal to slightly wheedling. "I had the nicest chat with Shana Leibowitz. Things are going well for you and Neil? You know me, I try not to pry."

Like hell.

"He's very nice, Mom, but—"

"So we'll see you both at Shabbat this Friday? Shana's making brisket."

"I can't make it, Mom."

"What are you—Myron, she can't make it to Shabbat at the Leibowitz's! What are you talking about, Libitz? It'll be very awkward without you there."

Oh, God. Did she have the strength to explain about Neil and J.C. tonight?

No. No, she did not.

"It's a work thing, Mom."

"Get out of it. What's the use of being the boss if you can't take off early when you want to?"

"You sound like Neil."

"What's wrong with Neil?"

"Mom, please."

"Please what? Please make me a grandmother before I die?" She sneezed again before answering her own question. "Yes, thank you."

"Maybe Neil and I aren't meant to be."

"*Meant to be*," muttered her mother. "Who's meant to be? You *like* Neil."

"I do, Mom. He's a great person . . . but I have to follow my heart."

Her mother sighed. "Follow your heart by all means, Libby, but you're not getting any younger."

Libitz finished her wine in a single gulp and poured another glass. "I love you, Mom. Maybe give Mrs. Leibowitz your regrets, huh? Stay home and nurse your cold."

"Now, Lib—"

"Tell Dad I love him too. Talk soon."

Before her mother could say anything else, she pressed the "End" button, and then, knowing her mother as well as she did, she powered down the phone completely. It'd be ringing all night if she didn't.

In the dim quiet of her apartment, she snuggled back into the couch and closed her eyes. Before long, she was asleep, her dreams mixed up yet vibrant—tangled musings about C.T., the model, and Camille, her mother's *grand-mère*. Jean-Christian cameoed in the role of Pierre Montferrat, and she saw herself, as a teenager, wearing emeralds and a yellow star as she ate brisket, vowing, in perfect French, never to speak it again for as long as she lived.

Arriving at his hotel room early had allowed J.C. to call Jessica English and catch up on the day's business. She'd sold the Anthony Primo chandelier in the gallery and had commissioned six more for a new restaurant in Philadelphia, in addition to finding a buyer for the Atroshenko ballerina who had so captured J.C.'s imagination before it had been stolen by *Les Bijoux Jolis*. He gave Jessica permission to sell it for a tidy sum and complimented her on her sales skills.

"It's hard to say no to a pregnant woman," said Jess, laughter thick in her voice.

"And even harder to say no to *beautiful* pregnant women," said J.C.

"You're a terrible flirt," she said, "but I'm immune. I married the worst of them and lived to tell the tale."

Alex English, Jessica's husband of almost two years, had once been one of J.C.'s biggest rivals, though J.C. was three years Alex's senior. They'd both dated casually, bedding the same women for sport without an iota of conscience or commitment. But Jessica Winslow had tamed her husband's wild ways . . . in much the same way that Libitz appeared to be taming J.C.

"Speaking of Alex . . . can I ask you something?"

"Sure. Anything."

"Were you ever scared about your feelings for Alex? Didn't you worry? About his reputation, I mean?"

"Of course," said Jess, laughter thick in her voice. "It was a problem at first. We had to move to England for a year because it felt like he'd screwed half of Philly."

And I screwed the other half, thought J.C. with a grimace.

"But you got over it?" he asked.

"You have to understand. I'd loved Alex since I was a little girl," she said, her voice tender. "I wasn't going to let him go when I was finally old enough to marry him."

"What about Alex?"

"What about him?"

"How did he . . . I mean, how long did it take for him to realize . . . to know that you two . . ."

"Asking for yourself or a friend?" asked Jess with a touch of sass, and he would have sworn she made mimed quotation marks when she said "friend."

Why lie? He was curious about how Jess and Alex had managed to mesh their lives together. "Myself."

"Ooo! Honesty!" she exclaimed. "How refreshing! And who is the lucky lady?"

"None of your business, *petite*."

"Fine," Jess grumbled. "Well . . . I can't speak for Alex, really. I can only tell you this: once we were together, there was no one else. I knew I wanted him the second I saw him. I think he'd say the same. We danced around it. He fought it to preserve my reputation. I backed away when I saw that the streets of Philly were *littered* with his conquests. We almost walked away from it, but we couldn't. In the end, we *had* to have each other and no one else. There was simply"— she sighed—"no other option."

Her words, albeit about her own marriage, resonated so strongly with Jean-Christian, he battled the urge to sigh along with her. Catching himself just in time, he straightened in his hotel desk chair. "What if it hadn't worked out? Wouldn't you have been devastated?"

"Yes," she said. "Shattered. But it did work out."

"What if it hadn't?"

"It *did*."

"What if—"

"We could go on like this all day," said Jess, her voice edging into exasperated, "but the fact will always remain: it *did*. And we'd never have known if we didn't take a chance."

It suddenly occurred to J.C., in blinding clarity, that while it felt like he was taking the bigger risk of the two of them, it was actually Libitz (by a thousand miles), and it made him profoundly grateful that she'd somehow been able to see through his bullshit and smarmy come-ons and daddy issues, and find something worthwhile underneath. He needed to do everything he could to convince her she wasn't wrong . . . and that meant staying in New York a little longer.

"Invite me to the wedding," said Jess. "But make it next summer, so baby English is here and I can wear something cute."

"No wedding on the horizon, Jess," he said.

She chuckled indulgently like Mad and Jax did when they knew he was wrong about something but didn't have the heart to call him out. "Whatever you say, boss."

"Speaking of being your boss, how do you feel about staying on for a little while longer?"

"Great," said Jess. "I love it here. I was sure I'd miss the museum, but I don't. I love this side of things, and it's keeping me off my feet, so Alex can't complain."

"Then get comfortable," said Jean-Christian, staring out the window at the traffic of Columbus Circle. "Because I just might open another gallery in New York."

As the clock ticked the day away, closer and closer to the gallery's closing time of six o'clock, Libitz became more jumpy. She'd get home by six-thirty and have half an hour to kill before Neil arrived to take her out to dinner, totally clueless about the fact that she planned to break up with him. She shuddered. Maybe she should throw back a couple of vodka shots in that half hour so she wasn't so edgy. She felt terrible about what she was about to do.

They hadn't dated that long—a little over two months. And they hadn't slept together, thank God. But Neil was, as her mother had pointed out in no less than eight e-mails and texts between last night and today, a "catch," and Libitz knew it. He was hardworking, thoughtful, kind, and stead-fast. He'd help her raise their Jewish children in a Jewish home, and their families would be overjoyed by their union. He was an organic choice—smart, seamless, and practical.

Jean-Christian Rousseau, on the other hand? He was, as he'd always been, a minefield. But more and more, he was *her* minefield, and she didn't want it any other way. He was sexy and charming, devilishly handsome, and a match for her wit. But it was more than that—the way he loved his fam-ily, the way he looked at her like she could give him the world, the way he made her feel when he touched her—it didn't hold a candle to the way she felt about Neil. Libitz wanted J.C.'s heat and passion. She wanted it forever.

When the security system beeped quietly to alert her that someone had entered the store, she looked up, half-expecting Jean-Christian to materialize from her thoughts, but her eyes widened in dismay. Standing just inside the door, holding two dozen roses pageant-style, with a mas-sive, beaming smile on his face . . . was Neil.

Two hours early, at her place of business instead of the privacy of her home.

Her stomach fell, and all the wonderful butterflies that had taken up residence there over the last few days flew upward, catching in her ribcage and compressing her lungs. She gasped unpleasantly, putting her hand over her heart. She wasn't ready. Shit. She wasn't ready to do this.

"Libitz?" said Neil, approaching her, a concerned look on his face. "Honey?"

His voice forced her feet forward, and she greeted him with an awkward hug. "Neil. You surprised me. You're early!"

He hugged her back, and Libitz took a shaky breath as he transferred the roses from his arms to hers. As she backed away, she had a ridiculous notion that she probably looked like Miss America and squelched the urge to wave.

God, I'm losing it.

"Are you . . . okay?" asked Neil, looking into her eyes.

"Yes!" she chirped. "Just . . . surprised."

"*Good* surprised?" he asked, cocking his head to the side.

Her lips parted, but nothing came out. She just stood there like a mackerel, staring at him.

"Lib?"

"These need water!" she said. "I think I have a . . . a vase. In my office."

"Let's go find out," he said, and if she wasn't mistaken, a touch of suggestion had entered his voice, as if he interpreted her quest for a vase as a ruse for alone time in her office.

"Stay here," she commanded him. "I'll be right back." But as she turned and walked away, she realized that if she was going to break up with him, her office would afford them the most privacy. She pivoted to face him. "Nope. Come with me."

He gave her a look, then grinned indulgently as he followed behind her. "Don't take this the wrong way, but you're acting a little funny, Lib."

Calm down, she told herself. *Calm down. You can do this.*

It's not that Libitz hadn't broken up with a guy before, and Lord knew she was a frank-spoken woman, but this felt mean somehow, because Neil had done nothing wrong. She dreaded hurting him. She wished there was another way to let him go, but there wasn't, and she hated the conversation they needed to have.

They entered her office and she closed the door, beelining to the bathroom in the corner of the room and finding a vase under the sink. She filled it with water, calling to Neil, "I'll be right there. How was Vermont?"

She plopped the roses in the vase, set it on the shelf behind the toilet, and then turned back to the room, surprised to find Neil blocking the doorway.

"I missed you, honey," he said, reaching for her. "That's how Vermont was."

Libitz lurched back into the bathroom, out of his reach. "Oh."

"Hey. Are you okay?" asked Neil, taking a step back.

She used the gap between Neil and the doorway to make her escape and crossed the room, sitting down in her office chair behind her desk. Gulping as Neil followed her and took a seat in one of the mod-style guest chairs, she nodded.

He chuckled awkwardly. "I feel like I'm interviewing for a job."

Libitz winced. This was the moment.

"Neil," she said. "You're amazing. You're kind and sweet, and you've been nothing but—"

"Holy shit," hissed Neil, recoiling in the clear-acrylic chair. "Are you breaking up with me?"

Libitz blinked at him, trying to retrieve her train of thought. "I just . . ."

"You just what?" asked Neil, leaning forward, his warm blue eyes taking on a cooler hue.

"I met someone else," she murmured, forcing herself not to look away.

"Someone else?"

She nodded. "Mm-hm."

"In five days?"

Her brows furrowed. "What—what do you mean?"

"You basically invited me to fuck you when we talked on Saturday . . . what changed in five days?"

She gasped at his language. Although she didn't mind cursing, Neil had never cursed in front of her, so it sounded extra angry coming from his mouth.

"Oh, wait," he said, nodding as he sat back in the chair. "It's been more than five days, hasn't it? In fact . . . oh, my God, I'm the biggest moron who ever lived," he muttered. He looked up at her, his eyes hurt and angry as he put the pieces together. "You already knew him. You finally said yes to going out with me *because* of him, didn't you?"

"Neil . . ." she started.

He sighed. "I couldn't figure it out. I thought . . . maybe she's sick of fucking random guys she meets in clubs. Maybe she wants something real; that's why she finally said yes."

Libitz winced. She honestly had no idea he'd known about her pre-Neil extracurricular activities, and it cast their time together in a new light to know that he did.

"No, honey," he said, as though reading her mind. "I didn't want to be a notch on your belt. I *liked* you. I saw something in you. I was willing to *overlook* your history."

"My . . . history?" she asked, sitting up in her chair, a defensiveness she hadn't anticipated somehow making her spine straighter.

"It never mattered to me!" he shouted. "I liked you for you!"

"I know that," she said softly.

"I thought there was more to you, but clearly, I was wrong." He paused, and his eyes narrowed. "Did you fuck him?"

"Neil!"

"Did you fuck the other guy?"

She stared at him in silence, unwilling to answer his vulgar question or be slut-shamed any further. Her heart ached for his hurt feelings, because they must be terribly raw for him to lash out at her like this, but Libitz Feingold knew who she was, and she refused to let anyone belittle her. For *any* reason.

"I'm very sorry about it," she said, standing up. "But you're being insulting. I need to ask you to leave."

Neil lowered his head, scrubbing his hands through his reddish-blond hair.

"I'm sorry, Lib," he said, looking up at her. His face was shattered and his voice broke on her name. "I had no right to—I just didn't see this coming."

"I know," she said, emotion making her voice shaky too. She'd hurt him, and it occurred to her that maybe she'd ruined him a little for the next girl. It would take him longer to trust, and that was her fault. She had surprised him and hurt him, and she felt awful about it. "You *are* great, Neil."

He looked up, his eyes bitter. "But not great enough."

She clenched her jaw because her own eyes were starting to burn.

He stood up and held out his hand, which Libitz took and shook.

"Neil—"

"Good luck, Lib. I hope it works out with . . . whoever he is."

And for just a moment, holding Neil's hand, she had an urge to tell him to stay. She was choosing Catholic, barely reformed manwhore Jean-Christian Rousseau over kind, solid, steady Neil?

Bad choice, screamed logic.

The only *choice*, whispered her heart.

"Thank you," she said, dropping his hand and giving him a slight smile. "Good luck to you too."

He nodded sadly, turned around, and left her office, closing the door behind him.

For a moment, she stared at the door before she realized that she was crying, tears spilling from her eyes in rivulets as she relived his ugly words. So she rested her head on her desk and cried—for Neil and for her, for the model in the painting and all those who shared her fate. The world had so much ugliness in it, and she'd just added to it.

I'm sorry. I'm sorry. I'm so sorry.

Once she was all cried out, she wiped her eyes and took a deep breath, reviewing their short, painful conversation in her head.

No matter how much it hurt her to hurt Neil, she quickly realized that he was absolutely not the right man for her. Whether now or later, her penchant for casual sex as a single woman would have come up. It would have been a way in which Neil felt superior to her, tried to control her, and made her cede to his judgment. It would have been a way that Neil kept them oh-so-slightly on uneven footing—him as the holier of the two, the absolute head of household, the de facto better person. For the rest of her life, she'd be made to feel inferior, and one day, she might have even believed it.

But right here, right now, Libitz *didn't* feel like she was inferior to Neil, and she certainly didn't feel inferior to Jean-Christian. She had made her decisions as a responsible adult and had always insisted on protection and safety. She didn't feel bad about her choices, nor did she fault Jean-Christian for sampling his fair share of women. And in a blinding flash of sweet realization, she knew that Jean-Christian would never judge her or belittle her as Neil just had—he would never, ever make her feel "less than" or "not as good as" him . . . and not because they had a history of casual sex in common, but because Jean-Christian wasn't a judgmental asshole. He was an adult with faults, just like she was. And he was the adult-with-faults that she wanted.

Buzz, buzz. Buzz, buzz.

She reached for her phone and opened the screen to a new text that made the growing smile on her face broaden with joy.

JC: One, I figured out something about LBJ.

JC: Two, are you ready for your convo with Neil?

JC: Three, in case you're having cold feet, let me remind you that I am crazy about you, Elsa. *All* of you.

JC: Four, I'm dying a little waiting to hear from you, so if you ever wanted to torture me, this is an ideal opportunity.

JC: Five, my offer to fuck you hard stands, but if you need something else from me tonight, just tell me. I can be whatever you need. I promise.

They came in quick succession, text after text buzzing in her hand, making her laugh and cry at the same time, her heart soaring with the kind of forever-love she hoped she'd only feel about one man for the rest of her life.

When she was sure no more texts were coming, she wiped her eyes and freshened up her lipstick. Then she grabbed her phone and threw it in her bag, asking Duane to lock up as she sailed out of her gallery and hailed a cab.

Chapter 13

J.C. checked his phone again, then threw it down on the bed in frustration.

He hadn't heard from her all day.

Not once.

Clenching his jaw, he picked up his glass of scotch on the rocks and crossed the suite to stare out the floor-to-ceiling windows. It was almost five o'clock, and late-afternoon shadows were setting in over Columbus Circle. With a fine mist of rain falling, New York looked gray and gloomy, and it matched his mood.

She'd been upset last night. Maybe he should have overruled her request for alone time and insisted that he stay with her?

"You're *shit* at this," he muttered, wondering if he should call Étienne for some advice. His little brother knew far more about relationships than J.C. ever would. But surely Kate had shared that they'd moved beyond flirtation, and he supposed Étienne wasn't thrilled about them upsetting her, so he couldn't imagine his brother would be a very sympathetic ear.

Maybe she'd decided that since he didn't stay with her last night, he didn't care about her on an emotional level. And maybe she'd thought about Nice Neil and how much more caring *he* was. And maybe she'd decided that she'd be better off with Nice-*fucking*-Neil in her life over J.C.

"*Fuck*," he cursed. "Nice Neil can suck it."

Crossing back over to the bed, he grabbed the phone again and unlocked the screen only to throw it back down with a grunt when he saw that there were still no messages waiting. He checked the time on the digital clock beside the bed. Five ten.

Five ten meant that she was still at work, meant that there were still about two hours before she talked to Nice Neil at seven. Making a quick decision to go plead his case, he grabbed his blazer and shrugged into it as he headed for the door. He'd explain that agreeing to give her space didn't mean he didn't care about her feelings. Not at all. In fact, he was trying to respect her feelings by—

Yanking open the door to his room, he gasped and stopped short. Libitz was standing in the hallway, her fist poised in midair as though she was about to knock on his door.

"Wait!" he demanded, blinking at her. "What are—you're here?"

"I'm here." She smiled at him, lowering her hand. "Are you going somewhere?"

"I'm going to you."

"To me? Why?"

He nodded, still stunned by her sudden appearance. "I'm going to tell you every reason why Nice Neil is wrong for you and I'm right."

"So tell me," she murmured, holding his eyes with hers.

"Come in?" he asked, taking two steps back, still turned around by her unexpected arrival.

She hesitated for only a moment, searching his eyes before stepping into his hotel room. As she untied the belt of her short, khaki-colored raincoat, he watched her, every cell in his body at attention, dread and hope fighting for dominion.

She could only be here for one of two reasons: one, to tell him that she'd broken up with Neil and she was free, but that was unlikely because Neil wasn't coming home until later . . . or two, to tell him that she'd decided not to take a chance on him after all and to let him know that she'd decided to stay with Neil.

His heart clutched as he considered option two, and he forced himself to take a deep, cleansing breath. Whatever it took, she was here now, which meant that some part of her still had feelings for him. This was his chance. Maybe his last chance. He needed to convince her that he was the right man for her.

Whatever it takes.

With a shimmy of her shoulders, the coat slid down her back, and he caught it, savoring the warmth transferred from her body as he turned to hang it up in the closet. Looking over his shoulder, he watched her pass by the bed and stop in the small sitting area by the windows.

"Nice view," she said, turning slightly to give him a small smile.

Was there sadness in the smile? Fucking *sadness*? Like she was here to tell him good-bye? Goose bumps rose up on his skin like falling dominoes, and he shut the closet doors, making his way to her.

"Yeah. Uh, yeah. It's good. The, uh, the circle." He sounded like an idiot, all the suaveness he'd perfected over the course of his lifetime failing him now when he needed it most. "You . . . do you want a drink?"

She turned to look at him again and nodded. "Sure. That would be good."

He turned toward the wet bar, his blood running cold.

Good? Why would it be good? Why did she need a drink? For courage? Probably for courage. Fuck. No doubt courage to tell him that she had come to her senses, and she didn't need a retired manwhore in her life when she had a good, decent man who hadn't fucked half of Philadelphia.

Squatting down, he opened the minibar and took out a small bottle of white wine, standing up to pour it into a stemmed glass. Bracing his hands on the black marble counter over the fridge, he looked up at himself in the mirror. His eyes were dark-green and wild, and he was holding it together, though he was certain he stood on the very brink of disaster.

I'm not losing her, he thought desperately. *She's the only woman who's ever been in color in a sepia world. I can't lose her now.*

Then you better talk fast.

He stood up and crossed the sitting area, handing her the glass.

"Ready?" he asked her.

"Umm . . . ?" She cocked her head to the side, pausing midsip. "For . . . ?"

"For the reasons I'm a better choice for you than Neil," he reminded her.

"Oh," she said, her cheeks flushing pink. "Well, actually, I have something to tell you first. It turns out—"

Talk fast. Now!

"I'm falling in love with you," he blurted out, cutting her off and effectively flaying his heart wide open with a verbal bisection he hadn't prepared for and had never seen coming. The words reverberated between them, coarse and jagged and painfully inelegant. And his heart bled out with every fast, throbbing beat as he stared at her, waiting for her to say something.

To say *anything*.

"W-what?" she sputtered, her eyes impossibly wide, her lips parted open. Her voice was soft and breathless when she followed up with a stunned, "*Whatdidyousay?*"

"I . . ."

Bewildered by his outburst, he couldn't form words and was left to stare at her helplessly. Furrowed brows. Brown eyes so deep and confused and shocked, they gazed up at him in disbelief. Her lips moved like they were trying to form a word, but she didn't say anything.

His heart was beating so fast now that his chest hurt. Ached. And his head. Fuck, his head throbbed like it had been repeatedly hit with a sledgehammer. He pressed a hand to his chest and forced himself to take a deep breath, reminding himself that he was a fit young man, and this wasn't a heart attack. It was just a panic attack brought on, he realized, not by the gravitas of the words he'd just uttered for the first time in his life, but by the crippling fear of losing Libitz now that he'd found her.

So do *something about it. Let her know that you meant it.*

He stepped around the coffee table between them and sat down beside her on the couch, holding her eyes. Unlike the rest of his body, which had been shared so freely, his heart was unused, untried, unsullied, and unspoiled, never having been given to anyone. And he hoped—God, he hoped with a desperation he'd never known—that if he gave her his virgin heart, it would be enough for her to choose him, to stay with him.

She reached for his hand, and a sudden burst of confidence made the ache in his chest subside. He reached out with his free hand to thread his fingers through her hair, the heel of his palm resting on her temple to force her not to look away. He watched, his heart in his throat, as she leaned into his touch.

"I'm falling in love with you," he said again, his voice soft but firm. "And I don't have much experience with fighting for the woman I want, but I will rip Neil apart if that's what it takes, and I swear to God, I will be the last man standing.

"Because *I* am the man for you, Libitz. I am the *right* man, no matter how deep my faults. I will keep trying, and I will not quit, and I will never, ever cheat. If you just give me a chance, you'll see. I'm not being an asshole giving you a line when I tell you that I can—I *will*—be whatever you need me to be. You said that people can change and people can choose. Well, I'm changing and I choose you.

"And—and—and you are the *right* woman for me, because you are the *only* woman for me. Because thirty-four years of playing the field tells me that you're a fluke, an anomaly, a mermaid, a fucking—a fucking *unicorn*. You know why? Because since you, I don't remember any of them. Not one of them matters. Because there is *only* you. My heart wants you. My heart wants to give itself to *you*.

"Let Neil find someone else. There are a million other girls who could make Nice Neil happy . . . but you're it for me. Besides, you don't belong to him. Whether you like it or not, Elsa, you belong to *me*."

"I like it," she whispered, her voice so soft, he almost wondered if he imagined it.

"You like it?"

She nodded against his palm, opening her eyes slowly. "I like it that I belong to you."

"Were you coming here to break things off with me?" he asked, slightly surprised by the efficacy of his clumsy, heartfelt, impromptu speech.

"No," she said, shaking her head. "Neil got home early. I broke up with him. I was coming to tell you that I'm free."

I broke up with him. I'm free.

If there were sweeter fucking words in the English language, he didn't know what they were.

"No, baby," he growled, untangling his fingers from hers so he could cup her face with both hands, "you're not. Weren't you listening? You're mine."

His lips crashed down on hers with a possessive kiss meant to brand her as his, to promise her that he was hers for as long as she wanted him, for as long as she would have him. Her fingers plunged into his hair, her nails razing his scalp as she opened her mouth to his, sliding her tongue against his with a moan of satisfaction. And because he wanted her—because he needed the affirmation of physical love after sharing his feelings with her for the first time, he scooped her up in his arms and made it to the bed in seconds, lowering her to the soft duvet without ever letting go of her lips.

Settling his body over hers, his elbows bracing his weight on either side of her head, he took his time kissing her thoroughly. Whether he knew it in his head or only in his heart, he was about to learn what it meant to love someone with his body—not just to give and seek physical pleasure but also to declare his feelings for her, to give and receive not just because his dick was hard but because his heart ached for the closest possible connection he could forge with her.

Rolling to his side, he gazed down at her bee-stung lips and glazed eyes with a grin. His fingers grazed the pearl buttons of her blouse, giving her a moment to protest, because he started unfastening them slowly.

"When did you know?" she asked, raising her arms over her head after he'd opened the silk so that he could pull it over her head.

"At Ten's wedding," he said, letting the fabric fall with a whisper to the floor.

"That early?"

He nodded. "I was jealous of you talking to your prep-school friends. I'd never felt jealousy like that before."

With a flick of his fingers, he opened the front clasp of her bra, gently spreading the fabric open to reveal her small, pert breasts capped with dusky areolas and large, light-brown nipples. They strained toward him, *small but fierce*, he thought, bending his head to take the top of one between his lips.

"Unh," she moaned, arching her back, her high heels hitting the floor as she bent her knees and slid her feet up the bed.

He drew back and flattened his tongue at the base of her breast then licked up, the erect nub interrupting the smooth sweep of his tongue. Sucking it strongly into his mouth, his cheeks caved at the same time Libitz's back rose off the bed, and J.C. repositioned himself between her bent spread knees. Licking his fingers, he reached for her throbbing nipple, rolling the slick flesh as he swirled his tongue around its twin.

"Fuck," she breathed in a guttural moan, trying to lower her hands to push him away. With his free hand, he grabbed her wrists and held them tightly, pinning them back over her head as he sucked her other nipple between his lips.

Her skirt had ridden up around her waist when she bent her knees, and now she pushed against his chest with her pelvis, whimpering as she squirmed beneath him. With one last flick of her distended nipple with his thumb, he flattened his palm under her breast and sucked hard on the other as he smoothed his hand down the soft, flat skin of her stomach and under her white satin panties.

As the heel of his palm pressed down on her soaked mound, she writhed in pain-pleasure and screamed out in her first orgasm, the muscles deep inside of her body convulsing as he finished loving her breasts for now. Using both hands to pull her panties away from her pussy, he raised her legs over his head and threw the damp fabric on the floor.

Leaning forward, he parted her lips with his fingers and dipped his head, licking her clit in one long, sustained stroke. She spread her legs wider, and he rested his hand on her thigh to keep them apart, nuzzling the hard, bright-red clit with his nose before sealing his lips over her. Flicking his tongue out over the sensitive skin, she started rolling her hips into his face, the muscles of her stomach undulating in waves as she rocked into his mouth. Leaning back, he flattened his tongue and licked slowly from the opening of her sex to her clit, lapping at the slick, throbbing skin until she started humming, whimpering, moaning, and finally crying out again, her fingers tearing at his hair and her hips bucking as she orgasmed for the second time.

Pressing his palm back over her spasming clit, he slid up her body, claiming her mouth with his, the taste of her juices mixing between them as her tongue tangled mindlessly with his.

"Fuck, this is hot," he groaned, slipping two fingers into her drenched sex and hooking them back against the wall, his fingertips stroking her still-trembling flesh. "Come for me again, baby. Three times."

"I can't," she whimpered, her tongue darting out to wet her lips as shocks and waves still rocked her body.

"Little and fierce," he said, sucking her nipple back between his lips as he slid a third finger deep inside of her.

"Jean—Jean—Jean-Christian!" she screamed, her entire body flexing and releasing as she fell over the edge of bliss for the third time.

He smiled as he watched her face, the way her neck extended back, the black of her hair buried in the snow white of the pillow as her fingers clenched the comforter. Withdrawing his fingers gently, he kissed her stomach before sliding off the bed. He leaned forward to unzip her short, black skirt and tugged it down her legs, dropping it to the floor and leaving her naked on the bed, riding out her orgasm as he quickly unbuttoned his shirt and tossed it to the floor. He toed off his mocs, and his jeans and boxers followed until he was as naked as she.

His cock stood straight up, waiting for its chance to sample what his fingers and lips had already tasted . . . and normally, he'd drag his partner to the edge of the bed, steady her hips with his hands and fuck her senseless at this point in the evening . . . because, hey! It was his turn now, right?

But this was Libitz, not anyone else, and it didn't occur to him to slide into her body without making sure she was present and ready, because he wanted her looking directly into his eyes the next time she came. He wanted—no, he *needed*—to know that everything that was happening in his heart was also happening in hers. So he slid back onto the bed and lay down on his side next to her, gathering her softly shaking body into his arms and pressing his lips to the back of her beautiful neck.

This is Libitz, he thought, holding her tighter as her body relaxed, melting into his. *This is love.*

Though she had been with more men than she could count on her fingers and toes, she had never experienced the sort of mind-blowing, overwhelming pleasure she'd just been offered by Jean-Christian. He was a master of the female form, playing her body like a Juilliard-trained virtuoso. She'd never been with anyone who'd made her come so fast, in such awesome waves of abandonment, her only focus the crest of the next surge, her only anchor the man who so lovingly attended to her body.

And now, despite the raging hard-on pressed against her back, he held her tenderly in his arms, his hands flat on her stomach, under breasts that were almost too sensitive to be touched, his legs bent into hers like a spoon.

He must be hurting like hell, she thought, her smile growing as she opened her eyes, gazed out the floor-to-ceiling windows, and found that it was twilight now, *and yet he's lying here beside me, waiting until I'm ready.*

If she hadn't felt such immense joy, she would have wept for this man who was changing right before her eyes to become a man she wasn't sure she deserved but would cherish for as long as he let her.

Turning in his arms, her tender breasts making her whimper as the hair on his chest rasped lightly against them, she looked into his eyes.

"Well . . . ?" he asked.

"That's never happened to me," she confessed.

"Multiple orgasms?"

She grinned at him. "Not three."

"So you're saying I'm the first?" he asked, looking cocky.

"Yep," she said, "that's what I'm saying."

"Want to know a secret?" he asked.

She nodded.

"We're only halfway done."

"Is that right?" she asked.

He raised his eyebrows and nodded. "Oh, yeah. My goal is at least six before tomorrow."

Her hands were flat on his chest, but now she skimmed one down over the ripples of his abs, tracing half of a pronounced *V* of muscle from his hip to his pelvis, finally brushing her fingers lightly over his straining cock and resting them there.

"Number four's all you," she said, using her other hand to push him onto his back.

"You don't have to . . ." he said as she pressed kisses to his chest, moving lower with each touch, her fingers wrapping around his velvet steel to stroke it up and down. "Ah . . . baby . . ." he groaned.

When she reached his stomach, she repositioned herself between his legs, crouching over him with her ass in the air, and bent her head to lick the tip of his cock.

"Fuuuuuck," he hissed as she opened her mouth and slid her lips from his tip to the base, one hand still clutching him tightly, the other playing with his heavy balls like marbles.

"Soon," she answered, taking him throat-deep again.

His hands found their way to her head, his fingers threading through her hair, though neither guiding nor forcing her head, which bobbed as she licked and sucked, tracing a vein along one side of his shaft with her tongue before licking the drops of salty pre-cum from the glistening top.

He groaned, sliding his hands to her face and stilling her movements. "I don't want to come without you."

"Yes, you do," she contradicted him, trying to lean forward to take him in her mouth again.

"No, baby," he said. "I want to be with you. I want . . ."

She stopped fighting him and sat back on her haunches, looking into his face. "What?"

He threw an arm over his eyes. "I feel like a kid."

She shimmied up his body, straddling his chest and pushing at his arm. "Tell me."

"I want . . ." He searched her eyes, then said, ". . . I want to watch you. I want to be, you know, looking at you."

"You want to watch me come?"

He nodded. "While I'm inside of you."

And suddenly it occurred to her that it was possible—just possible—that he'd never done so before. That he'd always closed his eyes, or looked away, or just not met his partner's eyes while fucking her. And here, now, with her, he wanted to change that.

Reaching for his cock, she held it firmly, positioning herself over the tip before sinking down slowly, so very slowly, onto his hardness. Sheathing it within her. And holding his eyes all the while.

"Lib," he gasped, his voice strangled.

"Look at me," she said, feeling the walls of her sex stretch to accommodate his thickness. She looked down at her pelvis, at the place where they were joined so intimately, so completely. "Look at us."

His almost-black eyes flicked down to where his cock disappeared into her body before trailing slowly back to her eyes. He put his hands on her hips and she moved up, then down, sliding her body on his cock, taking him deep before arching up again. As he pulled her hips forward, she leaned over his chest to kiss him and her clit rubbed flush against his pubic bone, which massaged her tight, throbbing nub. She found his lips with hers as she continued to grind against him, his tongue swirling around in her mouth as a fourth orgasm started building low in her belly.

She leaned back and he sat up, wrapping his arms around her and looking deeply into her eyes as he thrust upward, tighter and faster, the tip of his cock rubbing her inner wall and making her moan with pleasure. Her head started to fall back, but he reached behind her neck, forcing it upright.

"Don't close your eyes," he demanded. "Don't look away from me. I want to see you, Libitz . . . I want to . . ."

She panted in tandem with his thrusts, her breasts rubbing against his chest, tears welling in her eyes as the whirling in her belly exploded, sending fissures of heat throughout her body and making her muscles convulse with wave after wave of pleasure. And all the while, she stared into his eyes. Let him see what he did to her, how she felt about him, that he was her first in so many ways tonight.

And a moment later, when he found his own release, crying out her name like a prayer, she saw the same feelings in his eyes as he fought to keep them open and focused on her. She saw love. She saw passion. She saw forever.

She collapsed against him, limp and sated, her arms around him and his around her as their bodies rocked and trembled against each other. Resting her cheek on his shoulder, she heard him whisper it in her ear: the word "love" . . . over and over and over again like a litany, so softly it could have been a dream.

"Love, love, love, love love love love . . ."

It was the thing that had made tonight different.

It was the thing that had made tonight perfect.

Hours later, after making love a second time, ordering dinner, and taking a shower together, they lay side by side on their stomachs, cheeks on their own pillows, facing each other. They'd fucked and they'd eaten, and now they were closer and closer to falling asleep, but not before they told each other silly stories about past lovers who'd meant nothing, who could never compare with what they'd discovered in one another's arms.

"Shut up!" she exclaimed, hitting him on the shoulder.

"It's true," he insisted. "I dumped Alice for Bree."

"So that's why they hate you!"

"That's why *Alice* hates me."

Prim and proper Alice Story. It was the day she'd called him her "boyfriend" that had been the nail in the coffin. He'd gone home that weekend and run into Bree, who, not knowing about Alice, had been only too happy to distract him.

"Why does Bree?"

"Bree was friends with Alice, so she wasn't thrilled to find out that I'd stopped hanging out with Alice to hang out with her. I might not have volunteered that information."

"So Bree felt disloyal to her friend?"

"I guess that was part of it." He shrugged. "But I couldn't give her what she wanted. She wanted all of me. I could only give her a fraction."

"Maybe it felt serious to her?" asked Libitz.

"I guess. But I never gave her reason to believe it was." He reached out and cradled her face. "You're the only one I've ever offered my heart to."

"I know," she said, rotating her head just slightly to kiss his palm. "And I'll keep it safe. I promise."

He felt it again, deep inside—that burst of rightness he felt whenever he was with Libitz. It made him feel grateful and strong, and he loved her for it. He couldn't imagine how Neil must have felt today, finding out that he wouldn't have a future with her. Poor bastard.

"How'd Neil take the news?"

Her face clouded over, and she dropped his eyes for a second. "Not good."

A protective rush of emotion made him reach for her, rolling both of them to their sides so he could wrap his arms around her. "What happened?"

She shrugged. "He was upset. Hurt. Angry."

"He said things?"

She nodded.

"Fuck, baby. I'm sorry about that."

Her face brightened, and she leaned forward to kiss him slowly, tenderly, their tongues dancing for a moment before she pulled away. "I'm not."

"I'm going to make you happy, Libitz Feingold," he promised.

"You already do," she said. Suddenly her eyes widened. "Hey! Earlier, when you texted me, you said you found out something else! What was it?"

He rolled onto his back, pulling her with him so she was draped over his chest. She propped her elbows on his pecs and smiled down at him.

"I almost forgot," he said.

"Come on! Tell me!"

"What'll you give me if I do?" he asked, grinning at her.

She arched her back, rubbing her pussy against his hip. "Whatever you want."

"I called the art dealer in Marseille about the twins and found out that one of them is still alive. She's ninety-five. I called her nursing home and asked if I could talk to her. They said I'd have to come in person. I'm going to Marseille this weekend," he said in a rush, using one breath. "Let's fuck."

She started laughing, her breasts rubbing against his chest as she shook her head. "You're an ass."

"I can live with that," he said.

"Wait. Are you serious about the twin?"

"Yes, she's still alive. And yes, I'm going to go see her. My woman wants to know what happened to C.T., so I need to go find out for her."

"Your . . . *woman*?"

He nodded, grinning up at her. "My woman."

"Well," she said, rolling onto her back, "how do you feel about company?"

"Yours?" He hovered over her, parting her legs with his knee, the hardness of his cock slipping, without error, into her hot, wet sheath and pausing there. She lifted her hips to let him know she wanted more, and he obliged her by withdrawing and then thrusting forward again.

"Mine," she sighed, arching to meet his thrusts.

"I love it," he said, still deeply lodged within her body. "Are you saying you want to come with me? To Marseille?"

"I want to come with you," she whimpered breathlessly, sliding her hands down to his ass and digging her fingers into his skin with the next thrust.

"Give me about two minutes," he said between pants, making the most of the delicious double entendre she'd set up for him. "But do you also want to come to Marseille?"

She managed to nod and murmur a breathless "Mm-hm" before he bent his head and kissed her, making good on his promise to deliver orgasm number six before midnight and looking forward to this weekend a hundred times more than he had a moment before.

Chapter 14

Their flight left at six o'clock on Friday night from New York with a quick stopover in London before arriving in Marseille at nine-thirty on Saturday morning. It would be a quick trip, with them returning to New York tomorrow, but knowing how tired they would be, J.C. had arranged for their hotel room to be ready for them upon their arrival in Marseille.

En route to the InterContinental Mon Dieu, Libitz put her weary head on his shoulder and closed her eyes, giving J.C. a chance to call the nursing home where the surviving Gemini model, Madame Sylvia Comtois, was living. Told that she generally woke up for an hour or two in the midafternoon, the head nurse asked if he and Libitz could delay their visit until two o'clock, to which he gladly agreed. Libitz was snoring softly as the car negotiated late-summer traffic on the way to Vieux Port, and he was tired but content with his arm around her shoulders and the dead weight of her head on his shoulder.

They could check into their hotel and sleep for a few hours before exploring a bit of Marseille and finding a place for lunch before their visit with Madame Comtois.

He'd tried to convince Libitz to stay in Marseille for a few extra days, but her work ethic was fierce, and she'd soundly refused, telling him he'd have to go by himself if she had to miss more than a day of work.

Going without her wasn't nearly as tempting as having her in bed beside him, so he'd agreed to travel all the way to Marseille for a day and a night as long as she'd promise to return to France with him for a week at New Year's. Her answer—to suck his cock dry—he'd taken as a yes.

No wonder she was tired. They'd stayed up until early morning on Thursday, talking and making love, getting a few minutes of sleep between waking up to reach for each other again. He picked her up at work on Thursday evening and took her for dinner, after which they'd spent that night christening every room in her apartment. There was a fresh-ness, a newness, an excitement in finding the right person after knowing so many who weren't. And they were falling madly in love with each other. There was that too.

When he considered his siblings—Étienne with Kate, Jax with Gardener, and Mad with Cort—he knew that the only woman he wanted by his side was Libitz, with her sharp wit and voracious mind, her love of art and love of family. The faith she had in him when he had deserved none and the way she soothed his fears, leading his heart back to hers at every juncture of doubt, stripping away his misgivings until all that was left was his deep and constant yearning to be with her.

It was more than just her personality. More than her delectable little body, which he'd loved in wild ways that had both satisfied and challenged the sexual beast within. It was as though she'd been chosen for him, and he for her—he felt she was his fated mate in every way, almost like some-thing otherworldly had long ago decided that Jean-Christian Rousseau and Libitz Feingold should find each other in the big, wide world, and when they did, they should love one another. That's how it felt. Like the fulfillment of a promise. Like the manifestation of destiny. Like nothing in the world could ever feel as right as his growing love for her. And he never, ever wanted to go back to a life that didn't include her.

He wanted her forever.

And unlike his father, he would make the right choices.

And unlike his parents, he would do the work.

For the honor of knowing her, of loving her, of having her, he would do *anything*.

She stirred in her sleep. "Are we there yet?" she murmured.

"We're so close, love," he whispered, kissing her tenderly. "We're almost there."

Jean-Christian had let her sleep for a few hours, after which Libitz rose, showered, and dressed, feeling rested enough to tackle the remainder of their day in Marseille.

He'd left a note by the bedside: *Gone wandering. Back by two. Love, Jean-Christian.*

She'd held the note in her hands for a long moment, marveling over the leaps and strides in their new relationship and wondering if this was how it felt for everyone who met the elusive "one": the person they were supposed to be with.

In conversation and in bed, there was an openness, a complete trust, that she'd never known before Jean-Christian. It scared her, yes, but it would scare her so much more to lose whatever was growing between them. That said, there were so many details and decisions that would require their attention if they intended to make their relationship last forever.

They still needed to come clean with Étienne and Kate, though, when she considered Kate's personality, she felt strongly that her best friend would come around. Kate wanted for Libitz to be as happily settled as she—and to be sisters-in-law with her best friend? There was a sweetness to the notion that appealed to Libitz as it occurred to her. She'd be not only Noelle's godmother but her aunt too. Family, bound to Kate's child through both God and marriage.

There was the matter of where they lived: Jean-Christian in Philadelphia, near his siblings and gallery, and Libitz in New York, near her parents and gallery. Luckily Philadelphia and New York were only a two-hour ride away, but she wrinkled her nose as she applied her makeup in the bathroom mirror. She didn't like the idea of a long-distance relationship with Jean-Christian, even if the distance wasn't terrible. Would she consider moving to Philadelphia to be closer to him? Would it be forward to even mention it?

They were different people, to be sure: both raised in comfort, but Jean-Christian's wealth was stratospheric compared with hers, and their religions were, as they'd observed, different. Would that become an issue if they stayed together?

But as she closed up her makeup pouch and walked back into the hotel room to pull on some black linen shorts and a black-and-white-striped silk shell, her own words returned to her: *It's not a predetermined thing like your blood type or eye color. It's a choice. It's a choice to love someone and be faithful to them and do the work. We're all capable of that.*

And that's really all that mattered when contemplating forever, wasn't it? Nothing was guaranteed if they stayed together. There would be good times and hard times, bad and easy. They could have all the money in the world but lose a child. They could discover, as life went on, that their interests diverged. They could fall out of love. But at every upset, every intersection, they could take each other's hand and choose to do the work. Together. And if he was the person with whom she wanted to do that work? Then he was the man for her. No matter what.

As she slipped into black high-heeled sandals, the door to their room opened, and there he was: a little color in his cheeks, his green eyes sparkling with tenderness and promise, his lips tilted up into a smile just because he was looking at her.

I love you, she thought. *I'm going to love you forever.*

He crossed the room quickly and cupped her cheeks, kissing her gently. "Good rest?"

She nodded. "Thanks for the note."

"Didn't want you to think I'd run off."

"I wouldn't have thought that," she answered, smiling up at him.

His eyes flared with heat. "What makes you trust me like you do?"

"You're my person," she said simply. "On Wednesday, at your hotel, you told me that whether I liked it or not, I belonged to you."

He nodded.

"And you belong to me," she said. "That's just the way it is."

He leaned forward and kissed her forehead, and she closed her eyes, letting herself be held by him, letting her words surround them, letting them be the truth that they wanted and needed.

When he finally drew away, his eyes were warm and his smile blinding. "Are you ready to find out about C.T., my darling Elsa?"

"I'm ready."

"Then let's go," he said, taking her hand and pulling her out the door.

"*Madame Comtois, pouvez-vous m'entendre?*"

Her caregiver, a young nurse named Lizette, smiled up at them from where she crouched beside Madame Comtois' wheelchair.

"Her listen is . . . not, hm, so good," she said in heavily accented English. "*Madame?*"

Slowly, so slowly Libitz could see the immense effort it took, Sylvia Comtois lifted her head, the scattered snow-white curls bobbing as she tried to look up. "*Simone?*"

"*Non, madame,*" said Lizette in French. "*C'est moi. Lizette.*" She stood up and turned to Libitz and Jean-Christian. "The name of her sister is Simone. She, ah, she die two year ago."

Libitz reached for Jean-Christian's hand. "Maybe we should go?"

He sighed, giving her a pained look. "Let me try."

Kneeling down on the floor beside Madame Comtois' chair, he took her weathered, wrinkled, delicate hand in his and kissed it. "*Madame Comtois, je suis Jean-Christian Rousseau.*"

"*J-Jean-Christian?*" she repeated, lifting her head just a little to look into his eyes. "*Je vous connais?*"

"*Non, madame.*"

"She ask, ah, if she know him," whispered Lizette, leaning closer to Libitz.

"*Où est Simone?*"

"*Elle dort maintenant,*" he answered softly, gently petting her hand in his.

"He says zat, hm, her sister is sleep . . . ah, *sleeping*, right now."

Libitz nodded. "Thank you."

"*Madame,*" said Jean-Christian, his voice warm and smooth as honey in the sun. "*Vous souvenez-vous de la jeune fille juive?*"

"*La . . . Juif?*"

"*Oui,*" said Jean-Christian, nodding his head. "*La modèle de portrait juive.*"

"*La . . .*" she sighed, her eyes nodding closed. "*La Juif.*"

"Now he asks about a, ah, a Jewish girl? She model for a portrait?"

Libitz nodded but kept her eyes on Jean-Christian.

Jean-Christian looked up at Lizette and Libitz, his eyes widening like he had an idea. "Lib," he said, gesturing to her to come closer. "Let her see you."

Libitz lowered herself to the floor, kneeling down directly before the wheelchair beside Jean-Christian, her face turned up to the old woman, who drooled from her pale lips and stared blankly down at her lap.

He leaned closer until his lips grazed her ear. "Say this. Say: *Bonjour, Sylvia.*"

Libitz swallowed, focusing on his accent. "*B-bonjour, Sylvia.*"

Madame Comtois' lips moved as though she wanted to say *bonjour*, but no sound came out.

"I am, hm, *désolée*," said Lizette, hovering over them. "But she is very, hm, very sleep now. You can come back?"

Jean-Christian shot a glance to Libitz, ignoring Lizette. "Say, *Je vais être le modèle pour Monsieur Montferrat aujourd'hui.* Tell her you have a modeling job today. She has to look at you."

She nodded. "Tell me the words again."

He did, and she repeated them as best she could.

When Madame Comtois didn't respond, Libitz tried them again. About to give up, she braced her hands on the floor to stand up when the old woman opened her eyes. Though they were ancient and faded to an almost white-blue, they sparkled as her lips twitched, like she wanted to smile.

"*Monsieur Mont . . . ferrat,*" she murmured. "*Il est . . . trés . . . leste.*"

Behind her, Lizette gasped, then chuckled, clapping a hand over her mouth. Libitz looked up at her in question.

"She say he is . . . hm, ah, dirty? Dirty old man?" She giggled. "I think madame have secrets."

Libitz grinned at the young nurse, then turned back to Madame Comtois, surprised to find her eyes focused on Libitz with more clarity and awareness than she'd thought the old woman capable of.

"*C-Camille?*" she whispered, staring at Libitz like she was looking at a ghost. "*Camille . . . Trigére?*"

"Who?" murmured Libitz.

"*Est-ce . . . toi? Camille . . . Trigére?*"

Camille Trigére. C.T.

She heard her sharp inhalation of breath in her ears, but otherwise the entire world floated away, and all Libitz processed was the fact that Madame Comtois had just recognized Libitz as the model and given them the name they were so desperately hoping to find. And that name just happened to be the same as her great-grandmother: Camille.

Jean-Christian's voice in her ear grounded her. "Say, *Oui, Sylvia. C'est bon de te revoir.* It's good to see you again."

"*Oui, Sylvia. C'est bon de te revoir.*"

Madame Comtois reached out her hand, which shook like a lone brown leaf at the bitter end of autumn, and touched Libitz's cheek. "*Es-tu C-Camille . . . la jolie . . . juive.*" After expending such effort, her eyes fluttered closed and her head fell softly forward, her limp hand dropping to her lap.

"What did she say?" asked Libitz.

Jean-Christian whispered, "She says it's good to see you too, Camille . . . She called you 'the pretty Jew.'"

A small noise issued from Libitz's mouth as she braced her hands on the floor and slowly stood up.

"Now she sleep," chirped Lizette, pulling a blanket around Madame Comtois' shoulders and smiling warmly at Libitz. "*Oui?*"

"*Oui,*" said Libitz, vaguely aware that Jean-Christian had also risen and had his arm around her shoulder. "*Merci,* Lizette."

"*De rien.*" She nodded, taking her place behind Madame Comtois' chair, waving as she pushed the older lady back to her bed.

"Lib?" said Jean-Christian. "Are you okay?"

"My . . . my great-grandmother's name was Camille."

"I know," he said, searching her eyes, his expression warning her to be cautious.

"Camille Trigére," she repeated softly, wishing that her mother had known her great-grandmother's maiden name.

Camille. Camille like my great-grandmother.

"Hey," he said, guiding her toward the exit of the nursing home, "do synagogues keep records? Like, birth records?"

Libitz looked up at him and nodded. "Sure. Some of them keep meticulous records."

"Well, now that we have a first and last name . . ." he said.

"Yes!" she cried, her footsteps speeding up with anticipation. "Of course. Let's go!"

As Jean-Christian hailed a cab, she rolled the name over and over again in her head.

It's just a coincidence, she told herself, and yet her stubborn heart insisted it knew better, insisted that it was *far more* than mere coincidence.

Jean-Christian told the cabbie that they wanted to go to the Grande Synagogue de Marseille, and Libitz tried to steady her breathing.

Was it *possible*?

Was it possible that a portrait found in the attic of a mansion in Pennsylvania could have a direct tie to Libitz? She couldn't deny the profound connection she'd felt to *Les Bijoux Jolis* since the moment she'd laid eyes on it, but this? To be related to the model? It would be—

"Are you okay?" asked Jean-Christian, rolling down the window for some fresh air. "You're pale."

"I'm stunned. For her name to be Camille, just like my great-grandmother—"

"Lib," he interrupted. "Camille is a common name here."

"I know that," she snapped, suddenly feeling foolish. "I know, but . . . I *look* like her. *So much* like her. I just . . ."

"You *do*," said Jean-Christian, putting his arm around her and pulling her into his side. "I know how much it meant to you to find out if C.T. survived. Now that we know she shares the same first name as your grandmother, it must feel really . . . personal."

"It does," she admitted.

But he was right. The chance of the Camille Trigére in the portrait being her great-grandmother would be a next-to-no-chance coincidence. She sighed, the wind leaving her sails. "I don't even know where my great-grandmother was from. She could have been from Paris for all we know."

He nodded beside her.

"It was just . . . a surprise."

"Of course," he said, squeezing her a little closer. "We'll find out more at the Grande Synagogue, hopefully, and then I'm taking you out for a memorable dinner, followed by . . ."

She turned to look up at him, and he dropped his lips to hers in a sneak attack. "Lots of this."

"Hey," she said, drawing away from him so she could look into his eyes. "Who are you, anyway?"

"Jean-Christian Rousseau."

"No way," she said. "I heard all about him. Jean-Christian Rousseau is a dog."

"Jean-Christian Rousseau *was* a dog," he corrected her. "He's under renovation."

"A new and improved version?" she asked.

"Trying like hell, Elsa," he said, his eyes vulnerable as they looked into hers.

She kissed him tenderly. "I wasn't supposed to fall for you."

He sighed. "I know."

"We need to talk to Kate and Étienne at some point," she said.

"We will," he promised, nuzzling her neck with his nose, his lips pressing hot kisses to her skin. "But not yet. Let's just be you and me for now."

"You and me."

"Us," he said simply.

"So we're officially . . . *together*?"

"Hell, yes," he said.

"Exclusive?" she clarified.

"A hundred percent," he said. "No more Nice Neil . . . or anyone else for that matter."

"Except for you," she murmured, watching Marseille sail by out the window as her lover, her love, swept her off her feet.

"Except for me," he said, raising his head to kiss her again.

All too soon, the cab stopped in front of a large white building behind a tall, black wrought-iron fence, and the driver asked for the fare. Libitz opened the door and stepped out of the cab onto the sidewalk, looking up at the synagogue built in the 1870s, a place where Camille Trigére may have attended services as a girl.

"Can we go in?" Libitz asked Jean-Christian, looking at the fence.

Jean-Christian sighed. "There have been some anti-Semitic attacks on the local Jewish population in the past several years. It looks like the synagogue isn't open to the public anymore."

"A dead end?" asked Libitz, feeling frustrated.

"Well . . . hold on," said Jean-Christian, pulling out his phone. "Give me a second."

As he tried to figure something out, Libitz looked up at the beautiful building—the spotless white facade with a huge double door at the top of a small white-marble staircase. There was a round stained-glass window over the door, very high up, with a small clock on the middle. How she wished she could see inside, hear her feet on the marble floor as Camille may have once heard her own. See the colors of the stained glass, which were impossible to detect outside on the sidewalk in the strong Marseille sun.

". . . *merci beaucoup, madame. Au revoir.*" Jean-Christian took her hand as he tucked his phone away. "We can't go in. But the secretary was quite amenable and said she'd have a quick look at the birth records for us . . . see if she can find a Camille Trigére born in 1921 or thereabouts. I gave her my cell number, and she said she'd call if she can find anything."

Libitz beamed at him. "My hero."

He chuckled. "In the meantime, let's get something to eat?"

"I'd love it," she said, letting him lead her away from the synagogue. She took a deep breath of the brackish air. "Do we *really* have to leave tomorrow?"

"*Oui,*" he said. "You have a gallery to run, remember?"

"I remember." She sighed. "So do you."

As they each processed the fact that managing their respective galleries meant living in separate cities, a pall was cast over the lightheartedness of their walk.

Jean-Christian sighed. "I didn't mention it before, but on Wednesday and Thursday, I looked at some commercial properties in Manhattan."

"You did?"

"Mm-hm. I was thinking . . . I mean . . ."

"Thinking what?" she asked, her fingers tightening around his.

"Thinking that I might want to open another gallery in New York."

Her heart leapt with joy, and she jerked her head to look up at him. "You're *moving* to New York?"

"I didn't say that."

"Oh."

"I didn't *not* say that either."

"Oh?"

"Fuck, Lib. I don't want to go back to Philly if you live in New York. I want . . . I mean, I want to keep going forward. Fuck—how do you say this? I mean, I want to *be* with you. And I can't be with you if I'm in Philly and you're in New York."

Her breath caught with excitement, but she forced herself to be calm. "I want to be with you too, but we could still make it work, even if—"

"No. I don't want that. I don't want to just see you on weekends. Or twice a month when we can get away. I want to see you all the time. *Every* night. *Every* Saturday. *Every* Sunday."

"But your family's in Philadelphia."

"And I'd definitely keep a place there . . . and I'd go back a lot. But I want to spend my time with you. Near you." He cleared his throat. "So I thought . . . maybe . . . I don't know. I'd open a gallery in New York. Then I'd have a second reason to stay."

She had a wild idea that tried to flit quickly through her mind, but she caught it and squeezed it in her hand, wondering if it was bat-shit crazy or a viable idea. She wouldn't know unless she said it aloud.

"I have a gallery and you have a gallery," she said.

"Mm-hm."

"And a presence in Philly would benefit me as much as a presence for you in New York."

"Right."

"We worked on the Kandinsky together. It was a breeze."

"Where are you going with this?"

She stopped walking and faced him. "A merger."

His eyes widened as he stared down at her. "Are you serious?"

Libitz took a deep breath and shrugged. "Why *buy* real estate when there's room at my place for a few of your pieces and room at your place for a few of mine?"

"But a merger? That's serious."

"Feingold-Rousseau," she said, flattening her hands on his chest and grinning up at him. "Doesn't that have a nice ring to it?"

"Not as nice as Rousseau-Feingold," he said, wrapping his arms around her. "Are you sure about this?"

"No," she said, shaking her head. "For now, it's just a fantasy. I'd need for my lawyer to look at your business and my accountant look at your profit and loss. You'd need to do the same. If one of us isn't a sound partner, the other would have to withdraw the offer. No fault, no foul."

"I'm doing well," he said.

She nodded. "Me too."

His face, which looked so hopeful, so happy, clouded over. "But . . . what if—I mean, what if we don't work out, Elsa? This is all pretty new."

"First of all, it's a choice to work out," she said. "Do you want us to work out?"

He nodded. "I do."

"Then we will."

"Second of all, even if we don't, we're bound for life through Noelle. So we don't really have the option of not getting along. As I see it, you're an ideal business partner. I can never escape you, and you can never escape me."

"Is there a third of all?" he asked, smiling at her, his features relaxing.

"Hmmm," she hummed. "I don't think so."

"Good. Because fuck food. I'm so turned on by this conversation, I'm taking you back to the hotel and making love to you."

"Turned on by the idea of a long-term commitment to one woman?" she asked, grinning at him with delight.

"That is fucking right. So I'm going to take you back to our chateau and make love to you, my darling Elsa . . . my possible business partner, my goddaughter's godmother, my . . . my . . ."

"Your what?" she asked, holding her breath.

"My Libitz," he said, bending his head to kiss her. "Fuck. Wait."

He pulled his phone from his back pocket. "*Bonjour? . . . Oui. Oui, madame. Merci. Ah. Oui. Je vois. Uh-huh . . .*" He looked at Libitz, his eyes bright and excited. "She thinks she may have found something, but not a birth record. A marriage record!"

Libitz gasped, holding on to Jean-Christian's arm, staring into his eyes.

"*Uh-huh. Oui. Êtes-vous certaine?*" His eyes widened, and he nodded. "*Gilles Lévy. Oui. 5 de Septembre? Êtes-vous absolument—oui, madame. Merci. Merci beaucoup. Oui. Oui. Au revoir.*"

"Tell me!" said Libitz.

Jean-Christian tucked the phone in his back pocket, taking her hands in his, nailing her with his eyes. "She was married. Camille Trigére was married to . . . Lib, she was married to a man named Gilles Lévy on September 5, 1939. No death record on file."

She couldn't breathe.

She pressed her hand to her chest, staring up at Jean-Christian with wide eyes.

"Breathe, baby," he urged her.

She took a halting, gasping breath, her hands clawing at his arms. "Her name. Her married name was . . . Lévy?"

He nodded, his eyes as wide and shocked as hers felt. "Camille Trigére Lévy."

"My grandmother was—Jean-Christian, my great-grandmother was Camille Lévy."

"I know, baby."

"She was . . . do you think she was my great-grandmother?"

He looked away from her, started to say something, then shut his mouth and shrugged. "I don't know, but you look like her. You look exactly like her, Lib."

"Do you know what this means?" she asked, vaguely aware of tears falling down her cheeks. "She survived!"

He nodded. "It also means your great-grandmother modeled for my great-uncle."

"My God!" she cried, rubbing her forehead with her hand. "We've got to get back to the hotel. We've got to pack. There is only one person in the world—in the entire world—who can settle this mystery for us, and we're going to go see her first thing tomorrow! As soon as we land!"

"Whoa, Nellie! To pack? We don't leave until tomorrow morning. Slow down, baby. Let's explore Marseille for a little while, huh? As long as we're here?"

"Right. Of course. Sorry. Marseille it is."

"But as long as we're on the subject," he said. "*Who* exactly are we going to go see tomorrow?"

She turned to him and grinned. "My bubbe."

Chapter 15

J.C. put his arm around Libitz in the cab from Newark Airport to her grandmother's apartment in Brooklyn, but he could feel the tension radiating from her body.

Yesterday, they'd had a lovely walk around Marseille, drinking in the gorgeous port city as best they could with so little time and eating a seaside dinner of fresh fish, escargot, crusty bread, and an excellent Provençal wine. He was sorry to have to leave the country of his birth the following morning, but with the promise of returning in December and with the final part of their mystery almost solved, he was as anxious as Libitz to get to her grandmother.

They were 90 percent sure that Camille Trigére was her great-grandmother—what were the chances that another young Jewish girl from Marseille named Camille Trigére had married a man with the surname Lévy and escaped France shortly after the start of World War II? It had to be her. But only Libitz's grandmother could help them be sure.

The taxi stopped before a quiet doorman building across from a Catholic Church, and J.C. paid the driver, taking Libitz's hand as they entered the building and the concierge announced them.

"I'm nervous," said Libitz in the elevator, her brown eyes even wider than usual. "I want it to be her so badly."

"It is her," said J.C., running his fingers through her hair gently. "You look exactly like her, and your grandmother's name was Camille Lévy."

"Put 'Camille Lévy' into Google and there are almost five hundred thousand results. There could have been hundreds of women with that name in 1939."

"Who look exactly like you?"

Libitz exhaled deeply. "What if it's not her? What if the model in the portrait died a terrible death in France or, worse, in Germany? What if my bubbe can't come up with anything that connects her mother to what we know about Camille the model?"

"There's only one way to find out," said J.C., holding the elevator door for her.

Her grandmother, a small, gray-haired woman in a simple flowered apron and slippers, stood in the doorway of her apartment with her arms outstretched. "Libby! What a surprise, dahling!"

"Bubbe!"

Libitz ran down the hallway and threw herself into her grandmother's arms. J.C. followed behind, grinning at their reunion.

"Who's this?" asked her grandmother, looking at him over Libitz's shoulder. "He's very tall. Good looking."

Libitz released her bubbe and stood beside J.C. "Bubbe, this is Jean-Christian."

The older woman looked back and forth between them.

"What happened to Neil?"

Libitz shrugged, braiding her fingers through Jean-Christian's. "He didn't work out."

Her grandmother looked up at him. "Jean-*Christian*. Hm. You're not Jewish."

He shook his head. "No, ma'am. Catholic."

"Oy, vey," she muttered under her breath before lowering her chin and locking eyes with her granddaughter. "Your mother won't like it."

"I know," said Libitz, shrugging again.

"You know that Judaism is passed down through the mother?"

J.C. nodded at her. "So I've heard."

She still stood in her doorway, looking him up and down. Finally, she shifted her glance to Libitz. "As long as he knows what's what."

"He's learning, Bubbe," said Libitz, humor thick in her voice as they followed her grandmother through a hallway and into a sitting room.

J.C. and Libitz sat on a couch across from the older lady, who sat in a large, comfortable-looking chair, her tiny feet barely touching the floor.

"So? Are you getting married?"

They both gasped, looking at each other in unison.

"That's why you're here?" asked Bubbe.

"No!" said Libitz. "No. We haven't . . . that is . . ."

"We're not engaged, ma'am," said J.C. *Yet.*

Mrs. Metz looked surprised. "Well, Libby, dahling, I'm happy to see you, but . . ."

"Bubbe," said Libitz, leaning forward, one elbow resting on her knee, "what do you remember about your mother? About her childhood? About how she came over to the United States?"

"Well . . ." said her grandmother, sitting back in the chair, then looking suddenly like she'd remembered something. She turned her attention to J.C. "You want some coffee?"

"No, thank you, Mrs. Metz."

"Bubbe," she said. "You're the first man Libby's ever brought over to my apartment, dahling. You call me Bubbe."

He grinned at her. "No thank you, Bubbe."

She nodded once in satisfaction, then looked at her granddaughter. "Maman didn't talk about France. She didn't tell me stories about her childhood. She didn't share memories of her parents or brother, so everything I know about her I learned by mistake."

"By . . . mistake?"

"By watching her. I learned that she must have had madeleines at Chanukah because she made them every year. I learned that she spoke French fluently because she talked in her sleep. I learned that she loved art because any afternoon that she wasn't balancing the books for my father's butcher shop, we would visit the Brooklyn Museum or take the subway into Manhattan and check out the new exhibits at the Met. She took me to the Guggenheim in 1959, the year it opened."

"She loved art . . ." murmured Libitz, grabbing J.C.'s hand.

"She did." Mrs. Metz nodded. "She had no family here. Her brother was killed in the War, I think. Her parents . . ." Her voice drifted off, and her face grew cool. "They died."

"Cousins? Aunts? Uncles?"

She shook her head. "No one, dahling. Just her and my father."

Libitz's fingers slackened. "Anything else, Bubbe? Anything—any little thing—about France?"

"Hmm," she sighed. "Yes. One other thing. Wait here."

Slipping from her chair, she walked through the room and padded down a back hallway. J.C. turned to Libitz. "She loved art. It's the same Camille."

Libitz face was uncertain. "I just want to be sure."

"Your grandmother told me to call her 'Bubbe,'" he said, grinning. "She likes me."

Libitz smiled back, leaning forward to kiss his lips quickly. "Then don't let her down."

I don't intend to, he thought, looking up when Mrs. Metz shuffled back into the room, holding a framed needlepoint that she handed to Libitz before returning to her chair.

"That was my mother's."

Looking down at the old piece of handiwork, J.C. realized that the words sewn into the cloth were French, and his breath caught and held as he quickly translated their meaning.

"It was so strange," said Bubbe, "for her to have that because she never, ever spoke French. Even when the sommelier at the wine store tried to speak French to her, she answered in English. But that? She kept. I guess she brought it over from Europe with her, but I'm not sure."

Libitz shifted slightly to look up at J.C. "Do you know what it says? Can you read it?"

He nodded, swallowing over the lump in his throat. "It says . . . *Promettez-moi que vous aurez une bonne vie.* Promise me that you'll have a good life."

Libitz gasped, her lips parting in shock as her eyes widened. "Oh, my God!"

He nodded again. "A good life."

"*L'chaim tovim,*" whispered Libitz.

"Yes!" said Bubbe, somewhat oblivious to their massive revelation. "*L'chaim tovim.* She said it all the time when we complained. She promised someone that she'd have a good life and told us that we must do the same."

He knew what Libitz was thinking about because he was thinking of it too: life.

Life. The Hebrew letter in the signature. *Have a good life.* The French inscription on the back of the portrait. Pierre had wanted Camille to choose life . . . and somehow, she did.

"Now dahlings," said Mrs. Metz. "Tell me what all this is about."

They explained all about *Les Bijoux Jolis*, and Libitz promised to bring the portrait to her bubbe as soon as possible.

"My maman," said Bubbe, with tears in her eyes. "You'll give her back to me."

Libitz looked at J.C. with pleading eyes, and he nodded at her.

"Of course, Mrs. M—Bubbe," he said. "It's all yours."

Because after all, thought J.C., watching Libitz hug her grandmother good-bye, *the real thing is already mine. Or . . . almost mine.*

They held hands in the elevator, staring at each other with silly grins, each processing the magnitude of fate and forever, of magic and miracles, and the ways in which their families were entwined.

Outside, it had grown dark, and the September evening was chilly.

Libitz fastened her coat, then stopped to look up at him.

"You know . . . I was just thinking . . . if your great-uncle hadn't given my great-grandmother that advice . . ." She took a breath and held it as she stared up at him. "I mean, I might not be here today. Maybe she wouldn't have left France."

"I thought of that," said Jean-Christian, fingering the object burning a hole in his pocket. "It almost feels like—and I know this is crazy, Lib, believe me—but it almost feels like my great-uncle saved your great-grandmother's life so . . . well, so that you could save mine."

She giggled, shaking her head back and forth. "No. It's perfect."

"Is it?"

"That two cynics find out that they were meant to be before they were even born?" She shook her head and laughed. "The universe has some sense of humor."

He grabbed her around the waist and pulled her against his chest, his voice husky. "Did you know . . . I was drawn to you before I ever knew you? At Ten and Kate's wedding, I couldn't keep my eyes off you."

"I remember," she said, smiling up at him. "I wanted so badly not to fall for you."

"Baby, I had sworn off commitment for life."

"I honestly thought I was going to end up with Neil."

"Never," he said, the words almost blasphemous to his ears.

"Never," she agreed, standing on tiptoe to kiss the frown off his lips.

Grinning at her, he reached up to caress her cheek tenderly, smiling into her eyes. "You were chosen for me before I was ever born. I think—in the simplest of terms but with the most *profound* gratitude—you were meant for me."

As he said these words, his hand slipped from her cheek, and he lowered himself to a knee on the sidewalk, reaching for her hand, gazing up into her wide brown eyes.

"What are you doing?" she gasped.

"From Camille Trigére to Libitz Feingold . . . from Pierre Montferrat to Jean-Christian Rousseau. It took seventy years for us to find each other, and I don't want to wait another minute to be together." He grinned as her eyes brightened with tears and she took a step closer to him, her hand shaking in his.

Reaching into his jacket pocket, he pulled out the emerald he'd had set in Marseille on Saturday morning while she rested at the hotel. The emerald owned by his great-uncle. The emerald in a necklace worn by her great-grandmother. The emerald that symbolized their journey to find each other, and the emerald that would symbolize their love and union forever.

There was no panic in his head or his heart as he held the ring between his fingers, looking up at the woman who had changed the entire course of his life. All he felt was the soul-deep rightness of the question he was about to ask her and the fervent hope that she would give him the answer he so desperately wanted.

"You're my person," he said. "You've always been my person. Long before I was breathing, you belonged to me." He paused for just a moment, searching her eyes, and then nodded. "Marry me, my darling Elsa? Please?"

Laughing and crying, Libitz nodded as Jean-Christian slipped the emerald rock onto her hand. "Yes. Y-yes. God, I'm not a crier, but oh, God . . . this is so . . . so . . ."

"Perfect," he said, standing up to gather her into his arms.

He kissed her tenderly—this tiny, dark-haired, brown-eyed woman who he'd never seen coming but who now held the key to his happiness, and his heart, in her hands.

Both were safe there.

They were—finally, at long last—exactly where they were supposed to be.

EPILOGUE

September 9, 1939

Camille Trigére Lévy sat by the small window of her third-class cabin on the Holland–America SS *Volendam*, finishing the needlepoint she'd started in Boulogne-sur-Mer, watching the emerald-green coast of Ireland grow smaller and smaller in the far distance.

She was officially at sea.

Everything had happened so quickly.

Six days ago, France and England had declared war on Germany, and the following day, her parents had sat her down in their kitchen for a very serious conversation that they'd obviously been planning for some time.

Her father took off his glasses and rubbed his eyes. "We heard the whisperings about changes from our relatives in Poland, and now . . . now, as you know, the worst has happened. The Germans have invaded."

Camille *did* know, of course, but the news hadn't felt very relatable. The Germans had invaded faraway Poland. But France was France—strong and, in her opinion, superior in every way. More modern. More sophisticated. She was sorry for what had happened in Poland, but certainly it wouldn't have too great an impact on her, would it? France and England would send some soldiers to go sort it out, and everything would go back to normal, right?

"Several months ago, we took all our savings, everything we had . . . and we bought tickets," said her father, his voice low and urgent, "for a cabin on a Dutch ocean liner from Boulogne-sur-Mer to New York on September 9. Two tickets. One for you, and one for your brother."

"But this morning, your brother joined the army of *La Troisième République*!" her mother shrieked, balling her fists in frustration as tears poured from her eyes. "He's going to be a soldier. He wants to die! He wants to get himself killed by Germans!"

"*Non, chérie*," her father had said, standing to place an arm around his wife's shoulders and speaking gently. "No. He wants to fight for a free France. He's young, but he's a man and he—he has the right to fight for what's right." Swallowing as though it was painful, he turned back to Camille, his only other child. "Jules is gone. Your mother must go with you now."

Her mother gasped, turning to her husband with wide eyes and gaping lips.

"I'm not going to New York!" exclaimed Camille, putting her hands on her hips as hot tears scorched her eyes. "I'm marrying Gilles. We're going to Paris!"

"Paris?" her mother demanded, crossing the kitchen to grab her daughter by the shoulders and shake her. "We're at war, girl! You're not going off to Paris."

Camille's heart had raced with the sudden stark realization that life as she knew it was over. Dreams of modeling in Paris? Over. France was at war, and that war wasn't a make-believe, distant conflict that would be sorted quickly. No. In that moment, she felt her parent's fear and the lengths to which they'd gone to plan for her safety.

"Papa?" she murmured.

He nodded, rubbing his eyes again. "You'll be safe in New York. We've arranged for you and Jul—for you to stay with old friends from Provence, the Rosenbaums. They'll help you find a job and . . . and . . ." His voice tapered off, and his head bent forward in sorrow.

"I'm not going," her mother said softly to her father, wrapping her arms around his slim frame. "I'm staying here, Ira. I'm staying with you."

"*Non, chérie.* You will go. I will stay here to be a home for Jules. We will join you and Camille in America after the war is—"

"I'm not going," she said again. "It says in Ruth, 'Whither thou goest, there go I.'"

"That was the case of a daughter-in-law and mother-in-law," he said, caressing her cheek tenderly. "You're making a better case for going with Camille, *chérie.*"

"I'm not going," she said a final time. Taking a deep breath, she turned back to her daughter. "Has Gilles asked you? To marry him?"

Camille, who had taken a seat at the kitchen table, nodded. "*Oui.* We were supposed to leave for Paris tomorrow."

Her mother's eyes widened. "Were you going to tell us?"

"I was going to leave a note."

"*Merde,*" her mother murmured. "If things are that far along, you'll be married tomorrow."

"*Tomorrow?*"

"*Oui. Demain.* The rabbi will make a special exception. And you'll be on that train to Boulogne-sur-Mer on Wednesday as planned. There's an inn with a room booked for three nights. And then . . . on Saturday . . . you'll go to New York City. With Gilles."

"Maman!" she cried, "I can't go to New York. I can't leave France! I can't leave you!"

"You will go!" her mother commanded, her voice like steel, though tears ran down her face in rivulets. "I will *not* lose both of my children!"

"But you *will* be losing me! How do you know I'll ever see you again?"

"I don't," said her mother with a wince that made Camille's blood run cold. She stepped forward to sweep her daughter's dark bangs from her forehead and pressed her lips to Camille's warm skin. "But I know that you will live. You'll have the chance to make a good life away from this madness."

The world is going mad, petite. Leave France behind. Promise me that you will have a good life.

As Ireland slipped completely away, Camille wiped the tears from her cheeks and stepped away from the cabin window, turning as Gilles entered the tiny cabin with a huge smile on his face.

"Well, we're officially under way!" he said, excitement making his eyes shine with promise. "We could take a stroll on the deck before supper."

She nodded, hoping he couldn't tell that she'd been crying. Tying off the last bit of embroidery thread, she looked up at Gilles and smiled. "I'd love some fresh air."

Taking her hands in his, he kissed her forehead, and then her cheeks, and then her lips. "What an adventure, huh? Someday we'll tell our children's children how we left France behind and started a new life in America!"

No, she thought, *we won't tell them. We won't tell them that the France of our childhood was no longer our France. We won't tell them that the France we loved was no longer safe for us. No, my darling. We won't tell them anything.*

We will leave France behind, and we will have a good life in America.

"Are you ready for a new life, Mrs. Lévy?" he asked in French, offering his arm.

"Yes," she answered her handsome husband in stilted English, "I am ready."

THE END

*The World of Blueberry Lane
continues in 2017 with …*

THE STORY SISTERS
(Part IV of the Blueberry Lane Series)

The Bohemian and the Businessman
(Priscilla's story)
The Story Sisters #1

The Director and Don Juan
(Alice's story)
The Story Sisters #2

The Flirt and the Fox
(Elizabeth's story)
The Story Sisters #3

The Saint and the Scoundrel
(Jane's story)
The Story Sisters #4

Other Books by Katy Regnery

A Modern Fairytale
(Stand-alone, full-length, unconnected romances inspired by classic fairy tales.)

The Vixen and the Vet
(inspired by "Beauty and the Beast")
2014

Never Let You Go
(inspired by "Hansel and Gretel")
2015

Ginger's Heart
(inspired by "Little Red Riding Hood")
2016

Dark Sexy Knight
(inspired by "The Legend of Camelot")
2016

Don't Speak
(inspired by "The Little Mermaid")
2017

Swan Song
(inspired by "The Ugly Duckling")
2018

ABOUT THE AUTHOR

New York Times and *USA Today* bestselling author Katy Regnery started her writing career by enrolling in a short story class in January 2012. One year later, she signed her first contract and Katy's first novel was published in September 2013.

Twenty-five books later, Katy claims authorship of the multi-titled, *New York Times* and *USA Today* bestselling Blueberry Lane Series, which follows the English, Winslow, Rousseau, Story, and Ambler families of Philadelphia; the six-book, bestselling A Modern Fairytale series; and several other standalone novels and novellas.

Katy's first modern fairytale romance, *The Vixen and the Vet*, was nominated for a RITA® in 2015 and won the 2015 Kindle Book Award for romance. Katy's boxed set, *The English Brothers Boxed Set*, Books #1–4, hit the *USA Today* bestseller list in 2015, and her Christmas story, *Marrying Mr. English*, appeared on the list a week later. In May 2016, Katy's Blueberry Lane collection, *The Winslow Brothers Boxed Set*, Books #1–4, became a *New York Times* E-Book bestseller.

In 2016, Katy signed an agreement with Spencer Hill Press. As a result, her Blueberry Lane paperback books will now be distributed to brick-and-mortar bookstores all over the United States.

Katy lives in the relative wilds of northern Fairfield County, Connecticut, where her writing room looks out at the woods, and her husband, two young children, two dogs, and one Blue Tonkinese kitten create just enough cheerful chaos to remind her that the very best love stories begin at home.

Sign up for Katy's newsletter today: www.katyregnery.com!

Connect with Katy:

Katy LOVES connecting with her readers and answers every e-mail, message, tweet, and post personally! Connect with Katy!

Katy's Website: http://katyregnery.com
Katy's E-mail: katy@katyregnery.com
Katy's Facebook Page: https://www.facebook.com/KatyRegnery
Katy's Pinterest Page: https://www.pinterest.com/
    katharineregner
Katy's Amazon Profile: http://www.amazon.com/Katy-Regnery/
    e/B00FDZKXYU
Katy's Goodreads Profile: https://www.goodreads.com/author/
    show/7211470.Katy_Regnery

CPSIA information can be obtained
at www.ICGtesting.com
Printed in the USA
LVOW10s0343031216
515598LV00002BB/2/P